# SECRET SANCTUARY

Visit us at www.boldstrokesbooks.com

# By the Author

Cowgirl

An Alaskan Wedding

Secret Sanctuary

# SECRET SANCTUARY

*by*

Nance Sparks

2022

# SECRET SANCTUARY

ISBN 13: 978-1-63679-148-7

THIS TRADE PAPERBACK ORIGINAL IS PUBLISHED BY
BOLD STROKES BOOKS, INC.
P.O. BOX 249
VALLEY FALLS, NY 12185

FIRST EDITION: JULY 2022

CREDITS
EDITORS: VICTORIA VILLASEÑOR AND CINDY CRESAP
PRODUCTION DESIGN: SUSAN RAMUNDO
COVER DESIGN BY TAMMY SEIDICK

# Acknowledgments

I would like to acknowledge my sensitivity readers, Stacy Foss and Mioyshi. Input from these two women helped me honor a culture that I've admired all my life.

Mioyshi, thank you for making sure I described the rituals properly. The knowledge you've shared has been invaluable. Working with you on this book has blessed me with so much, including a new friendship. I sincerely appreciate you.

## CHAPTER ONE

Alex Trenton yawned and rubbed her eyes. She understood the need for the two o'clock in the morning transfers, but that didn't mean it wasn't hard on the body, especially after a full day of work on the ranch. She launched the app for the fence sensors. Everything was green. The transport team should arrive any minute. She flipped through the viewer app and inspected images from each camera strategically placed around the perimeter of the well-hidden safe house. All was clear.

She wasn't aware of the identity of the federal witness hidden on this stay, even though they'd been stashed there for almost three months. Keeping the circle of knowledge small was safer for everyone. The goal was always the same while waiting for the trial to start, and that was to ensure the witness didn't become tortured fish food before getting the opportunity to take the stand. Alex, a United States marshal, lived the job undercover as a ranch manager twenty-four-seven. She was the gatekeeper. The secrecy and the security of this post now rested solely on her shoulders. She used her cover to be the interface with the community. It was easy given that she'd been a part of the community since she was twelve. It also kept unfamiliar faces from being seen buying groceries and any other needed supplies, which meant she took care of whatever the witnesses and their protectors needed.

The twenty-four-hour a day protection detail was left to the two deputy marshals who shadowed the witness and any authorized family members throughout the entire process. Consistent faces allowed the witness to relax just a bit during what was most certainly a stressful time. Alex was grateful for the buffer. She knew the ones who testified weren't always the innocent who happened to be at the wrong place at the wrong time. Given her history, it was difficult for her to knowingly protect a criminal who was spared prison time simply by offering the next link or two up the chain. As far as she was concerned, the worst of the worst all deserved prison time, but she also knew that sometimes deals were the only way to take down the darkest souls at the top of criminal organizations.

Her phone buzzed quietly in her hand.

*Approaching gate one.*

Good, the transport team followed the instructions for the new network access. Alex pulled up the viewer for the cameras at gate one. The license plate, front bumper sticker, and the two canoes strapped to the top of the big Suburban matched the description of the vehicle details sent from the Billings office.

*Access code?* Alex typed into the phone.

*Chocolate milk tastes best ice cold.*

Alex smiled. Access codes were only used once, and because of this she liked to keep them light and interesting. She opened another app and tapped the screen to disengage the locks. An ordinary looking section of fence swung wide open. She watched the Suburban pass through and kept watch until the gate closed, and the locks engaged. Alex switched cameras as the truck crept along the inside fence line.

*Approaching gatekeeper for a drop-off.*

Alex waited while the vehicle approached. When it was close enough, she responded.

*Confirmed. Stop now.*

Alex stayed in the shadows and waited for the Suburban to come to a complete stop in front of her. The driver's door of the vehicle opened, softly illuminating the driver, US Marshals Service criminal investigator Candice Alvier. *Well, now, that's odd.* Candice was the last person she expected to see. A simple pickup was several tiers below her pay grade. She lifted a box from the passenger seat and quietly closed the door to the Suburban. The moon was high in the sky and Alex could see her as clear as day. She stepped out of the protection of the dense pine trees and walked up to Candice.

"Hey, stranger, aren't you supposed to be hot on the trail of some fugitive? How'd you get stuck with pickup duty? Piss someone off back at the office?"

"It's good to see you too, kiddo." Candice set down the box and held her arms open. "I came out because I wanted to give you a hug in person. You've been through a lot lately. First Hawk, and I am so sorry to hear about Mick."

Alex stepped forward and found comfort in Candice's embrace. She held her close and tried to keep her emotions in check. There weren't too many people she could step away from the script with. Scratch that, Candice was the only one left. She stepped back and looked into kind and understanding eyes.

"He doesn't recognize me much anymore. I didn't realize how bad the dementia was getting until after Hawk's death. He kept wandering around looking for him. Each time, I'd have to explain that Hawk had passed away and it was like telling him for the first time, over and over again. I can still hear him sobbing." Alex drew in a deep breath and let it out slowly. "Moving him to the memory care facility wasn't any easier. He forgot where we were going by the time we pulled into the parking lot. They say that to help those with memory issues, you sometimes have to 'live the lie' instead of correcting a false statement or arguing with them all of the time. Living the lie seems to be my reality."

Lying and making up new truths was one thing she was proficient at even though she struggled with the deception. It came with living day in and day out as an undercover agent. Her life was a lonely existence because everything about it was cloak-and-dagger. No one could know about her badge, just like no one could know that Hawk and Mick had also once held badges. No one could know about the four cabins hidden behind the trees, deep in the foliage, tucked off in the back corner of the five-square-mile ranch. All transports were scheduled in the middle of the night with very limited headlight use and the vehicles came through the national forest land where there were no official roads. Even then, nothing moved until a drone scanned the area for any threats because every witness kept on this site had such a steep price on their head. Sometimes literally.

"Why don't you take some time off? Consider what might be next for you."

"There's nothing to consider. This is my post. Hawk and Mick passed the torch to me. I owe it to them to continue the work here. I aced the programs. I know this land like the back of my hand. Besides, I promised Hawk that I'd look after Mary."

Ambrose "Hawk" Hawkins and his wife of more than fifty years, Mary, owned the thirty-two-hundred-acre ranch. A few nights before Hawk passed away, he'd begged her and her father, Mick Trenton, to keep Mary safe. Her father might have forgotten the conversation within minutes of leaving the room, but she'd honor the promises made that day. She owed the three of them her life.

"Mary isn't getting any younger and you can't be in two places at once. A site this big can't run with just one marshal. Alex, you don't have a backup."

She wasn't prepared for this conversation. This was supposed to be a simple pickup. Now she felt like someone was pulling the rug out from under her. Defensiveness flared up.

"This site has been running with one marshal for quite some time and you know it. I've added technology that sees more than the three of us ever could and it's working great. All of it is hidden behind redundant, next gen firewalls. I've set up segmented, isolated VLANs and it's over-the-top secure. Even the geeks at the main office haven't been able to hack it."

"Alex, you're missing the point. You can have redundant techno this and thats all you want, but—"

Alex's frustration grew. "I disagree. There are cameras hidden all around this area of the ranch with motion detection, audio pickups, and night vision recordings. There are at least two cameras dialed in on us right now, recording every movement and every word. The perimeter fences have pressure sensors and I'm alerted if someone so much as leans against it to tie a shoe. The interior fences that surround each of the safe house grounds can be electrified with a simple tap on my phone. Once it's energized, anyone who touches it would be knocked flat on their ass."

"We've always had an armed agent outside, minding the perimeter. What happens if there's a breach? What's your response time if you're in town? What happens if you're taken out?"

"The technology minds the perimeter. I'd know if there was an attempt well before they could get close to any of the cabins. And if I'm in town or taken out, the two marshals stationed inside with the witnesses have tablets with apps for perimeter sensors and controls for their assigned zone. They can operate gates, activate the electric fences around their cabin, open the gun safe, you name it. So, it could be said that I do have backup. I have all sorts of tricks up my sleeve. I take security seriously." Alex struggled to keep her voice soft. Yelling was the last thing needed on a pickup.

"No doubt you take it seriously. You've created a model setup." Candice stepped back and rubbed her face with her hands. "The truth is, your talents are wasted out here. It's been discussed that you could have your own team, jump up a few grades. We'd set up a shell company as cover and you could equip the other remote locations with your designs." Candice motioned to the box. "Speaking of which, here's the last of the gadgets you requested from the geeks at the office."

Alex's heart sank. She didn't want a team. She didn't care about jumping up a few grades. What she did here was important. Her life was here. She had friends and a community. She'd been safe here, and now she helped make it safe for others.

"First, one deputy isn't enough without backup, and then I've created the model site. Stop blowing sunshine up my ass and tell me what's going on. Are they pulling the post?"

"No, not yet, but it's a real possibility. This site is complicated because it was a first of its kind and the Marshals Service doesn't own the land. I don't know anything more than that. You should seriously consider your options. Team lead or division lead would be great for your career. Even if it works out to keep this post, you're under no obligation to stay out here." Candice reached out and squeezed her arm.

"What if I want to stay? This is my home." Alex tried to steady her breath.

"Please just think about it. Until then, run status quo. Let me see what I can find out from my end, okay?"

Alex nodded but felt little comfort.

"Occupant status after tonight's pickup?"

"All cabins empty. It makes sense now. I've never had all cabins empty." Alex suddenly felt just as empty.

"No matter what happens, you should be proud of what you brought to this site. The changes that you've suggested over the years have made a big difference and offered reassurance to those at highest risk. Some might not have testified without the security this place offered. The way you used the terrain along the ravine to stagger the additional cabins with half a mile of separation between each was very creative. The acre of fenced off outdoor space for each unit, well hidden beneath the treetops, was invaluable to deputies and witnesses alike. Being stuck indoors for up to three months would make anyone go crazy. I meant it when I said you've created the model setup. Makes me proud to have been a tiny part of it." Candice smiled faintly.

Candice had been more than a tiny part of it. She helped make all of it possible. It had been her rookie year when she'd brought Alex to this location for safekeeping twenty-five years ago, when Alex was just a scared little kid. Hawk and Mick were the two undercover US marshals who stayed at her side throughout the entire process. It took two months for the trial to start, and by then she'd become quite attached to the Montana landscape as well as the people who had taken her in. After the trial, she'd begged to return to the ranch with her new identity from the Witness Security Program. Her wish was granted when Mick Trenton broke all sorts of unofficial rules by taking her in as his long-lost daughter. Candice was the agent who had helped make that happen and there was a special bond between them because of it.

Hawk and Mick had been the best mentors she could ever ask for, and the thought of this sanctioned post possibly being pulled felt like a lead weight deep in her stomach, like she'd failed them after all they'd done for her. Once upon a time, this place had saved her, and once she'd earned her badge, she worked diligently alongside her two mentors to make sure every visitor and their protectors remained safe.

"Try to stay positive. Take a little bit of time to catch your breath, okay? I'll be in touch." Candice stepped closer and started to lift her arms for another hug.

"Status quo, understood." Alex stepped back, away from her extended arms, and picked up the box of equipment. She held it in front of her, creating a buffer.

Candice dropped her arms and stepped back. She looked at Alex for a moment and then walked back to the Suburban and climbed up into the driver's seat. The truck rolled onward up the fence line. Alex set down the box and checked the cameras and sensors again.

*Approaching cabin four for pickup.*

Was this going to be the last pickup? Alex shook the thought from her mind.

She opened a new text thread with the marshals in the cabin. *Truck is at the gate for pickup. All is secure.*

Dots flickered for a moment. *Thanks for the hospitality and the safe stay. We'll leave the devices on the table. Heading out now.*

Alex switched back to the thread with Candice.

*Team is heading out now.*

She tapped the screen to unlock and open the gate at cabin four and then connected to the camera app to watch the cloaked figures leave the cabin and head up the path to the gate. Once the last person was through the gate, she tapped the screen to close and lock access to the safehouse. She'd clean it up tomorrow. It wasn't likely to be occupied anytime soon.

*Package secured. Returning to gate one.*

She kept an eye on the cameras as the truck made its way along the fence line. Soon, the witness would be in court for a first day of testimony, and in the end, if all went well, they'd get a new identity, a new script to live by. It wasn't the easiest transition to make. She knew that from experience.

*Approaching gate one.*

Alex checked the sensors beyond the gate. Everything was green and no movement alarms. Another scan for heat signatures out in the foothills showed nothing but a small herd of elk grazing in the moonlight. She watched it closely for movement after she tapped the screen and opened the last gate. She stood there in the darkness, beneath the pine trees watching the Suburban leave the fence line and cut across the foothills heading toward the two-track road to the remote airport. She closed the gate and silently wished the witness luck in their new life.

## CHAPTER TWO

E lina Hawkins pressed gently on the brakes and then put her truck in park. She sat there behind the wheel knowing that the moment she opened the driver's door, the reality of a new normal would hit hard. This would be the first time in her entire life that her grandfather wouldn't be standing in the driveway to greet her. Cancer sucked. She called at one point last winter and he was his sassy ol' self, and then a couple of weeks later, he was too worn and tired to talk on the phone. By the time he was diagnosed, the cancer was everywhere and so aggressive that he chose hospice over treatment. He always said he'd go on his terms and somehow, she was sure he had. No doubt he knew something was up, but leave it to him to keep it to himself until it was too late.

He'd passed away five months ago, in the dead of winter. Elina still felt such guilt for not visiting more often, not being there in person to help or to say good-bye. She could make up a thousand reasons why she hadn't hopped right in her truck and headed north the moment she found out he was sick. She could claim that she wasn't yet in any shape to be around her family when that call came in. Even now, she was still healing. That last contract job had taken so much from her. She could claim it was the responsibility of being the division lead for the search and rescue operations covering the Grand Teton National Park, but then, that was one of the things she ended up losing because of that last contract job, or at least she would lose when her accrued vacation time ran out.

The mutual agreement was more than fair since she pretty much vanished for several months longer than expected. Then there was the responsibility of tending to her horses and dogs that aided her in her work, and yet, all the excuses in the world were bullshit and she knew it. The real reason, if she was ugly-truth honest about it, was as selfish as excuses came.

Her grandfather, known to most simply as Hawk, was the kind of man who was larger than life. He wasn't tall and yet he had a towering presence and a confident calmness about him. He might as well have worn a cape, and the truth of the matter was that she couldn't bring herself to see him being slowly devoured into a frail shell of his former self, even as fast as it happened. It wasn't the image she wanted in her mind's eye when she thought of him, and it was a decision she'd regretted ever since she received the call that he'd passed away.

A firm knock on the passenger side window startled both Elina and her two sleeping co-pilots. The Belgian Malinois dogs, Scout and Hunter, jumped up and lunged for the window in a moment of snarling panic barking. Elina's grandmother screamed and flailed her arms as she staggered backward.

"Knock that off before you give me a heart attack." She clapped twice and pointed at the dogs through the side window.

Scout and Hunter quieted instantly and sat at attention. Elina's heart was pounding with the sudden jolt of adrenaline. She reached over and ruffled the dogs' fur before opening the driver's door.

"Néiwóó, it's good to see you. How are you doing?" Elina asked, holding the door open for the dogs. She could speak the language of the Arapaho fluently and her grandmother had long ago shared how much she cherished the endearment, especially since she was a sassy woman of Irish decent and not an Arapaho elder like her late husband.

"Better, now that the beasts know who I am again." She patted the dogs' heads and then wrapped her arms around Elina's waist and rested her head on her shoulder. "Thank you for coming up to visit your old grandma. I knew you were getting close. I saw your beautiful face on the news."

Elina shook her head and rolled her eyes. "That reporter had no right to approach me while broadcasting live. I've spent my entire career avoiding cameras and the spotlight."

"Aw, live a little. It's not every day that Wolfbend makes the five o'clock news. My phone rang off the hook there for a bit because the gals from the senior center recognized you too. It didn't hurt that Ben Connor photobombed you and plugged Hawkins Ranch Bison either. I would have recorded it had I known you two would make us famous."

Famous was the last thing she wanted. There was a reason she didn't have social media accounts. It was better if people didn't know her real name or where her family lived. It was safer for everyone that way. Elina now wished she hadn't stopped at all, but her truck was running on fumes, and it was the only gas station for miles. She'd tried to duck out of frame and hide, but Ben had pulled her back into the frame and blabbed about the ranch. Punching him to get away would have only drawn more attention so she smiled and turned away as quickly as possible. Her only hope was that it stayed with the local news and didn't go national or post to the internet, not that a story about a centenarian movie star from a small town was big news. She'd have to remember to make a call and get any images on the World Wide Web scrubbed.

"Miss Ava must be over the moon for all of the attention." Néiwóó's eyes lit up.

"I had no idea who the birthday girl was, but I'm happy that she was able to celebrate her one hundredth birthday with all the limelight and fanfare. I still can't figure out why they were interviewing people at the gas station of all places." Elina leaned up against the side of her truck.

"Well, back in my day Miss Ava was a very famous actress. She was in films with Humphrey Bogart and James Stewart. Her daddy owned that station and she worked there as a kid. Hence, the autographed photos of her covering every inch of wall space inside. I'm glad they gave her a little attention. Us old folks get forgotten sometimes."

Elina wondered if that was a dig. If it was, it was likely deserved. She decided to ignore it. "I don't think I've ever been inside the gas station. I've always been a pay at the pump kind of gal. Besides, I drove out here to see you, not so I could be on the evening news."

"And now you've accomplished both. I'm glad you're here."

"Me too, Néiwóó, me too." Elina wrapped her arms around her grandmother's shoulders and exhaled. "Oh, how I've missed this place. So many memories came flooding back the moment I pulled through the gate."

"Good memories, I hope." She pulled away a bit and looked up. Her green eyes still had a faint sparkle, but there was such sadness behind her smile.

"Some of the best I have." Elina smiled back.

"I can understand that. My best memories live on this land too."

Elina squeezed her grandmother, unsure what to say. She knew that her grandmother had suffered the greatest loss of all, the loss of her best friend and soul mate. Perhaps the memories of their life together on the ranch gave her some peace, though she looked twenty years older than she had just a few months earlier at her grandfather's celebration of life. Even the last hints of reddish-brown hair surrendered to the now completely dominant gray. Loss had a way of aging those left behind, especially when they'd shared more than a half century with the one who was gone. Rustling and thumping in the trailer behind Elina's truck pulled her out of her thoughts.

"I'd better let the big beasts out of the trailer before they make their own door. I guess the six-hour drive up was enough for them."

"I imagine so. A six-hour drive would certainly do me in. Go and get them settled. I think Alex has the big paddock on the west side of the barn ready for your crew. The water trough should be full. If not, you know where the hose is."

"Indeed, I do." Elina smiled at the mention of Alex's name. She'd been looking forward to some time with her on this trip too. She wasn't sure why, but she found it comforting to talk with Alex. It was as if getting to know Alex was helping her heal.

Her grandmother took a few steps and then turned back. "I made your favorite, mutton stew. I'll let the dough rise and put the bread in the oven. I bet you're starving."

"Oh, that sounds delightful. Thank you, I won't be long."

Elina watched her grandmother walk into the house before she made her way to the back of the horse trailer. She released the latches and lowered the ramp. Four sets of ears perked up over the dividers. She'd thought about just bringing her primary horse, but two weeks was a long time to ask someone to babysit her brood, so instead, she shut down her cabin in Wyoming and loaded up the entire gang. It was probably better this way. The tiny herd was bonded, and change was always easier to adjust to when experienced amongst friends.

One by one, she led the horses to the back paddock until all four were stretching their legs in a soft lope around the perimeter. Elina leaned up against the fence and watched the elegance of her ponies in motion. Manes and tails flowed gently in the soft breeze while hooves drummed rhythmically against the hard pack. Pure serenity. She could do with a little more serenity in her life.

She looked beyond the paddock to her grandparents' herd of bison scattered about in a pasture of prairie grass along the foothills of the mountain range. Calving season was over and the red dogs bounded around playfully with their tails held up high while the adults grazed lazily in the late day sun. A few curious calves came up close to the pasture fence, sniffing and flicking their ears. Their coats were already losing the orange-red coloring that earned them the red dog nickname. It wouldn't be long before horn buds showed up and their shoulders would begin to develop the notorious hump. The herd looked good. It had easily doubled in size since the last time she'd been there.

A soft breeze blew strands of hair free from Elina's thick braid, tickling the side of her face. There were a few fluffy, white clouds scattered across the deep blue sky. It was a scene that belonged on canvas and yet it was more than that. If this picturesque moment could be a sound, she was certain it would be the songs of the tāhpeno, her grandfather's wooden flute. He had a talent for playing and could delicately switch notes like the winds wisping through the tall blades of grass. She loved to join in with a soft touch on the sacred drum, offering the heartbeat of the land.

Elina climbed the fence and sat on the top rail. She closed her eyes and listened to the memory of the music in her mind. She wished for the inner calm and peacefulness that usually came with her grandfather's music, though it was elusive today. She imagined his teepee standing tall just beyond the paddock fence. She pictured the trails of smoke wafting up from the opening at the top which would have offered the scent of campfire and the ceremonial herbs used for smudging. Whatever happened to the teepee? Was it still somewhere on the ranch? If it was, she'd like to try her hand at erecting it. Perhaps some time surrounded by her grandfather's spirit would offer her guidance. She could use the cleansing effect of a good smudging ceremony. When the time felt right, she'd ask her grandmother about it.

There was so much uncertainty in her life lately. She hoped this trip would offer clarity and help her define her path. She knew that her search and rescue career was over. She'd topped out some time ago and then started spending more and more time pursuing her contract work. The various federal agencies that hired her services had serious clout and could borrow her from the National Forest Service without affecting her seniority or accrued vacation. She earned a very nice compensation for taking a few unpaid days to hunt down an escapee or one of the most wanted at the federal level. It had been a sweet gig for a lot of years, but then last year happened and everything changed. Was her contract career over too? If she continued with that work, she'd have to establish much better ground rules. She wouldn't survive another job that tossed her to the wolves for fodder.

## CHAPTER THREE

Alex climbed the few steps and walked across the deck to the back door. A month or so after Hawk's death, Mary began inviting her to the main house for dinner more and more often, insisting that it was too hard to cook for one, though she understood Mary's loneliness too. It was difficult being in an empty house after you were used to sharing it with someone. The invitations quickly turned into a nightly event, and to show her appreciation, Alex made a point of putting away the leftovers and doing the dishes each night. Her life was a lonely existence too and she had to admit that she enjoyed the hour or so of company every bit as much as the food. It was so much better than eating out of a can while standing over the kitchen sink.

She knocked twice and turned the doorknob. The heavenly scent of traditional Irish stew and homemade bread, fresh out of the oven, made her mouth water. Voices and laughter drifted from the kitchen as if it were a holiday. She walked by the large family table which was already set for three. It was still odd to see the empty placemat at the head of the table next to Mary's spot. It reminded her of how uncertain her future was on this ranch. She shook her head and tried not to worry about that tonight.

Alex turned away from the table and gazed into the kitchen. Her heart did a little happy dance the moment she spotted her. Elina looked so relaxed, leaning against the counter in faded jeans and an untucked light cotton blouse with a few buttons undone at the collar. Her naturally brown skin had already been kissed by the early summer sun, or at least that's what the missing watch on her wrist indicated by showing off a band of skin several shades lighter than the rest of her. The floorboard squeaked beneath Alex's foot and Elina turned to face her. The unique coppery bronze color of her smiling eyes captured Alex's attention, just as it had every time she saw Elina. She'd known only one other person in all her life with a similar eye color and that was Hawk. It wasn't the only feature she'd inherited from her grandfather either. The high cheekbones and distinct nose and jawline created a perfectly feminine likeness of Hawk's face. Though, at eighty-four, his face was chiseled and distinguished with deep wisdom lines whereas Elina's face was silky sleek, elegant, and oh, so beautiful. Alex realized she was staring and tried to find her voice.

"Hey, stranger, it's good to see you. I hope your trip was uneventful." Alex stuffed her hands into the front pockets of her jeans. Shaking Elina's hand was absurd, but a hug seemed like overstepping at the moment, so she simply stood there. "Was everything okay in the paddock?"

Elina smiled sweetly, as if she could sense how nervous Alex was. "It's good to see you too. The trip was an easy haul, and my crew seems quite content in their new space. Thank you for having it ready to go. I appreciate it."

"It's about time you got here. Dinner's been ready." Mary bumped her elbow into Alex's ribs. "Elina, be a sweetie and grab the bread board and butter? Alex, would you carry the pot of stew out to the table? Let's eat, I'm starving."

Elina disappeared through the doorway with the bread board and butter.

Mary stepped up next to Alex at the stove and leaned in close. "Finished everything up in time to grab a shower before dinner tonight, eh? And don't you look dashing. Anyone in particular you might be trying to impress?"

Alex felt the color flush her cheeks and shook her head. There was no getting anything by Mary. At eighty-three, she was one keen cookie. It was true, she'd worked her ass off to get everything done so she'd have time to shower and put on nicer clothes. She'd never really spent any quality time with Elina on her previous visits. Instead, she and Mick used to take on extra work so Hawk could spend all of his time with the family while they were there. That said, it didn't mean there wasn't interest in impressing the woman she'd admired from afar over the years, especially given their phone conversations over the past few months.

Mary stood at the edge of the table and began dishing out the stew as soon as Alex set down the pot.

"How's your dad settling in up in Missoula? Are you still happy with the facility?" Elina sliced the warm bread and passed the bread board over to Alex.

"Thank you." Alex picked up a slice of steaming bread and buttered it. "The folks in the memory care unit have the patience of saints. I think being around people his age has helped. His spirit seems better anyway. He's not so despondent."

"This land just isn't the same without the two of them sitting out on that porch solving the world's problems. Hawk and Mick were like brothers, always egging each other on. I thank my lucky stars that Alex stuck around though. I don't know what I'd do without her." Mary reached over and squeezed Alex's hand.

"I can't think of anywhere else I'd rather be." Alex looked over to Mary and smiled. It was the truth and she hoped it worked out so that she could stay.

"So, you're thinking you'll keep the ranch then?" Elina asked. Her tone was neutral.

Alex focused on her bowl of stew but listened attentively. It seemed too soon and too self-serving to ask Mary about the ranch. She wasn't even sure what all Mary knew of the arrangement with the Marshals Service. It wasn't anything they'd ever spoken of. Did Elina know that Hawk and Mick were marshals? How could she ask without giving too much away? Moments like this made it difficult to calmly maintain the status quo. Too many things were up in the air. She watched and waited to see which option Elina supported.

"I don't recall suggesting otherwise. This is my home. Why do you ask?" Mary slurped stew from her spoon.

"It's just a conversation. Honestly, I can't imagine you living anywhere else either. I only asked because this place is a lot to take care of and you're not getting any younger. Have you thought about bringing on additional help?" Elina asked.

"I'm not entirely sure it's needed right now. Mick and your grandfather weren't much more than porch ornaments for the last couple of years. Acreage aside, this isn't a big operation. We recognized when it was time to slow down and stopped running cattle and sheep years ago. Anymore, there's just a couple of horses and a dozen or so laying hens. The bison are easy keepers outside of the roundup, and surprise, surprise...here you are, suddenly with free time at the beginning of your busy season, all too eager to be that extra pair of hands." Mary set down her spoon and folded her hands over her bowl. She turned her head and locked eyes with Alex. "What do you think, Alexandria? Do you think we need any additional help?"

Alex felt like a deer caught in the headlights. Mary used her full first name. That was never a good sign. She was certain she'd back herself into a corner with any answer she might give, so she chose a half shrug and remained silent.

Mary sat back in her chair and stared at Elina. "Maybe it would make you feel better if you spent some of your vacation helping Alex with the chores. That way you can see what the workload is really like?"

"I'd be happy to. I meant it when I said I'd help with anything you needed." Elina held Mary's stare.

Alex wasn't sure what was going on between Mary and Elina; all she knew was that she couldn't look away.

"Uh-huh, and your sudden availability has absolutely nothing to do with the fact that just last week I spoke with Alex about working the roundup alongside her?"

*Oh, holy fuck.* Alex choked on her mouthful of stew. She grabbed her napkin and covered her mouth just in time.

Mary narrowed her eyes and looked from Alex to Elina. "I've been on this earth longer than the two of you added together. What makes you think you know better than me as to what I'm capable of? Neither of you seemed to mind when it was Hawk and Mick out there with Alex last year. Or is it that I'm the sweet little old grandma and roundup is man's work? I'd hate to think I have to fight gender norms with either of you."

"How about none of the above." Elina sat forward in her seat. "When's the last time you were on a horse, let alone working the roundup? I know it's been many years because you were in too much pain to ride. I wonder what your ortho surgeon would think of you up in the saddle with that shiny new hip? What happens if you're out there with the herd on the move and you fall off the horse? Maybe you pop that new hip out of its socket or worse, break the other one? Maybe you can't get out of the way of the herd. How do you think Alex would feel if something happened to you? Are you willing to put that weight on her shoulders?"

Mary slouched in her seat and folded her arms across her chest. "So, I'm just supposed to park my ass in the rocking chair and wait to die?"

Elina chuckled. "Hardly, Néiwóó, if you want to go for a ride, I'm all in. All that I ask is that your first time in the saddle since surgery isn't on the bison roundup. I'm here. Let me help."

"I know what you two did was out of concern for me, but don't for a moment think you've gotten away with anything." Mary pointed her knotted arthritic finger from Alex to Elina several times. "How long have you two been in cahoots anyway?"

"It was at Hawk's—"

"We exchanged numbers at Neibésiiwóó's celebration of life. Don't be mad at Alex. It was at my request. You can sometimes sugarcoat things and I needed to know you were okay."

"Well, it's high time you two find something else to talk about."

Alex looked over the top of her water glass at Elina and smiled. Mary certainly hadn't been the only topic; as a matter of fact, finding things to talk about wasn't an issue at all. The issue, as of late, was ending the call. Her feelings for Elina were growing so intense that it was becoming more and more difficult to say good-bye.

Mary turned to Alex. "Work her ass off, you hear me?" She turned back to Elina. "Didn't sugarcoat that at all, did I?"

"Still as sassy as ever I see." Elina smiled.

Time to change the subject. Alex looked over to Elina. "How are your folks doing? Mary mentioned something about your dad being on a trip to Europe?"

"Oh, David. That child of mine has been such a disappointment." Mary rolled her eyes.

"Yeah, Dad is still following trust fund Sophie around like a lost puppy. Last I heard they were in France. I swear she's at least ten years younger than me, but I can't get a straight answer out of him about her age. I have a gut feeling she'll be my stepmom by the time they come home. She has some kind of huge following on Instagram or something, claims to be an influencer, like that's really her job, though I've never seen her suggest a single product. Instead, she's always posting kissy lip selfies." Elina set down her spoon in her bowl and tilted her head with puckered lips while framing her chin with interlaced fingers greatly exaggerating the pose. "I don't get why people waste their time with that nonsense."

Alex laughed. The antics made her wonder what Elina was like with her close friends. Was she the popular one that everyone looked up to and wanted to emulate or was she the quiet one who sat back and absorbed everything? She imagined that Elina was a little bit of both.

"And your mom? Have you heard from her at all lately? You look more and more like her every time I see you, especially with your hair so long," Mary said.

"I think she's finally finding her balance. The divorce was hard on her. She's moved back onto the Wind River Reservation and works at the clinic. Says she can finally put that social services degree to use. She's getting involved with the ceremonies again too. She'll be participating in the hoop dance competitions coming up. I think she missed the customs. She sounds good." Elina sopped up the last of the stew from the bottom of her bowl with the bit of bread she had left. She popped it into her mouth and Alex tried not to stare when she licked a drop of stew from the tip of her ring finger.

Alex cleared her throat. "Where is the Wind River Reservation?"

"It's a little southeast of the Bridger-Teton National Forest in Wyoming. Two tribes, the Shoshone and the Arapaho, share the land."

"Which tribe does your mom belong to?"

"She's Arapaho. All of our ancestors on my mom's side are direct descendants."

"Yeah, I'm the odd one out." Mary smiled. "The drop of Irish gave David freckles and a bright red tint to his hair. The boys all teased him, but the girls just loved it."

"You mentioned that your mom moved back to the reservation. Was she raised there or did your dad live there too? Is that how they met? I hope you don't mind more questions. It's just that I'm curious. Like, what are the requirements?" Alex was fascinated with the culture but talking to Hawk about it had felt intrusive. They'd been close, but she'd always been closer to Mick, and he never talked about what he said was Hawk's business.

"I don't mind at all." Elina leaned back in her chair. "They met at college, not at Wind River. The reservations follow a blood quantum law. Some tribes require only one-sixteenth native American blood while others, like the Wind River Reservation, require fifty percent blood quantum to establish residence. Dad could have lived there, but he had no interest. I could live there too because my blood quantum is seventy-five percent, thanks to both my parents being indigenous."

"Interesting. What's the hoop dance?" Alex asked.

"It's a dance ritual performed with hoops made from willow. It's performed to heal the mind, body, and spirit. At least, that's what my mom taught me."

"Have you ever participated?" Alex asked.

"No, like I mentioned, Dad was always interested in a more modern life. Occasionally, when he was out of town, Mom and I would dress up in our ceremonial best and dance in the backyard. She'd teach me the songs and the steps. We'd use hula hoops. I'm glad she's reconnecting with the tribe. Someday I'd like to participate with her." Elina took a sip of water and looked over at Alex. "What about your mom? Are you in contact with her at all? I don't know that I ever knew what brought you here. All I remember is that it was the summer before I went to college and suddenly there was this twelve-year-old who followed me everywhere I went and asked a million and one questions."

Alex felt the heat in her cheeks and knew she was blushing with the embarrassment of being that twelve-year-old when she'd been forced to relocate. Her chest and throat tightened up slightly. She hated answering questions about her youth. She hated the made-up stories and the lies, but it was what she agreed to and it was what she had to do to stay safe. Though, as time went on, it was as if part of her life was being erased from existence and soon there'd be no one left who knew she was someone else before she became Alexandria Trenton. *Stick with the script.*

"She died in a botched robbery at the corner store where she worked, so I came out here to live with my dad." Alex learned over time that the carefully scripted statement that she was forced to memorize typically shut down the conversation and for that she was grateful.

"I'm so sorry. I didn't mean to pry."

"It was a long time ago." Alex stood to collect the empty bowls from the table.

Elina's expression showed the depth of her sincerity and that look of sadness mixed with concern was exactly why following the script always felt so wrong. She could kick herself for asking questions that would certainly encourage questions in return, but the truth of the matter was that it was nice to sit and visit with Elina. She enjoyed the chance to get to know her better. At least now they could focus on events after the age of twelve and she'd be able to share anything she wanted to. Well...almost anything.

## CHAPTER FOUR

Cleanup occurred quietly in the kitchen. Elina felt bad for bringing up Alex's mother, and she certainly hadn't meant to embarrass her about the summer she'd arrived. Back then, Alex had been a wiry little thing with teeth too big for her mouth and soulful brown eyes. Their age difference had made Elina feel like she had a tiny tagalong, but now it was hard to tell which one was older. Alex had certainly grown up. She had soft lines around her eyes and the warmest and most welcoming smile. She was almost a foot taller than Elina with broad shoulders and a lean body created by years of working on the ranch. Her light brown hair was kept short, and she could tell that Alex wore a hat much of the time by the fact that her arms were ten shades darker than her face and ears. One thing that hadn't changed was her eyes. They were definitely the window to her soul, still so expressive.

Once the leftovers were in the fridge, Elina washed while Alex dried and put the dishes away. It didn't escape her how well Alex knew where each item went and exactly how her grandmother liked her dishes stacked. The attentiveness to those details made her smile. Even after the first few hours with her grandmother, it was also quite obvious that Alex's presence was the only way that she could continue to live on this land. She was grateful to Alex for all that she'd done over the years to help her grandparents, and yet she couldn't help but wonder why she stuck around. The pay for being a ranch manager couldn't be that good, even with the private residence. Elina finished wiping down the countertop and the stove while Alex put the last few dishes away.

"Enough cleaning, you two. The rest can drip dry. Come join me on the back deck." Néiwóó peeked through the screen of the window above the kitchen sink.

"We'll be right out. We've just finished." Elina tapped her nose through the screen. She wiped her hands off and turned to Alex. "Lead the way."

Elina followed Alex through the house. She'd picked up on an earthy, woodsy scent in the kitchen whenever Alex stepped close to pull a dish from the strainer and caught another whiff of it as they walked toward the back door. She wasn't sure if it was Alex's soap or lotion or some kind of cologne, but whatever it was, she couldn't get enough and it suited Alex perfectly.

Hunter and Scout were sitting on either side of Néiwóó enjoying a good scratching behind their ears. Each dog sat there with half closed eyes leaning into the attention. Elina was surprised there wasn't a puddle of drool on the deck boards in front of them.

"Thank you, girls, for cleaning up and putting everything away. You certainly know how to spoil an old woman." She motioned to the two wooden chairs on her left. Two small rocks glasses sat on the small table between the chairs. "Nothing like a nip of Irish whiskey while watching the sun drop behind the mountains." She picked up her glass. "As my daddy used to say each night after dinner, Sláinte Mhaith. It means good health."

"I'll toast to that, Sláinte Mhaith." Alex held up her glass.

Elina held her glass in the air too. "Sláinte Mhaith." She took a sip of the whiskey and enjoyed the warmth as it slid down her throat. "So, is this what you two do nowadays? Sit on the deck after dinner and drink fine whiskey? I may never want to leave."

Alex pulled the glass away from her lips. "It's a rough life."

Elina looked over in time to see a confident smirk flash across Alex's face. It was a side of her that Elina was certain she'd enjoy getting to know better.

"I'll never tire of this view, and for the next couple of weeks I get to share it with two of my favorite people on this earth."

"Five square miles of paradise." Alex lifted her glass again and sipped.

She couldn't have said it more perfectly. Indeed, it was five square miles of paradise, slightly larger than the average Montana ranch and yet a tiny peninsula surrounded on three sides by one and a half million acres of Bitterroot National Forest. It was sandwiched between the Sapphire Mountain range to the east and the Bitterroot Mountain range to the west on the western edge of the state. It was, in her opinion, the most beautiful spot in all of Montana.

Elina looked past the deck, out to the foothills of the Bitterroot Mountains where the sun had all but disappeared behind the peaks. Several creeks and small rivers flowed across the acreage, some offering alternative water sources to the bison herd, while others flowed closer to the houses where she'd been permitted to explore and play when she was younger. If she sat still enough, she could still hear the water in the closer creeks babble over the rocks. That water had been cold enough to steal her breath when she'd first stepped in with bare feet and rolled-up pant legs. She'd quickly get used to it and spend hours trying to mimic the craftsmanship of the beaver, though her attempts at a dam never held up as well as the real thing.

The creeks that ran across the land merged far beyond the house and disappeared into a deep ravine on the mid-eastern side of the property where the water flowed on toward the larger Bitterroot River. She'd been warned as a child, time and again on each visit, about the strength of the water currents down in the ravine and how it could easily sweep her away before anyone would know she was gone. It was the one area on the ranch that she'd always been forbidden to explore.

"You seem like you're a million miles away, child. What's on your mind?"

Elina looked over to her grandmother and smiled. "I promise that I stayed within the five square miles of paradise and I didn't go near the ravine. I've been away for far too long. I'm reminded why this place is so special."

"Your grandfather always said this land was sacred." She reached over and squeezed her hand.

"I can see why he'd say that." Elina held her grandmother's hand and watched the last hint of the sun disappear behind the peaks of the Bitterroot Mountains.

The three of them sat there in silence while darkness consumed the landscape.

"Well, you two, I think this old woman should call it a day." She slowly pushed herself up out of the chair.

"Do you need help with anything?" Elina stood up.

"Thank you, dear, but I think I can manage to put myself to bed. How about you bring in the tray when you two have finished up?"

Elina nodded and bent down to kiss her grandmother on the cheek. "Good night, Néiwóó."

"Good night, Mary. Thank you for dinner. It was wonderful as usual, as was the company." Alex stood and hugged her.

"Good night, girls. Tomorrow's a brand-new day."

It was a phrase that Néiwóó had said at the end of the day for as long as she could remember. Elina watched her grandmother disappear into the house. The evening had certainly been one for the books. She'd never been called to the carpet quite like she had during dinner.

"You got in trouble." Alex leaned over her shoulder and sang softly into her ear.

"And you just sat over there quietly choking on your stew. Way to hang me out to dry." Elina laughed and turned to face Alex.

"Can't have Mary upset with both of us." Alex stepped back to avoid Elina's playful swat.

"I can't imagine her being upset with you about anything. You're her rock now and I'm grateful to you for that. So, where's that hug you've been promising me?"

"I wanted to when I saw you in the kitchen, but I didn't know if Mary knew we'd been talking."

"She knows now." Elina smiled.

She caught a whiff of that earthy, woodsy scent again and a swarm of butterflies stirred deep in her belly. She took the next step forward and wrapped her arms around Alex's shoulders. Her head fit perfectly against Alex's neck. Being wrapped up in Alex's arms was better than she imagined. All that was missing was a slow song to keep it from becoming an inappropriately long hug and then Alex stepped back, and it ended way too soon.

Elina walked over to the tray and lifted the whiskey bottle. "Care to join me for another?"

"Sure, twist my arm." Alex smiled.

She poured a generous portion into the two glasses. She handed one to Alex and walked over to the steps that led out to the yard. Elina sat down on the top step and smiled when Alex sat down next to her.

"Talking with you on the phone these last few months has been nice, but I like seeing you in person just a little bit more," Alex said.

"Oh, is that so, just a little bit more?" Elina leaned over and shoulder-bumped Alex.

"Okay, maybe more than a little bit." Alex looked over and smiled.

"I've been looking forward to seeing you in person too. You're taller than I remember. I like that." Elina twisted her body and leaned her back up against the handrail post. It might be a little too forward to drape her legs across the top of Alex's thighs, so she drew her knees up to her chest instead. "How is it that you're single?"

"Excuse me?"

"Come on. You wrangle livestock by day and do dishes after dinner. You're sweet, thoughtful, tall, and good-looking to boot. So how is it that you're single?"

"Well, I work on a thirty-two-hundred-acre bison ranch and up until recently, I shared a two-bedroom, one-bath cabin with my dad. Doesn't exactly make me the catch of the year. Besides, there's not a big 'woman seeking woman' population in Wolfbend, Montana."

Elina laughed and sipped her drink. "What I'm hearing you say is that you'll be single forever. Maybe you could find someone to use you for your hot body once in a while."

"Ouch, thanks for the encouragement." Alex twisted and leaned up against the handrail post on her side. She stretched her long legs out on the next step down and crossed her legs at her ankles. She looked relaxed and sexy at the same time. "I'd like to think there's someone out there for me. At least, I now have a home all to myself. Why are you single?"

"Because I choose to be." Elina winked and hoped she'd kept it light. She was too guarded to share anything more personal. *Because I'm broken.* That was the answer that popped into her mind first. Or how about because she was a little to self-absorbed and self-important. Both of those could work too. She had a long list of reasons why it was best to remain single. The one thing she couldn't figure out was why she was so drawn to Alex. Something about Alex was different. Something about Alex called to her, and now Alex sat across from her, staring at her. Elina needed to change the subject before Alex asked any more questions about that. "I feel so much guilt for not visiting more often."

"How long has it been since you were last here?" Alex asked. "I tried to figure it out but there wasn't any event like a birthday to associate with a specific year."

"Hmm, how long has it been? Shit, maybe five years or more. Far too long, that's for sure. Suddenly, calling every once in a while seems like it wasn't enough to really convey what they meant to me."

"Time has a way of slipping by, doesn't it? I bet he knew. Mary sure lit up when you called to say you were coming out."

"Thanks, that's kind of you to say."

"Does it feel weird to be back?" Alex asked.

How did it feel to be back? Weird was a good word. She'd been looking forward to a couple of weeks of distraction. She hoped it would quiet her mind and offer some direction. But then, that was the selfish answer, wasn't it? Her grandmother and Alex had both gone through a lot too and yet they somehow simply carried on. Why was she having such a difficult time letting the events of the last year go?

"Earth to Elina."

"What?" Elina looked up at Alex.

"What are you thinking about?"

"Nothing much." Elina brought her glass up to her lips and sipped. She enjoyed the warmth of the whiskey as it slid down her throat. "It does feel different being back."

"In what way?" Alex asked.

"In every way. Néiwóó's aged more than I expected. I can't help but wonder how much longer she can live alone. The empty placemat at dinner was weird. Neibésiiwóó's death has certainly left a big void for everyone, and I'm sure you're adjusting to your dad's diagnosis as well as his new living situation. That said, I really enjoyed having you at the table for dinner with us. It's like you're a part of the family, maybe more so than me, and then there's all of the sweet things you do for Néiwóó. She appreciates having you here. I can see it in how she looks at you."

"I can't remember a time when I didn't feel like I was part of the family. Well, except for when you visited. Dad said that Mary and Hawk deserved to have time with you and your folks, so he insisted that I stayed closer to our cabin. The loss has been an adjustment for all of us." Alex turned and looked out to the foothills. The tone of her voice was filled with sadness.

"My words were wrong. I'm sorry. I never meant to imply that you weren't—" Elina turned to face her. "I wish he hadn't kept you away when I visited. We could have gotten closer so much sooner."

"No harm. Back then you didn't appreciate having a scrawny tagalong. I get that." Alex stood up and set her glass on the tray. "I should go. It's getting late and you had a long day." Alex squeezed Elina's hand and let it go.

"You could stay longer, if you'd like." It wasn't exactly what Elina wanted to say but it was close enough. She wanted time to find the words and make things right.

"I've had a long day too. I'll see you tomorrow," Alex said. "Sweet dreams."

"What time should I report to work in the morning?"

"Come on down to the barn whenever you're ready. How about a ride? We can check out the herd and make a game plan to bring them in." Alex's eyes were illuminated by the soft glow of the lights from inside the house.

"I'll be there." Elina picked up her glass and added it to the others on the tray. "Sweet dreams."

She watched Alex until she disappeared into the darkness. She heard a car door and then the engine started. It made sense that she drove down. The ranch manager cabin was probably a mile or more away. It was much closer to the ravine and was included in the area that had been off limits to her in her youth. Now, she wondered what Alex's place looked like, what kind of vibe it held. Elina could kick herself for not being more careful with her words. Yet another reason why she wasn't in a relationship. Hurting Alex was the last thing she ever wanted to do. She'd apologize tomorrow. While keeping her grandmother away from the roundup was the primary reason for her visit, getting some face time with Alex was certainly an added bonus, and she didn't want to screw that up. Elina picked up the tray and made her way into the house.

## CHAPTER FIVE

Alex cued her horse, Dutch, through the main pasture gate and then cued him to sidestep so she could close and latch the gate while remaining perched up in the saddle. Elina was a few horse lengths ahead, twisted in her saddle, watching. She looked relaxed and at home on horseback. She always had.

"Looks like you and Dutch are quite bonded. He respects you."

She gave Dutch a soft nudge with her heels and was riding at Elina's side in just a few steps. She'd daydreamed about riding with Elina for as long as she could remember and now that it was actually happening, she was a bundle of nerves. She only hoped she didn't do anything stupid that would land her on the ground.

"Dutch is a good guy. Dad and I went to auction a few years ago. Maybe it's been more than a few, six or seven years I guess. Anyway, he was in a pen off all by himself and came right up to me. He'd pin his ears at most everyone else, but time and again, he walked right up to me and nickered like crazy. I'd been saving for a new truck, but he was worth delaying the purchase a bit." Alex smiled and patted the horse on the neck. "Now which horse is this? I remember mention of a Mustang Sally because that's just an awesome name for a horse, but I'm guessing that he isn't Sally."

Elina looked over and smiled. "All four of my horses are mustangs. This one is Radar. He's the leader of my little brood and my ride for all operations. He and the dogs work miracles together.

I'm not sure if he hears the dogs or the people the dogs are tracking, but if I watch his ears and let him have his head, we're likely to locate our subject."

Elina didn't talk about her work much, but she lit up when she talked about the skills of her dogs and horses. According to a few articles Alex found on the internet about her rescues, she was the expert they called in when the weather was bad, grounding helicopters, and time was of the essence. She and her brood, as she liked to call them, had an impressive track record of successful rescues. It was just another thing for Alex to admire about her.

They crossed a good-sized stream where the water was deep enough to tickle the horse's bellies.

"The bison herd should be just over the next hill. This time of day they like the shade provided by the tall trees down in the draw."

Elina tapped Alex's arm. "I'm sorry if I made things awkward last night."

Alex pulled gently on the reins until Dutch was standing still.

Elina stopped her horse right next to Alex. "I shouldn't have brought up your mom or that time in your life. I didn't mean to upset you. It bothered me all night."

"Don't worry about it. It wasn't that big of a deal." Alex's chest tightened all over again.

"The look on your face says otherwise. It's the same expression I saw at dinner and later on the deck. I didn't mean to be an insensitive ass. It's just a natural talent. Can you forgive me?"

Alex was quiet for a moment. She knew exactly what it was about the conversation last night that bothered her. Elina easily recalled the twelve-year-old who would have followed her to the ends of the earth. Why couldn't they have been closer to the same age? Was it weird to have a crush on someone six years older? She didn't think so. She knew couples with much greater age differences. The bigger question was why on earth was she encouraging anything between them at all? Her life wasn't conducive to a relationship. Who was she kidding, conducive or not, she'd always been captivated by Elina. Even as that goofy twelve-year-old, the spell had been cast and she was enamored. There was something about her that instantly put

Alex at ease, and back then, she craved all the comfort and ease she could find. Over the last month or so, Elina had been asking to know more than the fluffy surface stuff.

Alex looked off into the distance and then brought her eyes back to Elina's. "Will I always be that pesky twelve-year-old kid to you? Is that what you see when you look at me?"

"Is that what you think? No, that's not at all what I see. Please believe me." Elina reached for Alex's hand. "I want to know more about your life, that's all. Mick always seemed like the kind of guy who would be a lifetime bachelor, a little rough around the edges and content with his solitary life here on the ranch. I can't think of a time that I visited and he wasn't around, so I wondered how it was that you came into the picture. What can I say? You've captured my attention and now I want to know everything about you."

Usually, it was easy enough to live by her regular script, but at this very moment it felt like torture. Alex craved the ability to be one hundred percent honest. Elina wanted to know everything and what she wouldn't give to be able to share everything. Didn't everyone deserve someone who knew everything and cared anyway? *Stick with the script.*

"I guess even lifetime bachelors have needs." Alex shrugged. "My mom and dad were never married but he wasn't the kind to walk away from his responsibilities either. He was there when I needed him most."

The nice part was that most of it was true. Mick had been there. He and Hawk both had, but it was Mick who turned his bachelor world upside down and risked a lot to give her a home. For that, she was eternally grateful.

"Is there an airport close by?" Elina's words pulled Alex out of her thoughts.

"No, but I hear what you hear." Alex twisted around in her saddle looking in every direction. "It's reverberating. I can't make out which direction it's coming from."

"It sounds low, like when the choppers come into a canyon for a med flight evac." Elina looked around too. "I don't see anything overhead. It's too loud to be so high up that we can't see it."

The engine noise grew louder and louder and then, suddenly, a single prop plane shot out of a deep valley on their left. It was flying low in the sky, too low, as if it were trying to land. Dutch stomped his hooves on the ground and spun around in circles, on the edge of bolting. The engine noise bounced around the valley amplifying it to a deafening decibel. The plane flew directly above their heads and Alex was sure she could have touched a tire if she weren't so busy trying to stay in the saddle. The plane banked hard heading off toward the ravine, still flying far too low.

The horses were finally settling a bit with the reduction in engine noise. The plane banked left again in a deep, sweeping one-eighty beyond the treetops and disappeared over the ravine. Even though she'd lost sight of it, she knew exactly where it was because her phone blew up with warnings. Moments later, she saw it again flying low out by the back of the property where it bordered the National Forest. Just when she thought it was headed away, it turned sharply and dropped even lower, heading directly at them once again. *What in the hell?*

Alex lost sight of it behind the draw and then she saw the belly of the plane appear as it climbed up and banked hard to the left, disappearing into the same valley it shot out of only minutes ago. Before the sounds of the plane had a chance to dissipate, the ground rumbled out a warning of what was coming next.

"Stampede!" Alex pulled on Dutch's reins to turn him around. "Go, go, go, run with the herd, don't look back! Try to get to the outside and watch the horns!"

Alex was blown away by how fast Elina's little mustang could go. She gave Dutch his head and urged him to keep up. If they could keep this pace, they might just stay ahead of the charge. Elina's horse maintained a full gallop through the deep stream they'd just crossed. Water splashed all around her with each step the horse took. Alex nudged Dutch to follow, tapping her heels into his flank, but Dutch shied at the last moment and made a leap for it instead. His landing was off, and once again Alex tried to stay in the saddle. Dutch struggled to get his hind legs beneath him. There wasn't time to worry about the landing. She nudged him with her heels and hoped he could stay in front of the herd.

Dutch tried to bolt, but his right hind leg buckled the moment he put weight on it. She looked around for a tree or a rock outcropping to shield them from the onslaught but there wasn't anything close by, and in an instant, she knew it was already too late. Staying on Dutch's back was her best hope of surviving and hopefully he'd survive too. The herd was closing in quickly and moved like a murmuration of starlings, running shoulder to shoulder. Bison were surprisingly fast for being so big and burly. It would be elegant to watch if she wasn't about to be trampled to death.

Alex held Dutch's reins begging him to stay statue still, hoping and praying the herd would make room for the obstacle in their path. She could feel him stammering his front hooves trying to lunge forward without putting weight on the injured leg. She pulled back on the reins and did her best to reassure him. If he turned, even the slightest bit, Alex knew they'd likely be gored or knocked down and pummeled beneath all those hooves. Shit, both could happen even if he stayed statue still. *This is how I go out? How fucking embarrassing.* She braced herself for impact and silently hoped they wouldn't overtake Elina too.

She looked up to check on Elina's progress and couldn't believe her eyes. Radar slid to a stop and turned on a dime faster than any reining horse she'd ever seen. Before they were completely turned around, Elina tucked her legs in tight and leaned forward. That little mustang might as well have been launched out of a cannon. They were coming back. Why would she come back? It looked like Elina was coming for her, but that meant running head-on into the stampeding herd. *What on earth is she doing?*

Elina dropped the reins around the saddle horn and waved her arms around like a big crazy bird flapping for lift. Her horse stayed true, blasting at a full gallop toward a sea of hooked horns. She held her stirrups out wide, screaming at the top of her lungs. Alex looked behind her and once again couldn't believe her eyes. The stampede splintered just as they hit the far side of the stream and started to fan out to either side, avoiding her and the oncoming flapping monster that was Elina. Once the divide started, it continued and grew wider as it went deeper into the herd, like a great big zipper.

Elina tucked tightly into the saddle and shot by Alex and Dutch. Between Elina and the herd, water splashed in every direction. Alex twisted in her saddle to watch it all unfold. She could hardly believe what was happening. Elina fanned her arms out again, still screaming like crazy and maintained the line until the stampede was completely split in two. She lowered her arms and legs, spun Radar around, and galloped back across the stream to where Dutch and Alex were standing on the far side. Elina circled her horse around Dutch until the last of the bison herd made it through the stream. Up ahead, the herd was already starting to slow to a trot and spread out. It looked like the worst of it was over, and thanks to Elina, they'd all survived. She'd always dreamt of being Elina's knight in shining armor and instead the knight had been rescued by the beautiful princess. Elina slid down to the ground from Radar's back and ran up, touching Alex's leg in the stirrup.

"Alex, are you okay?" Elina ran in a circle around Dutch. "It doesn't look like either of you caught a horn. What happened?"

"That was unbelievable! I can't believe you did that. What were you thinking?" Alex slid down from Dutch's back. She pulled Elina into her arms and held her close. "Thank you. I thought we were done for."

"I looked back and saw Dutch buckle. I had to try something. It looked like you were about to be mowed over," Elina said into Alex's neck. "What happened?"

"We were right behind you and then he shied and jumped. The landing was bad. It's his right hind." Alex let go of Elina and turned her attention to Dutch. She prepared herself for the worst.

Dutch stood with the tip of his back hoof barely resting on the ground. Alex ran her hands up and down his leg. It didn't feel like anything was swelling and he didn't flinch at all. She tapped the side of his leg, and he lifted his hoof up for her to inspect it. Relief washed over her. No wonder he buckled. A fist-sized jagged rock was wedged between his shoe and the sole of his hoof. It would have been like running barefoot on a floor covered in Legos. She tried to free it with her fingers, but it was jammed in there too tightly.

Alex gently lowered his hoof and unbuckled the saddle bag. She dug beneath his halter and lead rope and found exactly what she was looking for. She'd learned long ago to never ride without a hoof pick. She tapped his leg again and he held his hoof up for her. She angled the metal hook under the rock and used his horseshoe for leverage. A little wiggling and prying from each side of the rock, and it finally popped free. Alex inspected his hoof for any visible injury. Everything looked good. She massaged his sole a bit and he didn't pull away. Another good sign. She lowered it to the ground to see if he could support his weight. He was tentative at first, but it looked like he'd be able to walk on it without a limp.

"I'm sure that hoof will be bruised. Hopefully, nothing that a little ice soak and rest won't cure." Alex looked over to Elina. Fear was subsiding to the anger bubbling up behind it. "What in the hell was that pilot thinking? That stunt could have killed us."

"Did you get a tail number? I only managed to get N72." Elina asked.

"You did better than me. Dutch is a good guy, but being chased by an airplane isn't anything I've ever worked with him on. He was rearing up, bunny hopping, spinning in circles. It was all I could do to hang on and keep him from totally bugging out." Alex took off her hat and ran her fingers through her hair. "It doesn't make any sense. Why was he skirting down in the valleys of the mountain range? It's a clear day, visibility for miles. I mean, he had to have seen us on that first pass, and then to loop back around like that?"

"It didn't sound like engine trouble. He had plenty of power to pull up out of the draw. It's like he caused the stampede on purpose, knowing we were in the path. Has anything like this happened before? Have there been any issues with the ranch?" Elina asked.

"No, nothing like this, ever. What issues could there be? It's a bison ranch and you can't build a better fence. Not to mention that we feed them so well that they don't even test the fencing."

"The pilot could have tipped his wings to hide the tail number and kept on cruising. It's the loop around that has me baffled." Elina walked over to Radar and checked each of his hooves too. "I tell ya, Radar and I have been in some dicey situations, but today takes the cake." Elina lowered the last hoof. "Somehow he managed to avoid the rocks."

"You two are amazing. Fucking fearless. I still can't believe you charged into the herd like that." Alex drew in a deep breath and let it out slowly.

"Like you wouldn't have done the same thing if the roles were reversed."

"I like to think I wouldn't hesitate, but I'm not so sure Dutch would have been on board. Your guy trusts you unconditionally. He didn't so much as flinch. Maybe ol' Dutch will trust me like that someday."

"Without a doubt he trusts you. He was lunging forward even with that rock wedged in his hoof, and he trusted you enough to stand still and ignore the commotion behind him. You two are bonded spirits."

Alex slid the headstall over the top of Dutch's ears and let him release the bit. She replaced it with his halter and clipped the lead rope below his chin. Her hands were shaking from the adrenaline surging in her veins. The thought of being on the ground so close to a rattled bison herd, especially when the females were notoriously protective of their calves, kept her on edge.

The bison herd wasn't the only thing that had her on edge. Despite the sanctuary cabin's empty status, Alex felt an urgent need to deal with the onslaught of alarms. She was pissed that she hadn't gotten the plane's tail number. If she wasn't so worried about Dutch's hoof, she'd hop up on his back and make her way to the back corner of the property immediately. The more difficult task was coming up with a plausible excuse to go over there alone. Elina couldn't know about her badge or the sanctuary, so many secrets and so many lies. The sanctuary had always been the real reason she'd disappeared whenever Elina's family visited. She and Mick worked the perimeter and ensured the secrecy of the sanctuary by guarding the witnesses protected there. Her mind drifted back to the conversation on the deck the night before. This was why she was single. There were too many secrets that had to be kept, and Elina was going to want to help if Alex had some kind of task to do. She had to think of something good. Luckily, she had a two-mile walk back to the barn to come up with something believable.

# CHAPTER SIX

The following morning, Elina sat on the back deck sipping a cup of hot tea thinking about the pilot's motive for flying so low in the valleys of the mountain range. She was kicking herself for not focusing on that tail number. She wanted to believe it was nothing more than a sightseeing trip with a pilot who thought it would be fun to run the herd, but her gut told her that wasn't at all the case.

No, that type of flying was typical of smugglers who were trying to avoid radar detection. Money and drugs were the likely cargo and remote areas like the national forest preserve offered the perfect routes. She'd seen it before, planes ducking for cover in the deep valleys of the Grand Tetons. It wasn't all that uncommon for the ceiling to drop quickly and blanket everything in dense cloud cover or fog. On a few occasions, low-flying planes were caught off guard by quick moving weather fronts, and rather than climb up and risk detection, they'd try to navigate in the low visibility. She never knew how many were caught in the clouds and made it out safely because she was only called in to track down the crash sites of the few that didn't, all in hopes of finding a survivor who could provide valuable information. Maybe her work was making her cynical.

Her thoughts drifted to Alex. Something other than the plane had her rattled. Her demeanor shifted significantly once they were back. It was as if she couldn't get away fast enough. Maybe she was the kind of person who processed things alone. Maybe she didn't want Elina to see her emotions. Some strong women didn't like to appear weak or vulnerable. Elina could certainly relate to that. Alex hadn't even come down for dinner last night. The one thing Elina couldn't figure out was what was so important on Alex's phone. She was so focused on it the entire walk back. She tried to be discreet about it, but Elina spent her entire career noticing the little things. She was probably reading too much into it. For some people, their phone was a calming habit.

She tried to convince herself that yesterday's events had been a freak incident. Alex assured her that there'd been no previous issues and she spent a lot of time out there inspecting fences and checking on the herd. Elina decided to go with the fluke theory for now but with an ever-watchful eye.

The back door opened behind her and pulled her from her thoughts. Her grandmother must have finished her phone call.

"Elina, sweetie, would you be terribly offended if I abandoned you and Alex this evening? You're welcome to anything in the pantry or kitchen."

"Abandoning us for a hot date?"

"Hardly." Néiwóó rolled her eyes. "There's a bridge tournament at the senior center. We planned it a few weeks ago. I'd forgotten all about it when you called about coming up, and with such short notice, they can't find a fourth for our table. None of us want to forfeit the entry fee. It was a little steeper than most because it includes dinner and a couple of drinks. You're welcome to come along."

"I've heard stories about your card games. A little too high stakes for my blood. Thanks, but yesterday was enough excitement to last for some time." Elina set down her tea and stood up.

"Are you still chewing on that?" Her grandmother stepped out the door and walked up to Elina. She wrapped warm fingers around Elina's hand. "I should cancel. You traveled so far to be here with me."

"No, don't cancel. I'm here for two weeks. Go and have some fun. Besides, I think I'm done mulling it over. I've decided to give it the benefit of the doubt and go with a fluke incident."

"I think that's a fine place to start. Sometimes, people just do reckless, stupid shit." She gave her hand a gentle squeeze.

Elina chuckled. She always enjoyed her grandmother's way with words. "I couldn't have said it any better. Would you like me to drive you to the senior center?"

"There you go again. I'm old, not incapable. I pass my driver's test with flying colors on each renewal, thank you very much." She held up her car keys and shook them.

"I meant no disrespect. Please tell your friends I said hello." Elina followed her grandmother through the house and into the garage.

"The senior center closes around ten so I should be home by eleven." She smiled and wiggled her eyebrows.

"Party animal. Please call if you get sauced and need a ride home. No questions asked." Elina bent down and gave her grandmother a hug.

"I remember saying that to you a time or two." Néiwóó dropped into the driver's seat and started the car. She blew Elina a kiss and backed her car out of the garage, swinging into the turnaround spot. She beeped the horn twice and waved before turning to head up the driveway.

Elina pressed the button to close the garage door and walked into the house. Her mind was spinning with possibilities. She walked around her grandparents' home, taking everything in, room by room. It still looked much as it had all her life with little additions here and there. His and hers rocking chairs handcrafted by Neibésiiwóó remained side by side in front of the old woodstove with the window in the door so they could watch the fire dance. The rockers were covered in cushions Néiwóó made with fabric that matched the sofa. They were constantly crafting this and thats. Their love for one another always on full display throughout the home. It was like a living canvas garnished with a lifetime of cherished memories. She yearned to share a life like this with someone she was as connected to as her grandparents were with each other. While she welcomed the unexpected evening alone with Alex, it felt like an invasion of their space to entertain inside.

She wanted a neutral space where she and Alex could relax from the intensity of yesterday and enjoy each other's company. The back deck might just be perfect. It had a variety of furniture, soft lighting, and the beautiful weather was supposed to hold until later that evening. Now, what to do for food. There wasn't much time before Alex made her way over. Elina opened the fridge in hopes of some fun options. The vegetable drawers were desperately sparce. Apparently, her grandmother used most everything up in the stew because carrots were about all that was left. Nothing much was popping out at her. Leftover stew and toasted homemade bread were looking like the best bet. She'd run into town tomorrow and pick up some groceries. It had been a while since she'd cooked a full meal and it sounded like fun. Elina scooped some stew into a small pot and set it on the stove. She could warm it up when Alex arrived. Okay, so now they wouldn't starve. Hopefully, she had enough time to get changed before Alex pulled in.

The doorbell rang. The sound of it surprised Elina. Her grandmother wouldn't have gone to play cards if she'd been expecting company. She walked out of the kitchen and through the foyer to the front door. There was a floral delivery truck in the driveway. Elina smiled. Had Alex sent her flowers? What a sweet gesture after disappearing all afternoon yesterday. She ran into her room and pulled a ten-dollar bill from her wallet for the tip and then ran back to the foyer and opened the front door.

The driver had the back doors of the van open. It seemed as if the person had a full load to sort through. How many deliveries were there in the middle of nowhere Montana? Finally, she pulled out a beautiful bouquet of flowers in a clear glass vase. The arrangement was a mixture of all of her favorite shades of purple. What a thoughtful surprise.

"Is this the Hawkins Ranch?" she asked.

"Indeed, it is," Elina said.

"This place is way the hell out here. I thought I'd never find it. Cell signal is sketchy and the map app wasn't guiding so good either."

"Where are you out of?"

"Connor, and it was still over an hour. Good thing I had a great playlist."

Elina looked down at the ten-dollar tip in her hand. She should really tip more. "Hang on. I'll be right back."

She ran back up the hall and exchanged the ten for a twenty. No matter who the flowers were for, the driver deserved a decent tip.

"Hopefully this helps offset the mapping issues." She handed her the twenty.

"Hey, thanks for that. I hope you enjoy the flowers. Have a great day." She handed Elina the bouquet and turned back to the van.

"Thank you, you too." She backed up into the foyer and closed the front door.

What a beautiful arrangement. She spun the vase around and spotted the tiny envelope she was searching for. There was no name on it other than Hawkins Ranch, Wolfbend, MT. She'd apologize to her grandmother if the bouquet was meant for her. She lifted the flap and pulled out the simple card. Three words were written on the front. *See you soon.*

"Most definitely." Elina smiled.

She tucked the card in the envelope and stuck it back into the holder within the bouquet. If they weren't from Alex, then maybe Néiwóó had a secret admirer. Still, the flowers smelled amazing. She inhaled the sweet fragrance once again and then forced herself to go change. If the flowers were from Alex, the least she could do was look nice for their unexpected evening alone. Maybe Alex already knew they'd have the evening alone.

Was this a date? It sure felt like a date. She had that tingling feeling like it was a date. But then again, if only one party knew about it, was it a date or did it lean more toward seduction? Given all of the flirting during their conversations, either one was a natural next step. What was the age difference before she was considered a cougar? Hopefully not six years. Maybe it would be best to call it dinner and not a date. She wasn't entirely sure what she was feeling for Alex. Was it real? It felt real. When it came to matters of the heart, everything became so jumbled and confusing, especially after that last job. It would be best to go slow and feel all of the feels.

Elina stood in front of the mirror. She looked like she was going out on a tracking call. Her hair was pulled back into a braid and her face lacked makeup of any kind. She was wearing her typical T-shirt and cargo pants. Nothing about her work was glamorous. She'd gotten into a habit of wearing clothes that could tolerate mud, pine sap, and burrs. Over the years, she'd fallen into a bit of a rut and didn't much care how she looked or who found her attractive, but at this very moment, she cared.

Once upon a time, with a little bit of effort, she could turn heads. She reached back and removed the hair tie and used her fingers to shake her hair free from the tight braid. She watched herself in the mirror and admired the nice wave that the braid left behind. It was time to let her hair down and feel beautiful again.

## CHAPTER SEVEN

The previous day's events had thrown Alex's entire schedule off. More than that, her spirit was thrown a bit off the rails too. At least Dutch's rock bruise gave her a plausible excuse to break away after the long walk back. Elina had offered to help, and she wanted so much to accept the offer, but the pilot's antics triggered alarms all around the sanctuary, and dealing with that was a job she had to tackle alone.

The surveillance cameras captured the plane's breach in the air space over the cabins. At least now she had a complete tail number for the report. Sadly, none of the cameras caught a clear image of the pilot. The thermal cameras were all aimed out at the foothills and the perimeter surrounding the cabins, and nothing was aimed up at the sky, so she had no idea how many souls were on board. The fact that the Cessna's rear cargo door was open hinted at more than just the pilot. At least she didn't see any parachutes on her cursory scans of the footage, but the cameras missed so much trying to track through the dense cover of the tree canopy. As a precautionary measure, she sent the dual sensor drone up and scanned the area for heat signatures and then made sure nothing about the sanctuary was visible from above. Thankfully, there were no heat signatures anywhere in the protected zone, and the towering pines and other trees still provided a perfect cover.

Candice's words echoed in her ears. *You have no backup.* She realized that Candice had a point about the limitations of a single deputy on the ranch. She'd gotten so confident, cocky really, over the last couple of years about how the technology was better than an entire team of agents that she'd lulled herself into a false sense of complacency. The tech was useful in that it provided her with tons of data for both real time pickups and "after the fact, lessons learned" briefing, but it would have done little to stop the advancement of a real breach. Her arrogance had left the sanctuary much more exposed than she cared to admit.

Candice was also right about having an armed agent or two monitoring the perimeter. Agents close by and at the ready would have been able to react much faster than the two hours it took her to simply get to her cabin and deal with the alarms. Double that time to inspect each of the cabins and then another couple of hours to review the footage for each area and the main fenced perimeter. Everything took so much longer than she had anticipated.

It was late in the afternoon after the breach before she was able to upload the video from a few different angles to the Billings office. She hoped the super geeks could work their magic and come up with something on the pilot. She filed the mandatory report and uploaded the drone footage, as well as the new camera footage of the drone in the sky, all as supporting documentation. She was tempted to omit how long everything had taken from the report but in the end decided to be bluntly honest with her findings. Take the lessons learned and figure out how to make it better. Those who stayed in the sanctuary deserved that much.

As Mary liked to say, today was a new day and she wasn't about to miss another dinner with Elina. Once again, she was running late thanks to a shower. She knew she'd catch all sorts of shit from Mary for making her wait to eat again, but she'd felt Elina snuggle into her neck and draw in a deep breath when they'd hugged the night before last. A little bit of torment from Mary about being late and looking nice was worth a repeat of that hug. She parked in her normal spot by the back deck and hopped out of the truck. She realized she was almost skipping across the yard. She forced herself to walk normally and bounded up the few steps to the deck.

Alex stopped just shy of the back door, distracted by the sound of jostled chains. She retreated a few steps and leaned to the right.

"It's just me. I didn't realize I was so well hidden."

Elina stood in the shadows of the covered nook. The swinging loveseat rocked back and forth behind her. She must have been sitting back there waiting for her to arrive.

Elina took two steps forward and the setting sun bathed her in a golden spotlight. The sight took Alex's breath away. She'd always wondered what Elina's dark brown hair would look like free from the thick braid. It was much longer than she'd imagined and it sprawled down over her shoulders in soft waves. She'd never seen hair so full and lush, silky, and oh so beautiful. Elina's eyes glistened and shimmered and sparkled, framed by full, thick eyelashes.

She wore a short sleeve white cotton blouse as an unbuttoned overshirt. The soft pink tank top beneath was tucked into a pair of jean shorts that hugged her hips and upper thighs perfectly. While similar to her typical wardrobe, it was put together so completely differently. Come to think of it, Alex wasn't sure she'd ever seen her in shorts. She was attractive no matter what she wore, but damn, who knew she had such an amazing figure? Seeing her standing there and smiling like that was a breathtaking vision captured in a matter of seconds. One that she was certain she'd remember for the rest of her life.

"Your hair. I like it like that. Look at you, you're so beautiful." Alex stepped closer and reached for Elina's hand.

"Thank you. You look pretty amazing yourself." Elina reached for Alex's free hand. "I thought we could eat out here tonight."

The coffee table in front of the swing was set for two. Covered crocks and spoons hinted at soup or stew. A plate between the two bowls was covered with a baking towel.

"Mary?"

"Ditched us for a bridge tournament at the senior center. I don't expect her back until ten or eleven." Elina smiled. "Care to join me?"

Alex waited for Elina to sit on the loveseat swing and then took the seat next to her. It was a cozy space. It offered a vast view of the pastures and yet was protected from the glare of the sun. Elina removed the cover from the small crock and offered the bowl to

Alex. She lifted the baking cloth and uncovered several slices of buttered bread. She offered the plate to Alex and then picked up one for herself and lifted her bowl into her lap.

"Hopefully, it's still warm. I wish I'd had time to cook something for you. Néiwóó's cupboards are a little sparce. I'll put together a list and head into town for some groceries tomorrow." Elina dipped her bread into the stew. "What are some of your favorites? I'd like to make you something that you'd enjoy."

What were some of her favorites? Food was the last thing on her mind with Elina sitting so close. Honestly, she was only eating because she wanted to get it over with. Holding Elina's hand was much better than holding this bowl. Alex chewed the mouthful of stew and swallowed. "I'll eat most anything. I'm not all that picky."

"That wasn't my question." Elina smiled. "You're such an enigma, Alex Trenton."

"I feel like I should be insulted by that statement." Alex set her half full bowl on the table and leaned back. "What is it about me that you find perplexing?"

"Not perplexing…mysterious." Elina set her bowl on the coffee table too.

She leaned back and crossed her legs beneath her and then twisted in the seat to face Alex. Her shin pressed against Alex's thigh. Was her skin as silky as it looked? What she wouldn't give to find out.

"For all the conversations we've had these past few months, it occurred to me how little I really know about you. You have this way of getting me to do all the talking. I don't know what your dreams are or what you want out of life. I don't know your favorite color or your favorite food. Like, what do you drink besides Irish whiskey? What do you drink in your coffee? Do you even drink coffee or are you more of a can of Red Bull on the go kinda gal?"

Alex was still stuck on the first question in the series. She had dreams, didn't she? What were her goals? It was hard to answer a question that she'd never really asked herself. Candice had asked her similar questions the last time she was out. Was she supposed to want something more? She'd like something more with Elina, but was that even possible? Hawk had the same job and he got to enjoy a lifetime with Mary. Had Mary been privy to his secrets? Why hadn't Alex asked him about any of this when he was still alive? Who could she ask now? Candice? Maybe, but now that she had her badge, conversations like that felt like they would be crossing a professional boundary. She tapped her thumb against her thigh. She dreamed about someone knowing her, really knowing who she was, and she wanted Elina to be that someone.

"I like to listen." Alex could no longer resist temptation. She moved her hand off her own thigh and caressed the inside of Elina's bent knee. Her skin was warm and every bit as silky as she imagined. Why was Elina so irresistible? "My favorite color is midnight blue, ya know, the crayon color. It's the same color as a brand-new pair of jeans. I do drink coffee in the morning. I can drink it black if I must, but it's best with a splash of heavy cream and a touch of sugar. My buddy, Trapper, calls it sissy coffee. I've never tried Red Bull and wine is okay with some meals, but it isn't really my thing. I enjoy a nice sippin' whiskey or a cold beer. My favorite food is anything cooked by someone else, and if I go out, I enjoy Indian food. Spicy curry chicken and naan bread. I can cook. I grill a mean steak but it's a lot of effort if it's just me. I think that covers your questions."

"For now, anyways." Elina's smile made all the answers worth the effort.

"Now, there's something I'd like to ask you."

"Anything."

"What do you call the color of your eyes? I'm pretty sure that coppery bronze isn't technically accurate."

"Amber." Elina leaned closer and held her eyes open.

"Amber." Alex stared into Elina's eyes.

"Is that all you wanted to know about me?" Elina quirked one eyebrow.

Alex chuckled. She had thousands of questions, but at the moment, all she could focus on was how silky Elina's skin was. "I enjoy listening, remember. How's this? Your favorite color is purple. Not any shade will do, though. You used to listen to Prince as a kid and your favorite album was *Purple Rain* mostly because his outfit and the motorcycle on the album cover were the perfect shade of purple. You'll drink coffee but prefer tea. Cherry rooibos tea blended with a black tea is your absolute favorite. As far as alcohol goes, you're not picky. You enjoy wine, red more than white, but could just as easily enjoy an ice-cold beer. If it's a sipper, then your grandma Mary's influence shines and it's a top shelf Irish whiskey like we had last night. You love to cook and enjoy intricate recipes. Indian, Italian, Mediterranean, Mexican, American, and most any Native American cuisine. The more complicated the recipe is, the more your voice lights up when you talk about it. And I bet they all taste amazing. I look forward to trying anything you choose." Alex was rewarded with smiling amber eyes. "Shall I continue?"

Elina shook her head and leaned in closer and closer until Alex could no longer focus on her features. She let her eyes close and relished in the way Elina's hot breath felt against her cheek. Alex felt a warm hand cup her cheek and then Elina's lips delicately pressed against hers. Her breath caught. She lifted her arm that was up against the back of the seat and traced her fingertips up Elina's arm, over her shoulder and around the back of her neck and then she buried her fingers into soft, silky hair. She turned in her seat and wrapped her other arm around Elina's waist. Her lips parted and Elina rewarded her with the teasing tip of her tongue. When she nibbled delicately on Alex's bottom lip, it sent shivers up and down her spine. The moment, the kiss, was better than she'd ever dreamt it could be. The best really. The kiss intensified from gentle tenderness to passionate desire. Elina's hand brushed the side of her breast and then wrapped around her back and pulled her in closer. Alex's entire body buzzed and buzzed and buzzed—

And then the perimeter alarm sounded.

## CHAPTER EIGHT

A lex pulled back and stood up so fast that Elina had to catch herself to keep from falling forward into the now empty seat. Her heart was pounding wildly in her chest. That was one amazing first kiss, and she wasn't ready for it to end, not even close.

"Shit, I'm sorry. I've gotta go." Alex stepped around the coffee table and ran across the deck.

"What is it? What's wrong?" Elina jumped up and ran after her. "Can I help?"

"No, you can't be involved. Stay here, please."

Elina stopped at the top step. Alex was already in the truck. She pulled the driver's door closed and the engine roared to life. "Alex, wait, talk to me. What's going on?"

Without a word, Alex hit the gas and took off down the lane toward the ravine. Thoroughly confused, Elina stared at the plume of dust that billowed out from behind her truck. It sure seemed like Alex was enjoying the kiss as much as she was, well, at least until that damned alarm sounded. It was the same ringtone that kept going off yesterday on the walk back. Alex had checked her phone and disappeared then too. What was going on back there that demanded that kind of response? As far as she knew, the only thing in that corner of the property was the ranch manager's cabin and the ravine. Was there someone else back there? Trust didn't come easily for Elina, and she really thought that Alex could be one who was trustworthy. She'd just gotten her feet on semi-solid ground after falling down a dark hole. She'd been fooled into thinking she could trust back then, too. She wasn't going through that again. No way.

Elina ran into the house. She traded her shorts and white blouse for a pair of camo cargo pants and a long sleeve camo shirt. It was time for a little covert fact-finding mission. She pulled her hair back into a ponytail and snagged her truck keys and a pair of socks. Something was going on and she was going to get to the bottom of it. This woman was in her grandmother's house every day. If something was off about her, then she was damn well going to find out before things went any further between them, and before her grandmother got caught in some kind of crossfire. She wouldn't be caught off guard again.

Everything she needed was in her truck. She sat in the passenger seat and slid on her socks and then her lightweight work boots. Her backpack was stashed behind the seat and always at a ready to go status. She slid her arms into the shoulder straps and fastened the waist belt. Finally, she grabbed the dogs' vests and their leashes. Vacation or not, it was time to go to work.

The tire tracks that she'd followed from Alex's parking spot down the two-track road led to what she assumed was Alex's cabin. The truck was parked cockeyed in the driveway and the shotgun was missing from the gun rack in the back window. Elina had never seen this side of the property. It was completely different from the vast prairie land that they rode through the day before. She'd seen the treetops in the distance but had no idea it was so lush and dense with vegetation.

Elina knocked on Alex's cabin door. No answer. She turned the doorknob, but it was locked. She tried to peek into the windows, but the curtains were drawn, which seemed odd since her grandmother was her closest neighbor. She would have picked the lock and taken a look around if she hadn't been so intent on finding out where Alex was. She walked over to a large pole shed that was about twenty feet or so from the cabin. The small door as well as the large sliding doors were locked on this building too. Now, she was even more curious to know what was going on out here.

She returned to the driver's door of the truck. Alex had a unique stride and wore the heels of her boots unevenly. She dragged the left heel in the dirt for about an inch before landing her step, except when she ran. Elina was trained to notice these things. The first few steps out of the driver's door included the heel drag and then after that, Alex's stride changed to a full run. Elina followed her tracks for half a mile or so where it looked as if Alex ran right through a six-foot-tall fence. It surprised Elina to see a boot mark directly beneath the fencing. She walked from post to post and noticed that the fence left scrape marks in an arc pattern where the ground was mounded a bit too high. Somehow this section was a gate. There were small, fine wires running horizontal to the ground along every other row of diamonds in the fence. She'd seen this before and all of it was far too high tech for common livestock fencing. So much for simply climbing over. She looked beyond the fence and Alex was nowhere in sight. Now, how to get in without sounding an alarm and what on earth was she hiding inside? Suspicion built as to who Alex was and what she was into.

She followed the fence deeper into the dense vegetation until she came across a tight cluster of trees, one of which might just get her and the boys inside. She dropped her pack and pulled out three coils of rope. She clipped one end of each of the ropes to her belt. The other end of two of the ropes were clipped to the back of each of the dog's vests and then she clipped the last rope, which was knotted, to her pack.

Elina was able to use the nubs of broken branches to get up into the tree. Once she was perched solidly on the limb over the fence she motioned to Scout. He ran at the tree and jumped up. Elina kept the rope tight that was linked to the d-ring loop on his back. She heaved him up and pulled him above the top of the fence and then leaned forward and lowered him safely on the other side. She gave him the hand signal to stay and then disconnected his rope from her belt and dropped it next to him. She repeated the process with Hunter and then pulled up her pack. She released the clip from her belt and wrapped it around the stout tree limb. She tossed her pack, with the other end of the rope still attached, over the side with the dogs and then climbed up beyond the rope and carefully descended a few knots until it was safe to drop. She returned everything except the knotted rope to her pack and hoisted it up on her back. If worse came to worst, she'd have a way out.

She worked her way back to the small trail. Alex's footprints disappeared into the underbrush. Not sure what was out there, she kept the dogs on a short leash and gave a hand signal to track Alex's scent. Noses on the ground and in the air, they went to work. She spotted another fence with a heavier gauge of wire. It had the fine tracer wire weaved in it just like the last fence. This one ran for about three hundred feet or so and then turned ninety degrees and went on deeper into the woods. The dogs stayed on scent and passed the turn. What was this place?

Another half mile or so and then another fence appeared. Same gauge as the last run and once again, about three hundred feet in length. This time the dogs followed the scent around the corner deeper into the thick underbrush. Suddenly, the dogs stopped and lay down. Someone was approaching. While she still had time, she released the leashes and sent Scout off with hand signals to find and protect the scent, which was Alex. She gave Hunter a hand signal to give her space but be on the ready. He disappeared quietly into the underbrush. It still amazed her how talented her two dogs were. Elina stuffed the leashes into her pocket and remained crouched down out of sight.

A twig snapped close by. She didn't recognize the boots coming up along the back of the fence line. The leather was ripped in several places and partially held together with dirty, tattered duct tape. It definitely wasn't Alex.

"Like looking for a needle in a haystack. You got anything yet, Joe?"

"No, nothing yet. Hey—"

"Freeze. Show me your hands." Alex's distant voice came through the two-way radio.

Was Alex security for whatever this was? What was going on? At least she could assume that the man close by was an intruder and not a patrol guard working for Alex. Elina switched gears from investigation to apprehension.

"Joe, come in? Did you get away?" Duct tape man whispered into a two-way radio.

Static laden silence.

"Joe, goddamn it." He tapped the radio against his hand a few times. "Joe?"

The sound of a distant gunshot stopped him in his tracks. The two-way radio crackled and then snarling sounded through the speaker and an ear-piercing scream shot out of the tiny radio. The man turned away from Elina. She could see a handgun stuffed in the back of his jeans. His arm began to swing around the side as if he was reaching for the grip. She hoped Hunter was close.

"Look out! Grizzly!" Elina screamed.

The man spun around. Hunter shot out of the underbrush and latched onto his forearm just below the elbow. The man cried out. Hunter kept chomping down and thrashing his body. It gave Elina enough time to dart out of the underbrush and secure the pistol from his waistband. She backed up, quickly checked for a round in the chamber, and flipped off the safety. The man screamed and fell on his knees. Hunter twisted his body and whipped around, his jaw latched securely on the man's arm. He fell to the ground, flat on his back. Hunter released his arm and lunged for his throat. Ears pinned back, he stood on the ground next to the target, jaw wide open and teeth grazing the skin on the man's neck.

"Don't move a muscle. He's all too eager to give you a new airway." Elina stood more than an arm's length off to the side and aimed the pistol at his forehead.

"Please, no more biting. I won't move."

"If you do, you'll regret it for the last five seconds of your life." Elina unzipped the side of her pack with her free hand and pulled out a handful of zip ties. She signaled to Hunter. He lifted his head away from the man's neck, though he continued the deep growl and curled his lips to reveal a mouth full of teeth. He was one intimidating beast.

"Slowly roll over on your stomach and then rise up on your knees." Elina stayed back, well out of reach. "Now, cross your feet at your ankles and put your hands behind your back. Lace your fingers together." Elina put the safety on the gun and tucked it into her belt. She snugged up a zip tie around each wrist and then zip-tied his wrists together.

Alex came around the corner at a full run and made her way up the fence line. She had the shotgun slung over her shoulder and a pistol in her hands trained on the kneeling man. The way she carried herself was not that of a ranch hand. She'd had training of some kind. Her stance was spot-on, and her eyes darted around to take in the entire situation. Damn, she looked hot in a badass kind of way and then she looked directly at Elina. Her eyebrows furrowed and jaw clenched. Now, she just looked pissed.

"His radio and weapon." She offered the handgun to Alex. "The safety is on."

"Keep it for now. Walk with me." Alex looked down at the zip ties and then looked up at Elina. She shook her head. A faint smile touched her lips. At least that was something. "Up you go." Alex cupped her arm under the man's armpit to steady him while he got to his feet.

"That dog mauled me. I need to see a doctor."

"All in good time. Come on now, walk." Alex nudged him forward.

Elina followed Alex and the target around the fence into a more open area. They walked up a wide path covered by treetops for a mile or so, when they came upon another man with his arms cuffed around the trunk of a small tree. Scout sat in front of him growling. Alex cuffed Elina's target with one side of a pair of cuffs and cut the zip ties from his wrists. She grabbed his free hand and handcuffed him around another small tree.

"Would either of you like to tell me what you're doing out here?" Alex looked from one intruder to the other.

"I'll sue your ass for letting that dog attack me," the man who Alex apprehended said. Elina assumed he was Joe. "I ain't saying shit without a lawyer."

"Just call the sheriff and let us get on with our day."

"Shut the fuck up, dimwit," Joe said over his shoulder.

"Fine, if that's the way you want to play it. Not one word from either of you." Alex stepped out of sight of the two men. She looked over at Elina and then down to Hunter and over to the man she'd just cuffed to the tree.

Elina nodded. She signaled to Hunter to sit at the ready in front of her capture. The man whimpered when the dog sat directly in front of the crotch of his pants. Alex pulled out her phone and moved a few feet away. So many questions swirled around in Elina's mind. What was this place and how was Alex involved? How long had it existed? Did her grandparents know about it? This had to be on the Hawkins' land because the ravine was still to the east. She had a litany of questions to ask when the time was right. Right now, she had to display a united front and a commanding presence. It was what she was trained to do. A tap on her shoulder pulled her from her thoughts. Alex motioned her away from the captured men.

"I know you have questions. I'll figure out what I can and can't share." Alex looked down at the ground and then, slowly, brought her gaze back to Elina's eyes. "If you want to be left out of this, now is your one and only chance. You'll need to backtrack and pull the knotted blue rope that you left in the tree. My only ask is that you leave Scout with me, so I can explain the bite marks."

"I steered clear of all pressure sensors on the fence. How do you know where I crossed and that I used a knotted blue rope?" Elina was impressed.

She usually spotted cameras before anyone else. Whoever designed the security for this area had skills. Whatever this was, Alex was a key player with much more tech than what was visible. She hoped like crazy that Alex wasn't doing anything to put the ranch at risk.

"Did they teach you about pressure sensors and intrusion detection systems in search and rescue training?" Alex asked in a hushed whisper.

"Who said I've only ever been to SAR training?" It wasn't really an answer.

"Now who's the enigma? What do you *really* do for a living? Is it routine to carry heavy-duty zip ties in your go bag? What about the dogs' vests? Since when did tactical military grade vests replace the simple blaze orange SAR tracking harness? I'm guessing you swap patches depending on the job. Scout took that guy down and disarmed him better than any SOG dog I've seen—he's efficient as hell and not one command was needed from me. Gauging by the other guy's arm, I'd say Hunter is every bit as effective."

"Not one command from you was *needed*. Scout did exactly what I asked him to do." Elina held Alex's stare.

SOG dog. Only one agency used that term. Alex had tipped her hand, but was it on purpose? It didn't seem like it was. Either way, it gave her a little peace of mind. Elina removed her pack and set it down next to a log. Alex had secrets, that was for sure, hell, so did she, but it seemed Alex was on the right side of the law and that made a world of difference. "When you call it in, please use my full name and include each of the dogs' names after my last name."

"What? Where are you going?"

"I'm going to get my rope. I'm staying."

## CHAPTER NINE

The team, dispatched from Missoula, came in nice and quiet, exactly as Alex requested. No dust plumes, no helicopters, no badges, or jackets identifying the agency. The two intruders were secured in a caged back seat of the Suburban. The quads that they used to access the back of the property were loaded in an enclosed toy hauler. She'd love nothing more than to get back to her evening with Elina. Hell, she'd love nothing more than to get back to that amazing kiss, but somehow, she knew that moment had passed.

"We're all set. We were instructed that a second team was dispatched for the third intruder."

"If I'd known, I would have called off the second team. She's not an intruder," Alex said.

"A breach is a breach. They'll have to take her in." The driver closed his door.

Elina looked up from the log she was sitting on and smiled as if she were the proverbial cat that ate the canary. It was a bit unnerving. What did she know that Alex didn't? Hunter and Scout sat quietly on either side of her. Alex was glad she'd been able to convince the first set of agents that cuffs were unnecessary. She feared for the safety of anyone who tried to handcuff Elina in front of those dogs.

Alex checked the cameras and the sensors. All was clear. She opened the back gate and motioned the SUV out, toy hauler and all. A tall shelf of dark gray clouds was rolling in. There was supposed to be a heavy rain tonight. It would help hide the tire marks in the dirt and any evidence that the two men were ever there. She wanted the team on a main road and out of the area before anyone reported them missing.

"I wish you hadn't followed me. Things are already complicated enough for me ever since…shit, and now I've got to explain your presence. Are you always so impulsive and headstrong? You had no idea what you might be walking into, and you weren't even armed." Alex stood with her back to Elina.

"I'm sorry if I put you in a bad position. I know you asked me to stay put, but really, how could I not follow you tonight? Especially after you disappeared all afternoon yesterday. Your phone chirps and then you bolt. It was suspicious as hell."

"Past tense? You're no longer suspicious?" Alex turned to face Elina.

"Oh, I still have plenty of questions when you're ready to be honest with me."

"Ditto." Alex folded her arms across her chest. "Do you want me to come with you when they take you in?"

"I doubt I'll be taken in. Let's see what plays out." Elina stood and brushed off her pants.

"Can you tell me who you work for?" Alex asked and then her phone buzzed in her hands. It was becoming a constant interruption. "God damnit!"

*Approaching gate one.*

*Passcode?*

*It's time for a stiff drink.*

Yup, at this point she'd welcome several stiff drinks. She checked the cameras and then opened the back gate. The SUV used for pickups crossed through the gate and approached slowly in the waning light, same canoes, same bumper sticker. She closed the gate. Her heart sank with the prompt arrival. She was hoping for five minutes alone with Elina. She wanted to talk. She wanted to ask questions. She wanted to explain something, anything, well, everything really. It was probably best that the team arrived before she betrayed her oath.

Standard operations called for at least two agents on any apprehension. Alex was confused to see the outline of a single shadow in the SUV. What was going on? The vehicle pulled in behind the tree line and parked. The driver's door opened. Scout and Hunter stood, tails wagging like crazy and then darted toward the driver. *What the fuck?* Elina turned and smiled that broad, welcoming smile that Alex had started to crave more and more as time had gone on, except this time the smile wasn't for her. It was for the driver of the Suburban. Alex walked around the side of the vehicle to get a better look. She wanted to know who she should hate for the rest of her life.

She stopped cold in her tracks. "Candice?" She turned to Elina. "How do you know my Candice?"

"Your Candice? Huh." Elina quirked her eyebrow and smiled. "I guess you'll have to share."

Not the reaction Alex expected. She felt sideswiped.

Candice bent down and scratched each dog on the head. "I've missed you two and your mama."

"Excuse me?" Alex wasn't accustomed to feeling jealous or protective, but at the moment, both feelings were running wild. Candice was her friend, her rock, and the last remaining link to her past, and here she was talking about missing Elina and the dogs? The dogs ran right up to her. Had they dated? Were they once a couple? Is that why she'd missed them? *Don't jump to conclusions.* She had to get a grip.

"Are you ever a welcome sight. I wasn't sure who'd be sent out. I'm glad it's you." Elina took a step toward Candice and gave her a brief hug. "The last team wanted to cuff me."

"Will one of you please tell me what in the fuck is going on?" Alex looked from Candice to Elina. She was five seconds away from blowing a gasket and had never felt so invisible.

"Not out here. The rain's not far off and it's going to be a doozy." Candice turned to Alex. "Do any of the cabins have a place to hide my truck?"

"Cabins? What cabins? What is this place?" Elina spun around in a circle. "I have so many questions. For starters, does Néiwóó— Shit, Néiwóó. She could be home any moment. Alex, our dinner is still sitting on the back deck. She'll be worried sick if she finds that mess and us missing."

Concern for Mary calmed Alex's emotions instantly. "Let's put the Suburban in the pole shed at my place. Candice, would you wait there while Elina and I run up to the main house, clean things up, and touch base with Mary? We won't be long and then we can all talk. Does that work?"

Candice nodded and opened the back door of the Suburban. Elina made some sort of hand signal and both dogs jumped up into the back seat. She tossed her pack in, climbed in next to the dogs and pulled the back door closed. No need to call shotgun. Alex climbed into the front seat next to Candice.

"Candice, is this truck secure?" Elina asked from the back seat.

"Yes."

"Alex, are you a US marshal?"

Alex looked over to Candice for some guidance. She nodded once and Alex breathed a sigh of relief.

"Yes, I am," Alex said. Three words had never felt so freeing.

"Does Néiwóó know about you, about this place back here? Did Neibésiiwóó?"

Alex caught Candice's quizzical look. "Mary and Hawk." So, maybe Candice and Elina weren't so close after all. It made her feel marginally better.

"She's been thoroughly vetted. Probably has a higher security clearance than either one of us. You can answer those specific questions," Candice said to Alex.

Alex twisted in her seat so she could look into Elina's eyes. She hoped like hell she'd say this correctly. "'Ine hee'ino' yonootiinoo niiteco'onhonoyeit."

Elina smiled and nodded. "Impressive."

"Translation, please?" Candice looked across the seat.

"She said, and I quote, 'Yes, he knew about it. I am hiding it. I am always on the lookout.' Her pronunciation was perfect." Elina rested her hand on Alex's shoulder. "Did you pretend to not know about the Arapaho culture at dinner the other night?"

"The questions I asked were genuine. There's always plenty more to learn."

"You spent a lot of time with him, didn't you?"

Alex nodded, suddenly unable to speak because of the emotion that bubbled up. She'd been able to share a bit of her truth. She could admit how close she'd been with Hawk and their common interest to protect the sanctuary. Rain began to splash on the windshield. It was fitting, almost cleansing. She reached up with her free hand and covered Elina's.

"You mentioned cabins. What are you hiding and protecting back here?" Elina asked.

Alex wanted to answer. She wanted to blurt out all of her secrets, but she knew better. She was not authorized to say a word and to do so in front of a superior would certainly terminate her position at this post. She wasn't even sure Candice could or would answer.

"What I'm about to share with you is classified top secret. I received prior authorization to read you in when your name popped in the system," Candice said.

Alex held her breath in anticipation. Was Elina really going to be read in? Could she be the person who not only knew about her badge, but also the work that really happened on the ranch? Was this really happening?

"It was your grandfather's vision and now it's his legacy. It was the first of its kind. Alex took over operations and security years ago. We call it the secret sanctuary. It's where the US marshals hide the most at-risk witnesses while waiting for a trial to start. Once they leave here and testify, they earn a new identity and a new beginning."

"So, Neibésiiwóó carried a badge too? He was a US marshal?" Elina asked.

Candice stopped the truck and twisted in her seat. "He and Mick were both marshals."

"Why wouldn't he ever tell me he was a marshal?"

"He didn't tell you for the same reasons that Alex couldn't tell you. He wasn't authorized to tell you or anyone else about his badge or this place. To the best of my knowledge, your parents don't know either. Hawkins Ranch raises bison, period."

"I've known you all these years and you never looped me in? You know me. You know my security clearance."

Alex listened to Elina's words and tried to ignore the pangs of jealously that crept up all over again. How many years had they known each other? How did they know each other?

"Elina, stop. This is a dark site and I know you know what that means. It's strictly need to know, and until you jumped that fence, you didn't have a need to know. You're only being looped in now because of your security clearance and your relationship with the USMS. No one, not even local law enforcement, can know this site exists or we might as well shut it down." Candice turned around and dropped the truck into gear.

Alex spun around in her seat and looked at Elina. "Do you work for USMS?"

"No, I—"

"Is there a secret phrase when we reach this fence?" Candice asked.

Alex turned back to face the front of the vehicle. "Let's hope this is a one and done." She launched the app on her phone and opened the gate. "Before we drop this beast in my pole shed, is there anything in here that identifies USMS? Who's it registered to? Any badges, jackets, weapons?" Alex asked.

"The Suburban is registered to Hawkins Ranch, LLC. Insured that way too. I, however, came right from the office and have my badge, security ID and service weapon. I'll need a place to stash those. I do have my alias with me, so I guess Aunt Candice is here for a visit."

"Aunt Candice, do you have any idea who's behind the breach today? Or the flight yesterday?" Elina asked. "They can't be unrelated."

"To be clear, I'm Alex's aunt, not yours, sweetheart." Candice twisted in her seat and smiled at Elina.

"Can we get back to the breach, the plane?" Alex made every effort to conceal her annoyance, but the look on Candice's face told her that she'd failed miserably.

"They're still peeling back the layers, but the plane is owned by a series of nested shell companies. Our people are digging into it. We're hoping to learn more when we interrogate the two guys captured today. Honestly, I'm still trying to come up to speed. I wasn't pulled in until Elina's code name threw an alert in the system."

"Code name?" Alex had called it in herself. She hadn't used a code name. "Shit, of course, that's why you asked me to mention the dogs. I should have known."

"Elina, I know you're taking a break, but USMS would like to contract your services until this is resolved," Candice said.

"No need. I'll do it for free, and quite frankly, I'll have more freedom if I'm not contracted."

"Contracted? More freedom? What exactly do you do?" Alex twisted in her seat and looked at Elina.

"Noowuho' nootikoninoo heniinoo'eihiininoo."

"English version, please?" Candice looked at Alex.

"She tracks people. She scouts for enemies. She's a hunter."

"That's a bit of an understatement. Elina, it's not negotiable. I need you contracted so I can read you in on the case. Besides, you need to color inside the lines on this one. Deputy director's orders."

"Who *are* you?" Alex looked over her shoulder.

Elina grimaced and shrugged.

"Candice, pull over, there, on the left." Alex had had enough. She needed out of the car.

She opened the door before the truck completely stopped. Her head was spinning. Had Candice really called Elina her sweetheart? She knew so few people, so how was it that two of her favorites not only secretly knew each other, but somehow had history? Alex unlocked the large sliding door. Her mind was still spinning out of control. For a brief moment, she thought that most of the secrets had been shared and then to find out that Elina was what, a sanctioned killer? Who claimed to be a hunter...of people? She pushed the large sliding door open with so much force it almost popped off the upper track. She should have known that a life lived in secret could only include those who also lived with secrets. The bigger question was, who could she trust?

# CHAPTER TEN

Rain fell from the sky in big, assaulting drops. Elina was soaked to the skin in the short run from the pole shed to Alex's truck. She hopped inside and waited while Alex let Candice into her cabin. The familiar earthy, woodsy scent of Alex tickled her nose and warmed her heart. She leaned back in the seat and absorbed what she'd learned so far. The driver's door opened, and a whoosh of wind and rain swirled around in the cab. Alex hopped up into the seat and yanked the door closed. She put the keys in the ignition and the engine roared to life.

Alex whipped the truck around and started up the two-track road toward the main house. She was quiet, which was unusual. Elina looked across the seat and wished she could read Alex's mind. She knew they needed some time to talk, some time to clear the air. Hopefully, they'd have a little time before Néiwóó came home.

Elina caught movement out of the corner of her eye. "Alex, could you point the headlights at the back deck. Someone's up by the house."

The deep red reflection of two pairs of eyes glowed in the headlights. It was difficult to make out any features through the driving rain. Alex hit the gas, closing the distance to the deck, and turned on the high beams. One of the heads turned again to face them and Elina released her breath. At least these masked bandits wouldn't be a threat.

"Looks like a couple of raccoons have helped themselves to what was left of our dinner." Elina shook her head.

Alex parked the truck and shut off the engine. "I'm okay with that. I've had enough adrenaline for one day."

The furry thieves sauntered off as soon as Elina and Alex exited the truck. Elina was once again drenched in the short time it took for them to pick up the mess that had been made. She flipped on lights with her elbow and made her way into the kitchen with the tray full of dishes. Alex followed behind her with the items that wouldn't fit on the tray.

"Go ahead and set those down. We can wash the dishes in a minute. I'll grab us some towels and dry clothes."

"Since we have a few moments alone, can I ask you something?" Alex followed her to the edge of the hallway.

"Sure, I'll answer anything I can." Elina pulled a few towels out of the linen closet. She walked back up the hallway and handed a couple to Alex.

"Thanks." Alex rubbed the towel over her hair and then wiped off her face. "Were you really search and rescue or were the articles on the internet just part of a cover story?"

"My search and rescue career was very real, though over time my expertise evolved. While I'm technically still the division lead, my role will end when my accrued vacation time runs out." Elina pulled her hair free of the ponytail and wrapped it in a towel. She used the second towel to dry her face and dab at her clothes.

She walked into her room and rummaged through her suitcase. She found a pair of black sweats and a Henley shirt that looked like they might fit Alex. She leaned out her door and held the clothes out.

"If you'd like to change, I can throw your clothes in the dryer."

Alex took the clothes from her hand. "What did Candice mean when she said you had to color inside the lines on this one?"

Elina stripped in her bedroom. Coming back to the half-eaten dinner and the swing in the nook brought back the rush of that amazing first kiss. After the adrenaline of the day, her body craved a release, craved fulfillment of primal need, a distraction. She'd become an expert at compartmentalizing while on a job.

Silencing the cautionary voice and living one hundred percent, hyper-focused, in the moment. It kept her senses sharp and gave her a keen awareness of her surroundings. It was a useful skill while on the job. She could act on instinct and impulse when there wasn't time to think. A talent that kept her alive more times than she wanted to think about, it was also a curse that invited reckless abandonment when allowed to bleed into the off hours.

She never would have imagined that physical gratification could become an addiction every bit as powerful as drugs or alcohol. The need for release transcended the drugs that created the new compulsion and heightened the experience. It still blew her mind how one contract job could turn her entire world upside down. The insanity of that job bled into all hours and blurred every line until it had nearly consumed her soul. The entire operation had gone sideways from the get-go and became a cluster fuck that tossed her smack dab in unfamiliar territory. The cravings for that erotic release still taunted her at times too. It was a hard habit to break, and the temptation for fulfillment tonight was almost overwhelming. She drew in a deep breath and exhaled slowly. She needed to feel like herself again, and the only way to do that was to move beyond that toxic time in her life.

She'd seen Alex at her grandfather's celebration of life and was instantly drawn to her. She'd been a cute kid, but she was something special as an adult. She was certainly attractive, and also attentive, kind and had a strength to her character that Elina admired above all else. The more they talked, the closer she felt to her. There was something about Alex that was helping her emerge from the hazy darkness.

"Are you ignoring me or trying to come up with an answer I'll believe?"

"Neither. I'm sorry. What was your question?" Elina finished dressing in dry clothes and stood just inside the doorway.

"Is being a tracker, scout, and hunter another way of saying contract killer? Is that what Candice meant when she said you had to color in the lines?" Alex appeared in the doorway. She had wet clothes in one hand and her phone, wallet, belt, and keys in the other.

She looked adorable in sweatpants, even if they were a little too short for her. The look on her face, however, was pure skepticism and a far cry from the look in her eyes just a few hours earlier.

Elina collected the wet clothes and added them to her own. She tossed the sopping lot into the dryer and set it for thirty minutes. She filled the dogs' bowls with food, removed their vests, and toweled them off so they could eat. It had been a long day for them too.

"We both have secrets, Alex, things we can't share with most anyone in our lives. The nice part is that it seems we've chosen to walk similar paths, on the right side of the law, without even knowing it. If anything, it gives us a common bond that others wouldn't understand. Don't you agree?"

"Yes, I agree, but it didn't answer my question."

Elina walked into the kitchen and filled a tea kettle with water. She set a back burner to high and rested the kettle on top of the flame. She walked over to the sink and turned the faucet on to fill the basin. Sharing didn't come naturally, and she had to figure out what she wanted to say.

"My last contracted job, for an agency other than USMS, didn't go as planned and I—well, I tested the limits of some boundaries. What is it they say? Screw up once and word travels fast. That's all I can share about coloring in the lines. No, I'm not a contract killer. I prefer to capture whenever possible, but if my hand is forced, I'll always hope to be the last one standing. I don't know of anyone who would choose anything different." Elina looked up into Alex's eyes, eager to see a touch of understanding. It wasn't there, not yet. "Now it's my turn. Have all of your secrets been revealed, or will I learn more once I sign that contract?"

Alex's face softened and she looked away. Okay, so she had more secrets too.

"I don't know what all you'll be read in on." Alex pulled a clean dish towel from the drawer and picked up a bowl from the strainer.

"And I don't know what all I can share right now either, but I promise to share anything and everything that I'm able to. Can that be enough for now?"

Alex nodded. "And here I felt all this guilt these last couple of days, like I was misleading you and lying to you. It's weird to find out that you live with the same curse of omission. How can there be trust between us with so many secrets?"

Elina looked at Alex. She was the last one to offer any answers about trust. It didn't come easy to her. She answered as honestly as she could. "I hold out hope that trust can evolve like all of the other emotions. The need for omission is what we signed up for when we chose this life. Can that understanding be the thing that brings us closer instead of pushing us apart? I'm still me, you're still you."

The softness around Alex's eyes was back. Elina hoped that it meant they were making headway. The tea kettle whistled, breaking the silence. Elina set the last dish in the strainer and wiped her hands off. She pulled two cups from the cabinet and made tea.

"What I wouldn't give for something a little stronger than tea," Alex said, standing directly behind her.

"Me too, but I want to be clear when we talk with Candice." Elina leaned back, up against Alex's body. She drew in a deep breath and exhaled slowly. It felt good to be so close to her. The grounding effect she had was still such a surprise.

"Other than the clandestine career, is everything else that we've talked about true?" Alex asked.

"Yes, everything I've shared has been true." Elina reached behind her and found Alex's hand. She pulled it around her waist and smiled when Alex reached around with her other hand and pulled her closer.

"I've dreamt of having someone close to me who can know about my badge. I'm glad it's you." Alex's breath tickled the side of her face. "There is one more thing I'd like to know."

"Ask."

"What's with Candice calling you sweetheart? The dogs ran right up to her too. Did you two date at one point or something?"

Elina laughed. "No, we've been friends for years, but we've never dated. The dogs are close to her because she watched them while I was on a job last year. The sweetheart thing has been an ongoing joke since shortly after we met. There was this guy in her office who wouldn't take no for an answer, who thought he was God's gift to women and wanted to be God's gift to Candice. So, I dressed extra sexy and went with her to the Christmas party as her date. We called each other sweetheart all night. His friends ribbed him something awful, and after that, he quit asking her out."

"How about you two? Care to explain 'my Candice'?" Elina turned her head and tilted her chin up until her cheek rubbed against Alex's face.

"She really is like an aunt to me. Beyond that, we're back to omissions," Alex said into her ear. "Can you accept that?"

"You know I can." Elina felt hope that they'd find a path forward. Granted, her last foray into trust hadn't worked out, but Alex was different. She was working with the good guys, and that meant something. Her phone rang. She stepped out of Alex's arms and picked it up. "Hey there, are you on your way home?" Elina asked when she saw her grandmother's number come up.

"She's already been home and gone again. Her car is in the garage. Go ahead and check. I'll wait," a male voice said into the phone.

She spun around to face Alex and mouthed the word "track." Alex nodded and grabbed her phone off the table. Elina ran through the laundry room and opened the garage door. Néiwóó's car was parked in the same spot it had been earlier that day. She ran out and rested her hand on the hood of the car. It was already cooled quite a bit. It had been parked there the entire time she and Alex were talking. What a careless mistake to make. She should have cleared the house. She'd wasted so much time. She walked back inside.

"Who are you? Why would you kidnap my grandma?" Elina asked the question loud enough for Alex to hear. Her heart hammered in her chest, and she forced herself to focus.

"Kidnap is such a strong word for a short-term problem. Grant me use of your expertise and you'll have her home before you know it."

"My expertise?" Elina needed to keep this person on the phone for as long as possible. She strained to listen for any background noise that might provide insight as to where he was. "Is she unharmed?"

"She is unharmed. Your truck and horse trailer say search and rescue. I happen to have a few items that need to be located. Find my items and return them to me, I will be happy to let your grandma go on about her business."

"What's missing and where?" Elina asked.

"Right to business, I like it. It appears some items were dropped in the northeast corner of your grandma's property. It looks like rough terrain, right up your alley. I sent a couple of guys in to retrieve them, but now they are missing too. Find my items and my guys and I'll give you back your granny."

"What makes you think your guys haven't already found the missing items and called finders keepers?"

"Because they know that there would be dire consequences."

"People get greedy," Elina said, watching as Alex went about tracking the call.

"Not those two, they knew their place. Find my guys, find my stuff, and your granny lives happily ever after."

"What am I looking for?"

"Four large red and black duffel bags."

"That doesn't mean shit to a dog's nose. If you want me to find your stuff, then you have to tell me what I'm looking for. Cash, drugs, weapons? What *scent* do I give the dogs?"

There was silence on the line for so long that Elina wondered if she'd lost the call. She looked at her phone and the call timer was still ticking away. Good, it gave Alex more time to pinpoint the location. She wanted to push him, put him on edge, but not with Néiwóó's life in his hands.

"Cash. There are locks on each of the bags. Fuck with 'em and I'll know. Call the cops and I'll know. Involve anyone else and I'll know. You'll be the reason your granny doesn't come home. You have twenty-four hours to find my missing items."

"Okay, now that I know what I'm looking for, where do I deliver them?"

"I have your number. I'll call you with further instructions."

There was a beep and the words "call ended" popped up on the screen.

"Tell me you have a location!" Elina turned to Alex.

"We do. The call was stationary, no direction of travel. Highway Ninety-three, in the middle of nowhere and then the phone went dead. Likely tossed out a window. No way to know if they went north or south from there. What are we looking for?"

Elina's blood boiled. She had to get her head in the game. It was time to focus. She'd track every last one of them down if it was the last thing she did.

## CHAPTER ELEVEN

Alex's eyes burned from staring at the screen. The lack of sleep was taking a toll. She refused to give in to the exhaustion until Mary was home safe. She guided the drone into the next sector after marking the last one off the list. Candice sat at the other end of the desk watching the drone's belly camera for any sighting of a black and red duffel bag.

"The sanctuary is clear. I'll start scanning the sectors in the ravine."

"Hopefully, they pushed them out of the plane together and not staggered. They've got to be out there somewhere," Candice said.

They'd called Candice as soon as the call with the kidnapper had ended, but Elina had refused to call in any other help. Alex wasn't sure why, but she hadn't pushed. "Might be floating down the Bitterroot River by now. That was a hell of a rain last night and the water is rushing into the ravine from all directions. Wouldn't the rain wash the scent away?"

"Let's hope not. The canopy is a saving grace. The rain doesn't hit beneath the canopy like it does out in the open. Hopefully, it was protected enough to refresh the scent, not destroy it."

"Do you know a lot about working with tracking dogs?" Alex asked.

"Only what Elina has taught me over the years. Fugitives think they can run upstream, and it will throw the dogs off the scent. The stream hides their footprints, but the scent lingers for some time as long as there aren't high winds. If I need K-9 help, she's who I call. She's trained those dogs better than any of our Special Operations Group dogs."

"That's what I said." Alex shook her head. "So much has happened since then. It seems like a week ago."

"Hopefully, it will be over soon." Candice squeezed Alex's arm.

Alex landed the drone for a moment and looked at the screen on her right. Three blinking red dots showed the progress that Elina and the dogs were making. They'd started at the northernmost point of the ravine just inside the property line. The way the water flowed from the north and the steep change in elevation on the far side created the deep gorge that leveled out about four miles down on the southernmost side of the property. It created the most secure outer perimeter fence she could ever dream up. The bottom of the ravine was narrow, and the water rushed with such force that it was impossible to swim across. Elina insisted on searching at the same time as the drone instead of waiting for coordinates. At least she'd agreed to wear a tracking device and to search from the less steep inside track. Alex also begged her to not attempt a water crossing. It looked like she would honor her word and work along the inside. Watching the dogs work, even if they were red blinking dots on the screen, was impressive. Alex turned back to her screen and put the drone back in flight.

"If Elina contracts with all sorts of different agencies, why isn't the FBI or whatever crawling all over this town? You think she'd call in every favor under the sun to get Mary back."

"There's no doubt that she'd call in the calvary if she was certain it wouldn't get Mary killed. We don't know who's behind this and we have to assume that taking Mary's life wouldn't be an issue for them. We do have a few things working in our favor without calling in extra lights and sirens. For example, they don't know that Elina isn't simply search and rescue. They also don't realize that she has two highly trained US marshals already on site without making a single phone call and we have every resource at our fingertips. The small circle and the element of surprise could work in our favor."

Candice turned away from the screen and looked into Alex's eyes. "Lord help them if they harm Mary in any way."

"Will she kill them?" Alex couldn't stop herself from asking the question.

"Not unless she has no other choice."

"How did you meet her? Was it because of Hawk and Mick?" Alex focused on the screen. The underbrush was so thick in this area that she didn't want to risk crashing the drone. This task was too important.

"Hawk had talked about her, but I met her by chance. Her name is so unique, that's the only reason it clicked on that first day who she was. There was a transport en route to the Billings office. An elk, of all things, ran out of the thicket, directly in the path of the van. The dash cam caught the entire thing. They hit the elk head-on and went off into a ditch. The van rolled. The driver was killed on impact and the guard with the prisoner was knocked unconscious. The prisoner came to first and got ahold of the cuff keys and the guard's gun. Our chopper got us from Billings to the crash site, but a quick moving storm grounded further flights. I called the Grand Teton SAR team and asked for a volunteer."

"So, she helped you track him down?" Alex asked. She marked off the sector she just finished searching and moved on to the next one.

"Elina showed up with four horses and two hounds. Ken Smith was on that call with me."

"He's a stick in the mud and the toughest instructor I've ever had."

"If he pushed you, it was because he saw potential. Anyway, we might as well have been invisible. She insisted on being out front so she could work with the dogs. The hounds weren't trained like her dogs are now. They closed in on the target as if he was a lost tourist. Elina couldn't pull them back fast enough. Shots were exchanged between Ken and I and the fugitive. He was killed but not before she took a bullet and lost one of the dogs. Ken was hit in the vest." Candice tapped on the table. "Back the drone up. Hover a bit to the right. Pin it. We found one of the bags."

"Fuck yeah, one down, three to go." Alex landed the drone. She picked up her phone and texted the coordinates to Elina. Dots flickered on the screen.

*I'll head in that direction with the dogs and work from that scent. Thank you.*

*We'll keep searching from the sky too.*

Elina sent back a thumbs up emoji. Alex set the phone on the table and returned to the drone's controls. "So, what happened after she was shot?"

"I stopped by the hospital a day later to see how she was recovering. She asked me what kind of dogs we use for tracking fugitives and how she could get training to be better equipped for the next call."

"That sounds like Elina." Alex laughed.

"That was twenty years ago. Now, we're all completely different versions of ourselves, aren't we? You were what, seventeen back then, still trying to figure out a new normal."

"Do you ever stop trying to figure out a new normal after something like that? It took forever just to remember my new name." Alex looked over.

"I never thought of it like that."

"Did she go to training?"

"Not right away, she came here, to this ranch for a couple of weeks, to heal. Hawk worked with her, taught her stillness and how to track with patience. She had no idea it was training. She was simply healing at her grandparents' ranch. She still gives me shit for waiting another year before I helped her with the next step. Truth is, there was no holding her back."

Alex thought back. She had a vague memory of Elina coming to stay just before school let out for the year. It was one of the few times they actually got to hang out a bit and visit. She knew she'd been injured but she hadn't realized she'd been shot. There were times that she felt like she could know Elina the best because she'd known her for so long, but then, she realized that she'd only known of her and there was a difference. Maybe she'd get a chance to really know her, someday.

"Who all does she contract with?"

"Besides USMS, I honestly couldn't tell you. I have hunches, but we've never talked about it. That's Elina's business, but I know she's always busy."

Alex's phone chimed. An incoming text from Elina. She grounded the drone and picked up her phone.

*Found the second duffel bag. Attaching a tracker and securing it to a tree.*

*Two down, two to go.* Alex typed into the phone and hit send.

*Halfway there.*

Alex looked at the clock. Halfway there and only six hours remaining of decent daylight. She shook off the looming deadline, more specifically the thoughts of Mary held somewhere against her will, and focused on getting the drone back up in the sky.

"Are you going to force me to ask you about your feelings for Elina?" Candice asked. "We won't find a better time to talk one-on-one."

"I'm still trying to figure out if what I felt yesterday is the same as what I feel today." Alex wanted to look over at Candice. She wanted to see if there was any reaction to what she said, but she didn't dare look away from the screen. She'd feel awful if she took out the drone.

"Tell me more."

"Is she the same person I've been getting to know these last few months? She seems so kind and tender. She seems interested in me. She asks what I like to eat or what my favorite color is, but now I'm meeting this whole other side of her. She says she's a tracker, a scout, and a hunter. You say that's an understatement. What does that mean? What does she really do?"

"I consider her a dear friend and I'm certain that she's the person you've been getting to know these last few months. She cares for you. I can see it in her eyes," Candice said. "I don't have the authority or the clearance to give you specifics on what she does. All I can say is that over the last twenty years she's become the absolute best of the best."

"Why didn't you ever tell me that you knew her? I mean, you knew I lived here, with her grandparents. And you knew she came to visit and that we knew each other. Why didn't you say anything?" Alex asked. "Does everything have to be so secretive?"

"It was never meant to be a secret. I know a lot of people and in many capacities. Some I develop a friendship with while others remain colleagues. Besides, I've seen you more in the past few months than I have in ten or even fifteen years. It doesn't mean I don't care about you. Life just gets busy. If it makes you feel any better, I never talked with her about Hawk or Mick or you either. I couldn't because it creates too many questions that I know I can't answer. Some things do have to be kept secret and you know it." She gave a wry smile. "But I did wonder if a situation might ever arise where the two of you would have an awkward conversation."

Candice was right. Elina was right too. It was the path she chose, and it required that secrets be kept. Alex sat there navigating the drone through the brush. Candice said that there wasn't a better time for them to talk. She still had a few questions to ask.

"Could I tell her? Do you think she can know everything about me?" Alex swallowed hard. The words were out before she realized it.

"If anyone could be trusted with that information, it would be her, but as a senior agent, I'll add that your truth prior to coming here should never be shared. It's what keeps you protected and in the program," Candice said, and without looking over she reached across the table and squeezed Alex's arm again. It was a comforting touch.

"Last question, for now anyways. Do you think they'll pull the post because of these events?"

"Let's see how it all plays out first. So far, nothing has been compromised. The two that did gain access, never saw infrastructure, just security from hell. For all they know, you were protecting the bison herd."

"Yeah, but ranch managers don't typically call the marshal service for trespassers. Those guys didn't seem all that smart, but they'll be smart enough to wonder about that."

"We spun that a bit and let them overhear a conversation about why there were marshals on site. We used Elina's position and said something about a training exercise. So far, they're buying it and they won't come to this place again because of the dogs, if nothing else. Besides, they won't see daylight for a while. Firing at a federal agent is a serious crime."

There was hope on all fronts. Alex focused on navigating the drone within the sector. The sooner they found the last two bags, the sooner this could be over. Well, they'd get Mary back. But beyond that, it seemed like there were an awful lot of questions to be dealt with.

# CHAPTER TWELVE

Elina couldn't help but feel like she was disobeying her grandparents by being down in the ravine. It wasn't an easy area to navigate, especially after such a heavy rain. Mud and leaves collected on her shoes making traction almost impossible. Swollen creeks and streams seemed to pour over the steep side walls from every which way. The water cascading down into the gorge was thick and murky with leaves, tree branches, and other debris that had been swept up along the way. The roaring water at the bottom of the ravine rushed by with such force that she certainly understood why she wasn't allowed to explore the area as a child. They were right to keep it off limits, because with currents that strong, her tiny body would have been two towns away before anyone knew she was missing. While dangerous, the ravine was also quite beautiful and when the extra water from the rains moved farther downstream, she imagined that the area would offer gentle tranquility.

The dogs located the third duffel bag shortly after finding the second one. One last duffel bag remained to be found and the light was dwindling fast. Scout and Hunter were still on scent, which was encouraging. At least something was still upwind. Once she had all four bags, she'd have leverage to bring Néiwóó home and that was her focus.

The dogs cued a find. Elina climbed up through the dense foliage. No wonder they caught such a strong ink scent, the bag had snagged on a tree branch and ripped open. Bundles of cash were scattered all over the area. She pulled out her phone and took a few pictures as evidence, not that mystery man would accept it. Elina attached one of the photos to the text thread with Alex.

*Found the last bag. It's unusable. I'll collect what I can find. Won't fit in my go bag. Don't suppose you can toss down a suitcase?*

Slipping and sliding in the wet muck, she began the task of collecting the bundles of cash and stacked them together. Thank goodness they were bound and hadn't gone all over the place.

*I have an idea. Hold tight.*

Elina finished collecting all of the bound stacks of cash that she could see. It was quite a pile. She checked her phone and found nothing new from Alex. Movement caught her eye and she spun around. The roar of the flowing water was so loud that she hadn't heard the drone approach. Alex was one crafty character. The drone had a strap hanging down with an oversized empty backpack clipped onto the end. Elina looked into the camera and gave her a smile and a thumbs up. Brilliant! She removed the backpack from the strap and stuffed it full of bundles. She pulled out her phone and typed a quick message to Alex.

*Do you have a drone big enough to haul these bags out of the ravine?*

Elina watched the dots flicker. It felt good to stop and be still even if it was just for a moment. She was exhausted. Her stomach grumbled deep in her belly. It was a reminder that she hadn't stopped to eat. She thought back and realized that she hadn't had anything since the stew that the racoons finished. Suddenly, she was starving.

*If only I had a cargo drone. I'll add to wish list.*

*Can you have the drone bring me a granola bar?*

*Look in your go bag, side pocket.*

Elina unclipped the waist belt and pulled her low profile go bag off her back. She found two granola bars stuffed in the side pocket. It was one of the sweetest things anyone had done for her. Alex was so different from anyone else she'd ever been attracted to. Alex was thoughtful and sweet. This one simple gesture felt as warm and genuine as her hug had the other night. She ate one of the bars and then split the second bar between the dogs. She wasn't even sure they chewed the treat. She used a carabiner clip to secure her go bag to the side of the large pack.

"Okay, pups, let's find a way out of here." Elina pulled out her phone and typed out a text to Alex.

*Is there any way for me to exit from the south? The climb back to the north will be all uphill.*

*Sadly, no. The ravine gets very narrow to the south and the water will be raging.*

*Roger that. I'd better get moving.*

*Candice and I will come in from the north. With any luck, we'll meet up by the third bag. The three of us can pack it all out. See you soon.*

*Sounds good.*

Elina tucked her phone in her pocket and hoisted up the pack. The waterlogged cash made the pack much heavier than she anticipated. It took a moment for her to get her balance. She navigated the underbrush trying to find the path of least resistance, which wasn't easy given the equivalent of a medium-sized suitcase on her back that seemed to attract every low-hanging branch.

Her legs shook with fatigue. It had been much easier to work her way down into the ravine, but the lack of sleep and the lack of fuel had her body protesting the physical demands of climbing her way out. She slid more times than she could count. The dogs kept stopping and looking back as if annoyed that they had to wait on her. Her shoes felt like fifty-pound boat anchors, each caked with mud and leaves.

Elina pushed ahead. Néiwóó wouldn't give up on her and she wouldn't quit until her grandmother was home. Darkness was coming quickly in the ravine. Alex and Candice shouldn't be far off. She knew she needed help and while she wasn't the best at asking, she silently wished they'd hurry.

The ground all around her was so saturated with rain that a few small trees uprooted when she pulled on them for leverage to climb. She heard a thunderous whoosh from somewhere on the ravine wall above her head and looked up just before being devoured by a cascading landslide of debris. There was no time to react. Her legs were swept out from beneath her and she went down hard. Rocks and trees that would help slow her descent flashed by with such speed that she was unable to reach out fast enough to grab ahold. The avalanche of muck picked up pace, racing toward the raging water at the bottom of the ravine and there was little she could do to stop the momentum.

She knew she should have created an anchor system along the way. She wouldn't be in this mess if she had rigged up ropes to clip on to for security when the area was extremely steep. Her training had taught her better, but in her haste to beat the timeline, she'd decided against it. She had allowed the emotion of the situation to cloud her judgment and now it seemed it would take her to a watery grave. She felt sharp punctures in her outstretched arms. The searing pain brought her back to the present, all senses on high alert. She looked up and saw Hunter and Scout digging in, tugging on the backpack, tugging on her arm, trying desperately to pull her from flow of the landslide, but there wasn't much footing to be had. She turned and looked down the hill. The raging water in the river below was closing in fast, all too eager to suck her in. She knew what she should do if she fell in, but she wasn't sure she could get the pack off before the weight of it pulled her under water.

A sudden jolt stopped her murky slip and slide ride. Muddy debris rushed around her and, at times, over her head. Hunter and Scout tumbled into her body. She managed to grab the loop on one of the dogs' vests and held on with everything she had. The other dog was pinned up against her shoulder, putting pressure on her neck and head. The thick mud rushing over her body made it difficult to breathe. She flailed her arm trying to find something, anything to grab ahold of. Panic filled her soul when the dog pressing against her shoulder slipped and disappeared. She pulled the other dog up on her chest and held on tightly. She tried to free the waist belt from the large backpack, but the clasp wouldn't release. She couldn't move. The weight of the pack had her pinned in place. Elina strained for a breath of air and sucked in mucky water instead. Her lungs burned and tried to reject the invasion. She choked and coughed and lifted her head one more time hoping for some air.

Warmth encased her forearm. Elina looked up into concerned, soulful eyes. Alex had ahold of her and pulled up, heaving her away from the raging waters tugging furiously on her legs.

"Let go of Scout. Give me your other hand. I've got you."

Elina released her grip on Scout's vest, and Alex lifted him off her chest. She offered her free hand to Alex. Her lungs continued to burn, but at least she could fill them with air again. She pulled herself up into Alex's arms, or maybe it was Alex who was doing the pulling. Either way, she wasn't about to drown.

"Can you stand?" Alex asked.

"I think so. I lost my footing and there wasn't anything to grab," Elina said, but she didn't try to move. It felt too good to be in the safety of Alex's arms. "My arms. The dogs tried to stop my slide."

"Pinched, more than anything. I'm sure it hurts, but it doesn't look like they broke the skin."

If her words sounded callous, her embrace certainly wasn't. She pushed wet, mud-caked hair out of Elina's eyes. The gesture meant so much more than the granola bars, and that was a tough one to beat. Alex reached down and released the clasp on the waist belt.

"Can you pull your arms out of the straps?"

Elina nodded and tried to free her arms. She was completely drained, but now was not the time to give up. She wanted this to be over. Mystery man could have the money, all she wanted was to have Néiwóó home safe. Everything else could be figured out once she knew her grandmother was all right.

# CHAPTER THIRTEEN

A lex heaved the saturated backpack out from beneath Elina. It was so much heavier than she expected. She slid her arms into the straps and fastened the waist belt. Darkness was creeping in quickly, and the roar of the water rushing through the ravine was almost deafening. The way it reverberated off the ravine walls seemed to echo in her skull. It was unnerving to have her senses completely overrun. Elina was still on the ground, sitting off to the side of the still rushing water and debris, coughing up the last of the water trapped in her lungs. She was a mud-covered mess. Twigs, leaves, and pine needles stuck to the side of her face and poked out every which way from her hair. Alex wondered how on earth someone covered in muck could look so beautiful.

"Can you stand up?" Alex held her hand out for Elina again.

"Scout and Hunter?" Elina asked. She rose to her knees and then slowly up on her feet. "Are they okay?"

"Yes, they're both fine. I had Candice call them up to higher ground." Alex pulled out a two-way radio and cued the mic. "Elina's okay. Do you have a visual of us?"

"Negative."

"Is my rope still anchored?"

"Rope is secure."

Alex wasn't taking any chances. She'd almost been to Elina when she'd been swept away by the landslide. Water was rushing in from the heavy rains and at times carving out large chunks of the upper ravine walls with it and sweeping up anything or anyone unlucky enough to be in the path. The longer they stayed down here, the more dangerous it would be for them. The sight of Elina slipping away was one of the scariest things she'd ever experienced. She vaguely remembered holding the cam open on her rope and running down the slope as fast as she could, consequences be damned. She'd caught the strap of Elina's go bag that happened to be clipped to the larger pack and closed her cam seconds before she ran out of rope. They'd both snapped to a stop, and she'd prayed that all the clips would hold until she could pull her out of harm's way. She used a tree as an anchor and tugged on Elina's arm and the shoulder straps of her pack to get her out of the water flow. Now, she had to focus on getting the two of them back up the steep, muddy slope. She removed the extra gear from her harness.

"How are you doing? Have you caught your breath yet?"

"Getting there."

"Can you hold onto my shoulders so I can get you in a harness?"

"Normally, I'd crack a joke about you wanting me in a harness, but I'm too tired to think of anything funny." Elina wrapped her arms around Alex's shoulders.

Alex smiled and secured the harness around Elina's waist. She pulled the leg straps from the backside around the inside of each leg before connecting them completely around her leg and clipping the leg straps to the front waist strap. She flipped the side of a progress capture pulley open and lined the slack in the rope up into the channel and then flipped the cover closed again and secured it to the belay loop on Elina's harness. Any other time, it would have been sexy. Right now, she just wanted to get them out of there.

"I know you know how to use this. I also know you're exhausted, so humor me and climb up ahead of me. I'll be right behind you. Okay?"

Elina nodded and then leaned forward and kissed Alex. "Thank you, for coming after me."

"Let's not make this rescuing each other thing a habit between us." Alex leaned her forehead up against Elina's. "All right, up you go."

"Stay right behind me, or I'll be back for you. Understood?"

Alex nodded. She had no doubt that Elina would risk everything to come back for her. All the more reason to buck up and make sure she could rise to the occasion. Alex let Elina get about a third of the way up before she started up the slope. The pack was so heavy that it quickly wore her down. She thought about tying a rope to it and pulling it up once she was up on solid ground, but there was too much underbrush for it to snag on. Elina was one badass warrior for having hefted this thing for as far as she did. What she wouldn't give for the time to set up a double pulley system or any other means of getting out of this hell without this enormous effort. At least the rope and pulley kept her from losing ground each time she slipped and lost her footing in the muck. Climbing wasn't her area of expertise. She only had the gear because of a training course. Well, that and the cute blonde at the outdoor sporting goods store.

"Elina's up with me." Candice's voice crackled through the two-way radio.

She planted her feet and rested for a second. Her arms and shoulders were burning from the effort.

"Roger that. I shouldn't be too far behind," Alex said into the mic.

"She says the path up from there is fairly clear. We're tossing down a rope for the backpack."

"I won't say no to that." Alex clipped her radio and watched for the rope.

Once the waterlogged bag of cash was off her back, she was able to complete the last leg of the climb. Elina had cut down a couple of green saplings about two inches in diameter and stripped them of the branches.

"You suddenly have the energy to whittle? How did you even cut those down?" Alex asked while stepping out of the climbing harness.

"I keep a small, folded saw in my go bag. I almost left it behind. Now, I'm very glad I didn't. See, carrying poles. It will distribute the load between the three of us. One of us in front, one in the middle, and one in the rear and a pole on each shoulder. A cash bag between each of us on each shoulder. It's the only way I can think to get all of the bags out in one trip."

Elina fed the handles of the two duffel bags close by onto the stick and spaced them out. It was a brilliant idea and much easier than trying to heft out those large bags with just the three of them. Alex's admiration for Elina continued to grow.

"It's how I was trained to haul an injured person out if we were on foot and transport couldn't get in the area. I'll take lead since I'm the shortest and we'll still be walking up an incline. Candice, you take middle and Alex, since you're so tall, you get the rear. We can collect the other two bags as we make our way out."

"I don't know how you two are even standing. I'm exhausted and I haven't done anything." Candice stepped into the middle position.

"I want Néiwóó home safe and all of this to be over, then I'll sleep for a week."

Alex took her spot in the rear, and when Elina counted to three, she lifted the poles up onto her shoulder. It was much easier with the distribution of the load. At least the trail from their position to the north edge of the ravine was an easier hike. The steep, evil cliffs were behind them and now all they had to do was get to the truck. Thank goodness, because Alex wasn't sure how much more energy she had to give.

## Chapter Fourteen

The twenty-four-hour window was drawing to a close. Elina heaved the last of the four bags into the back of her truck. Her body ached from exhaustion and exertion.

"We need a game plan." Alex leaned up against her truck which was parked next to Elina's.

Before Elina could say a word, her phone rang. The caller ID was an unknown number. It had to be the kidnapper.

"Hello."

"I hope you had a successful search," the male voice said.

"I have the money. Let me talk to my grandma."

"Drive to the end of Dry Gulch Road. Go through the gate. We'll make the exchange there. If you leave now, you'll make the half hour deadline. No games and everyone will go home tonight."

The phone beeped, signaling the end of the call.

"I have a half hour to get to the end of Dry Gulch Road. Alex, do you know the area and how to get there?"

"I do."

Elina considered options. "Are there any high vantage points around there that are accessible by road? We don't have time to use the horses."

"I'm sure that was the point of the deadline," Alex said.

"Toss Candice your keys. She can follow us in your truck." Elina opened the back door of her quad cab truck. "Candice, are you still a crack shot with the long gun?"

"Yes, ma'am. Certify every year," Candice said.

Elina lifted the rear seat and then pulled back the carpeting. She typed her six number code into the keypad and the floor panel popped open. She released the clasps and lifted a scoped rifle out of the cradle and then handed it to Candice along with two, five round magazines. She lifted another panel and pulled out a small case, a holstered pistol, and then grabbed her bag of tricks before she dropped the panels down, folded the carpet over and then lowered the seat. She cued the dogs into the truck and closed the back door.

"Holy shit, you have quite the arsenal. I can shoot too, ya know," Alex said.

"I have no doubt, but I don't need you to shoot, I need you to be me." Elina tossed Alex the keys. "I want you to drive my truck. Candice, you'll need to follow us lights out. There's a night vision headset to use once you turn away from our taillights. It's a cloudy night, so you should be invisible unless they're also using night vision. See if you can find any vantage point, even if it's standing in the bed of the truck. Let's go, let's go."

Elina climbed into the passenger seat of her truck and pulled the door closed. She unlaced her mud-caked, waterlogged boots, and dropped them on to the floor. She unzipped her bag and set it on the seat between her and Alex. Stealth was the goal for this mission. She lifted a rolled-up pair of knee-high, leather soled moccasins from the bag. It was the last thing that she and her grandfather had made together. It seemed fitting to wear them tonight when the goal was to bring Néiwóó home. She crisscrossed the leather straps around her leg several times and then tied them off. She tucked a sheath, holding a three-inch arced knife, into a fold of leather on the outside of each knee. The way it was positioned, the sheath would stay in her boot when she pulled on the handle of the knife.

"Do you want to clue me in on the game plan?" Alex asked.

Elina turned her attention to Alex. She looked nervous and understandably so. She was a gatekeeper, not a hunter.

"The pistol is for you. Hide it wherever you feel comfortable. Magazine is full, chamber is empty. Do you see this button here?

When we get close, push it up and open the window to the bed of the truck. The dogs and I will exit that way. Drive normally on your way through the gate. Close the window after we climb out."

"He's going to know I'm not you. Our voices are completely different."

"We're both covered in mud. Trust me, you look as bad as I do. Call Néiwóó grandma, she'll play along. He'll be focused on the money, not what you look and sound like. Besides, if I have anything to say about it, he won't be standing long."

She tucked her arms into the shoulder straps of her go bag and then clipped a separate waist belt in place. She closed her eyes and opened each pouch on the waistbelt, touched the object, and closed the pouch. Everything was where she expected it to be.

"What are you going to do?" Alex asked.

"I'm going to keep you safe. If I'm successful, Candice won't need to fire a single shot."

"Okay, but who's going to keep you safe? I don't like this. We should have a tactical team. We should not be going in blind. Fuck, we're already at the gate."

"Alex, take a breath. Trust me, it will work out." Elina leaned over and kissed Alex's cheek. "Turn the radio on. Don't super blast it, but you know, enjoy a song. Give me as much time as you can before you shut off the truck. I need you to be the distraction that allows me to remain hidden."

She climbed over the seat and then out the window into the bed of the truck. She looked through the thermal scope. Just as she expected, there were a few guys with guns spread out around the area. She tucked the scope into the pouch and then climbed over the tailgate and stood on the bumper. She lowered the dogs to the ground by their vests and released them, then sat down on the bumper and stepped off herself.

The way the road angled in, Elina used the truck as cover for a hundred yards or so. She'd be difficult to spot from this vantage point even with night vision. The headlights lit up an old cabin and a shed. Elina pulled out the scope. She could make out the top half of a person at the ready peeking around the corner of the shed. Luckily, his finger wasn't on the trigger. She went wide so she could come up behind him.

Always grateful that dogs could see well in the dark, Elina gave Hunter and Scout the hand signal. They came in from the side. It was amazing how quietly they could move. They launched into the air in unison with perfect timing. The man went down hard with little more than a loud puff of air escaping on impact. Elina had a rope around his neck and a knee in his back before he knew what hit him. She crossed the ends of the rope and pulled on the small wooden handles, restricting the blood flow in his carotid artery until he went limp. She checked for a pulse. Good, he was still alive. Alex would approve. She retrieved a small bottle from her pouch and tapped a single tablet into her hand. She tucked it in the man's cheek and then zip-tied his arms behind his back and bound his feet at the ankles. She had an hour or two before he'd wake up.

Alex parked the truck in front of the cabin, the radio playing but not too loudly. *Way to go, Alex.* Elina watched for activity, but no one approached the truck. She worked her way to the next target. He went down as easily as the first. She zip-tied his hands and feet and then gave him a nice little sleepy tablet. Onward.

The third man was hiding on the far side of the house. The car the men traveled in was parked up against the same side of the cabin. The engine was still warm. Elina used it for cover and watched him through the scope. He was a jumpy mess. His head snapped in the direction of every little sound. Gauging by the way his hand was positioned, he had a finger on the trigger too. This would be a little more challenging. She didn't dare risk him firing his weapon. She had no idea if anyone was hiding in the shed or the cabin. She remained still and watched him for a little longer. There was something glowing just an inch or so in front of his face and then his hand moved away from the trigger and pulled the item away from his face. He dropped it down to the ground and stepped on it. Bingo. He was smoking. Now, she had an in.

She moved in closer and signaled to the dogs to be ready. His hand reached for something in his shirt pocket. Hopefully, it was another cigarette. She crept closer. He propped the rifle up against the cabin. Elina gave the signal and the dogs launched at him. They hit him directly in the back, and he fell forward, face-first. She moved in and had the rope around his neck before he could get up onto his hands and knees. She applied the pressure into his back and exhaled a sigh of relief when he finally went limp. She drugged him and tied him up like the others.

A car pulled into the driveway. Elina tugged on the man until she was certain the headlights wouldn't reveal his slumbering body. She stayed back and waited for the car to park before she crept back to the front corner of the cabin. The headlights from the car illuminated the driver's side of her truck. Alex was still seated in the driver's seat, holding her hand up to shield her eyes from the light.

The dome light clicked on in the car when the man opened the driver's door. The car's headlights stayed on too. He stepped out of the car and left the door open. He was wearing a suit and tie. Pompous ass. Another man, with a neatly trimmed beard, sat in the back seat next to Néiwóó. Elina couldn't see a gun, but it didn't mean that either of the men weren't armed.

"Kill the engine. Get out of the truck nice and slow. Where's my money?"

The radio shut off when the engine did. Alex opened the driver's door and stepped down out of the truck. She stayed in the headlights and walked toward the back. She lowered the tailgate and lifted one of the large duffel bags.

"Let my grandma out of the car. I want to know she's okay."

The man in the suit looked back at the car and nodded. The back door opened, and the bearded man stepped out first and then tugged on Néiwóó's arm until she was standing next to him. Elina looked through the thermal scope to see if he was holding anything in his free hand. It didn't appear he had anything at the ready. Perhaps they were counting on the three who were now unarmed and unconscious.

"Grandma, are you hurt in any way?" Alex asked.

"I'm okay. I just want to go home, honey."

"Working on that now."

Néiwóó looked tired but she was standing on her own and that meant Elina could focus on taking these guys down. Elina gave the signal to the dogs. They came up from behind the car, fast and quiet. Scout latched onto the bearded man's arm. The impact pulled his hand free from Néiwóó and he staggered away from the car trying to shake the dog off. Before the man in the suit could turn around, Hunter shot up along the passenger side of the car and hooked onto his arm just above the elbow.

Scout thrashed wildly and the bearded man cried out and fell to his knees. Scout whipped his body around and tugged on the man's arm. He fell onto his belly and Scout moved in quickly to the man's throat. Elina glanced ahead to the man in the suit. Hunter had him down too, with his jaw wrapped around his throat. My, oh my, how she loved her dogs!

"Tounin." Elina instructed both dogs to hold their targets. "Either of you move a muscle and I'll let them rip you into tiny pieces."

"I won't move," the bearded man said. "Get it off me."

"Hands behind your back. Cross your feet at your ankles." Elina zip-tied his hands and feet, checked for a weapon, and then ran up to repeat the process on the man in the suit. Alex stood firm and had a pistol to his head.

"The dog has him. Will you go check on my grandma?" Alex tugged the zip ties out of her hand. "I can secure him."

Alex had her game face on. She looked hot holding a gun. Candice pulled into the driveway in Alex's truck. Elina ran back to Néiwóó.

"Are you all right?" Elina wrapped her arm around her grandmother's shoulder and smiled when her grandmother lifted her arms and held her tightly.

"I'm better now." She leaned in closer and whispered, "Am I ever happy to see you two and the puppies."

Elina held her grandmother close for a long moment. When she pulled away, she glanced into the back seat of the car and spotted Néiwóó's purse. She leaned in and grabbed it off the seat.

"We'll get you home here in a minute." Elina walked her grandmother over to the truck and helped her up into the front seat. She leaned in close. "I'll leave Scout with you, okay? He misses his scratches."

"Sounds good, dear. Please, don't be too long. I'd like to be home."

Elina leaned in and kissed her grandmother on the cheek. She closed the passenger door and jogged back over to join Candice and Alex on the far side of Alex's truck.

"How is she?" Candice asked.

"She's tired and wants to get home."

"What's the situation down here?" Candice asked.

"Five captures, zero escapes, zero kills, and two vehicles for impound. All weapons secured. The shed and cabin are padlocked from the outside. Unlikely that there's a threat inside, though I've yet to clear those two buildings." Elina rattled off the status as if it were any other job.

"Great work, both of you. The apprehension teams are about an hour out. Alex, do you recognize anyone?" Candice's voice was just above a whisper for the last question.

"Yeah. The guy in the suit is a local. He's in real estate but I couldn't give you a name. I've seen his picture on advertisements. I have nothing on the other three that Elina took down. I'd have to go and take a look at their faces."

"Don't worry about it. Your post is still active, and I'd like to keep your cover intact. Why don't you take Mary home? Elina and I will wait for transport and then I'll head back to the office with the team and see what all I can learn. Elina can head back in your truck as soon as the transport teams arrive."

"Roger that. I'll leave the duffel bags of money on the ground." Alex turned to leave.

Elina reached out and caught Alex's arm. "Before you go... thank you. I can't thank you two enough, for everything."

Alex nodded once. "I'm glad it's over and everyone's okay."

"I'll second that." Candice smiled.

Elina watched Alex make her way to the truck. Words didn't seem to be enough to convey the gratitude she felt. Candice and Alex had risked their lives to get her grandmother back safely. Candice had been a good friend for some time. Elina recognized that she didn't have too many people in her life that she could count on. Now, at least, she felt like she had a few.

## CHAPTER FIFTEEN

"Wait, go back. Elina." Mary turned in her seat and looked out the rear window.

Alex wanted nothing more than to turn around and go back. She should be there. She was the one with the badge, after all. And she would turn back in a heartbeat if it weren't for the sanctuary. She understood why Elina and Candice had sent her away, but it didn't mean she had to like it.

"She'll join us in about an hour or so." Alex glanced up in the review mirror and then back to the road ahead.

"Why would she stay behind? It's not safe back there. Dan had three guys with guns head up there and hide prior to the meet. He called them the clean-up crew. None of us were supposed to leave that property alive."

"It would seem that a pissed off granddaughter and two highly trained dogs trumps three guys with guns. They were captured before your car pulled in and Elina has Hunter out on patrol."

"I'd be lying to say I wasn't grateful." Mary leaned back in her seat. "I hope they went down hard, arrogant pricks."

"Seriously? You too?" Alex looked across the seat. "Why aren't you more upset? You were kidnapped, for Christ's sake."

"Maybe I'll be upset later, but right now I'm pissed as hell! If Hawk were alive, he wouldn't rest until every one of them paid the piper." Mary slammed her palms onto the dash.

"I have a feeling that Elina is very much like Hawk when it comes to protecting the ones she loves." Alex still wondered what it meant for Elina to color in the lines. She never really got an answer.

"I certainly hope so. That fucker will be sorry he screwed with this old lady."

Alex tried not to laugh. She'd never before heard Mary say the word fuck, and it was both shocking and funny, regardless of the circumstances.

"What happened? How'd they even get you?" Alex asked.

"Dan and Carl, the two in the car with me, were hiding in the house when I got home from the bridge game. Apparently, they saw Elina on the news and the search and rescue stickers on her truck. He said he needed her expertise but then decided that I could be useful to persuade her to help. Carl had a gun and forced me to go. All the way out to their car I kept thinking about Hawk. Time and again, he'd tell me I had to learn to shoot. I should carry a gun or at the very least, bear mace. He'd tell me that I needed to know how to protect myself. I'd tell him that there was no reason. What would anyone possibly want with an ornery old woman? Besides, he'd be around to protect me. Looks like karma gave me a swift kick in the ass."

Alex's heart tugged and guilt washed over her. She should have been there to protect Mary. She'd promised Hawk that she'd keep her safe, that she'd take care of her.

"I'll teach you to shoot." Alex looked across the seat into Mary's eyes. Then it registered that Mary had names. "Dan, Carl? Which one is which?"

"Dan was in the suit. Carl was in the back seat with me."

"Last names?" Alex asked. She flipped on the blinker to turn left. The case might be over, but maybe she could gain helpful information for Candice.

"Well, how the hell would I know? I played the feeble old lady card and pretended to be asleep most of the time so I could listen in. They were as talkative as old hens."

"Wicked smart." Alex couldn't help but smile. "Tell me everything. What did you learn?"

"Apparently, Dan's in a pickle. He cleans money for some cartel and used some of their money for an investment that didn't pan out. Now, he has to get the money deposited before the cartel notices that it's gone. Here's where it gets weird. There was a shipment of money that was stolen from the cartel, by the crime boss's sister no less. The cartel found the pilot hired to drop the money and tortured the coordinates out of him. Dan was supposed to get the money back and clean it, but he figured that he could skim enough to cover what he needed and blame it on the sister, the pilot, or Elina."

"That's some first-rate detective work." Alex looked over and smiled. She wanted to ask more questions but wasn't sure Mary knew about her badge, although that cat seemed pretty much out of the bag now. "We know about the money. We spent the last twenty-four hours finding it and then carting it out of the ravine so we could trade it for your freedom. Why do you think we're all so muddy? He called for the swap just as we got up to the truck."

"I appreciate the risk you took. I've been down in that ravine. The water had to be rushing in from every which way after the storm."

"Understatement of the year." Alex looked across the seat. "It was a community effort. Elina was down there with the dogs. Candice and I ran the drone."

"Candice is here?" Mary asked.

"Jesus, you know Candice too?" Alex shook her head. "Does everyone in the Hawkins family know Candice?"

"Sweet Alex, I know. Just because we don't talk about it doesn't mean I'm oblivious. Like I keep telling Elina, I'm old, not senile. You forget that I was married to Hawk for a lifetime. I will always be the wife of a US marshal. I had two of them to deal with on this ranch, and then you earned your badge and I had three of you to love. So, yes, I know Candice. The work that's done up here is important."

Alex felt a lump form in her throat. Mary knew. All this time, Mary knew about everything. They could have talked. She could have asked questions. So many secrets she kept close to the vest that weren't necessary. Or was it best to keep it close so she didn't slip up?

"You know about my badge?"

Alex could feel Mary's eyes on her. She was tired, wired, and she was a bundle of emotions. She'd gone too long without sleep and her eyes burned like they were on fire.

"I've known since the day you earned it. You don't know how proud I was of you and for you. I'm still so very proud of the work you do. You've been a part of this family since well before Mick adopted you. I'm sure your mother would have been proud too. I know she made some mistakes in life, but she did her best to protect you in the end. She gave you up to keep you safe."

That was one tidbit too many. Tears fell and Alex could do little to stop them. She clenched her jaw to keep from sobbing. Mary remembered. Mary knew all of it. She finally had someone to talk to about all the things she kept bottled up inside.

"Is my mom still alive?" Alex asked. "Was her death faked? Is she in WITSEC somewhere else? It's something I've always wondered."

"Sometimes, not knowing is better than knowing. You can make up any version you want if you don't know what really happened." Mary's words were hard, but her tone was gentle.

Alex's breath caught and a fresh round of emotion bubbled up. She wanted to know. "Knowing the truth is always better than making stuff up. I'm sick and tired of the lies and the memorized reinventions of my life. Just this once can I please know what really happened?"

Alex pulled into the driveway and parked the truck in front of the house. Her grip remained tight on the steering wheel as she braced for the worst.

"Can we go inside, or do I have to sit out here until I talk? I don't know about you, but it's been a long twenty-four hours and I could use a nip of whiskey to calm my nerves."

"Shit, I'm sorry. Let's get you inside." Alex pulled the keys from the ignition and ran around to the other side of the truck to get Mary's door.

Mary used her key to open the front door and stepped across the threshold. She stopped and turned back to look at Alex. "Aren't you coming in?"

"I'm a filthy mess."

"The house can be cleaned. I'd rather not be alone right now. Can you wait for Elina to get home before you clean up?"

Mary's eyes pleaded her case more than the words. Alex nodded and stepped inside. She'd stay crunchy and muddy for as long as it took if it helped Mary feel safe.

"Be a pal and pour us a drink. I have to use the ladies' room."

Alex looked over to the liquor cabinet and noticed a bouquet of flowers on the dining room table. The assortment seemed to have been selected for color more than the type of flower. Each bloom was Elina's favorite shade of purple. How long had they been there? She wanted to open the small white envelope but decided against it. She retrieved Mary's bottle of whiskey and two glasses.

She poured a heavy shot into a glass and tossed it back in one gulp. It burned a little going down, but the warmth felt good on her throat and in her belly. She poured each of them a drink and set the glasses on the dining table. Would Mary finish the conversation about her mother or was that a topic for another day? She decided not to ask any more questions about it tonight. She pulled out her normal chair and sat down. Her legs felt like lead, and it was nice to sit for just a few minutes.

The chair across from Alex scraped on the floorboards. Mary flopped down in her seat and picked up her glass. She tossed it back in one gulp.

"That's the ticket. Did you bring the bottle over?"

"It's easy enough to grab." Alex retrieved the bottle and poured Mary another.

"Well, aren't those pretty. Did you send Elina flowers? They sure smell nice."

"I wish I could take credit for them, but no, it wasn't me. The last few days have been a little hectic."

"Isn't that the truth." Mary sipped on her drink. "Does the card say who they're from?"

"They aren't my flowers. I didn't open it."

"You're such a rule follower, live a little." Mary stood up and pulled the card from the holder. "Hawkins Ranch is all that's on the outside." She lifted the flap and pulled out the small card. "All it says is 'see you soon' and there's no signature. Huh, I wonder who sent them." Mary put the card back in the envelope and stuffed it back into the holder. She sat back down in her seat. "Such a bizarre couple of days. I don't think I could make anything up quite that crazy."

"If I hadn't lived it, I wouldn't believe it."

"Will you stay up here? I'd feel better if we were all together, maybe a day or two?"

Since the sanctuary was empty, Alex didn't feel the need to rush back to her cabin. Candice could call her up here. She nodded. "I'll stay. I need to check on the horses and then I'd like to pick up a few things from my cabin, especially some clean clothes."

"Sounds like a plan. Thank you for humoring the old woman."

Alex nodded and smiled, knowing that Mary was anything but just an old woman. Mary reached over and squeezed her hand. At that moment, she realized how much Mary meant to her. As much as she missed her mom, she couldn't have asked for a better adoptive family. They had all welcomed her with open arms and helped her feel safe when she needed it most. Now that Hawk was gone and Mick recognized her less and less, Mary was the last of that generation. If anything had happened to her, she'd have never forgiven herself. They didn't share the same bloodlines and it didn't matter. Mary was her family nonetheless.

# CHAPTER SIXTEEN

The house was eerily quiet after the insanity of the last couple of days. The sun had peeked above the horizon bringing life to the dark landscape below. Fitting, given the recent events. Elina peeked in on Néiwóó one more time. She seemed to have handled the ordeal better than expected. The heavy towels that Elina hung up over the windows were doing the job of keeping the room dark so her grandmother would sleep as long as possible. She pulled the door closed behind her and stopped by the laundry room to feed the dogs.

Elina was so tired that she could barely stand. She removed the dogs' vests and tossed some food in their bowls. Hunter sniffed it, took a bite, and then flopped down on his large dog bed and yawned loudly. Scout was more of a foodie and finished both bowls before he surrendered to the exhaustion. She couldn't agree more. Not so much about the food, but certainly about the need to surrender to the exhaustion. A shower and sleep were next on her list too.

The mud had long ago dried on her clothes and her hair was a tangled, matted mess. She stripped off the grimy clothes and stepped into the strong stream of steaming hot water. It felt good to scrub the last two days away from her skin and hair, as if she was washing the insanity away. She soaked beneath the water while the conditioner worked its magic. It was far too relaxing, the way the water pounded on her back. It was tempting to curl up beneath the spray and sleep right there. Well, it would be tempting if there were an unlimited supply of hot water. Since there wasn't, she rinsed her hair, turned off the faucets, and stepped out of the shower. The room remained a steamy warm bliss while she toweled dry. She wrapped the towel around her body and picked up her hairbrush. A hazy mist covered the mirror making it impossible to see her reflection. She stared into the blurry void and worked on combing the tangles out of her long mane. Suddenly, there was a whoosh of air that tickled her exposed skin.

"Oh shit, I'm so sorry. I should have knocked. It was so quiet, I thought you were sleeping. I knew I should have just showered at my place." Alex's voice filled the small room. "Mary insisted I come back as soon as possible."

Elina slowly turned around. Alex stood in the open doorway with bare feet peeking from beneath her muddy pant legs. She held a small stack of clean clothes in her hands. She had the cutest shocked expression on her face. Elina could tell she wanted to look, wanted to stare, but she averted her eyes anyway. There was that throbbing need again. She wanted nothing more than to drop the towel and see Alex's reaction. Would she want Elina as much as she wanted her? Would this insatiable need for release ever go away? Then again, was it really all that wrong to crave someone you cared for? Alex's face was still smeared with mud and bashful embarrassment looked adorable on her, maybe more so because of the mud. The need would have to wait. It wasn't a good idea, at least not today. They were both too raw and too exhausted. Rather than complicate the moment, she kept her towel in place.

"Nonsense. There's plenty of hot water. I'll step out and let you get cleaned up." Elina picked up her hairbrush and hair ties. "Can I talk you into a drink after?"

"We'll have to see if I can keep my eyes open. Probably would be good to share what we've learned, although, I may fall asleep holding the glass."

Elina smiled and stepped closer to the door. Alex didn't move at first. Encouraging. Maybe she needed a little release too. Her eyes dropped to the towel and then came back and locked onto Elina's gaze. Super encouraging. And then Alex averted her eyes again. She smiled sheepishly and stepped off to the side. Elina drew in a shaky breath and then let it out slowly. She scooched past Alex and forced herself to walk across the hall to her room.

She made it through the doorway but didn't actually close the door. Instead, she stood there, leaning up against the doorjamb. She imagined Alex stepping out of the muddy clothes. She tiptoed across the hall and stood outside the door, her hand hovering above the doorknob. No, Alex made it clear that she was exhausted. Elina pulled her hand back and walked back across the hall to her room.

After a long moment, the water turned on. She imagined Alex tilting her head back and what the water would look like cascading down over her broad shoulders and streaming down her back, dripping off her breasts. Her body pulsed and she wondered how she'd ever fall asleep given the relentless throbbing between her thighs.

Elina set the brush and the hair tie on the dresser and crept back across the hallway. She turned the bathroom doorknob. It wasn't locked. She pushed it open a few inches and peeked inside. She could just make out Alex's sexy silhouette. She felt ridiculous and quietly pulled the door closed and turned back. What was she doing? Did she really want their first time together to be a lust filled moment in the shower? Then again, there was something to be said for shower sex. It could be extremely intense. *Stop it!* She had to get a grip.

She walked back across the hall and into her room. The sounds of the steady stream of water beckoned her back, though, and she ignored the warning bells in her mind as she once again made her way back to the bathroom door. She stood there, her hand on the knob. The water shut off and she knew the moment of opportunity was passing. Elina stared at the doorknob. Was it turning or was it her imagination? She heard the latch click and pushed ever so gently on the door. It swung wide open. Alex stood on the bathmat. Water glistened on her naked body and dripped from her hair. Elina leaned against the doorjamb and stared at Alex's sexy body.

"Do you know that the floorboards squeak super loud every time you walk back and forth and back and forth? Was there something you needed?" Alex raised her eyebrows in a questioning expression. A touch of arrogant sass looked good on her.

Elina looked Alex up and down, admiring everything she saw.

"I realized that I took the last towel. Though, if I stand here staring long enough, you'll eventually drip dry." Elina released the towel wrapped around her body and held it out to Alex. "Or you could use this one if you'd like."

She stood there, completely exposed, watching Alex's eyes for a reaction. She was rewarded with a sexy, seductive smile. She held each end of the towel in her hands and swung it up over Alex's head, around the back of her neck.

"Come to think of it, there is something I need."

She gathered the two ends of the towel into one hand with every intention of leading Alex across the hall, but Alex stepped forward, bent down slightly, and lifted Elina into her arms before she even had the chance to turn around. Her breath caught and she wrapped her legs around Alex's waist.

"Take me to bed?"

Silently, Alex carried her across the hall. Elina had no idea how she closed the door, but she was grateful when the latch clicked. Alex lifted a knee onto the bed and then gently lowered her onto the mattress. Elina released the hold her legs had around Alex's waist and stretched out alongside her. Alex's naked body felt incredible. Strong, firm, and fit. Alex pulled the towel from behind her neck and tossed it onto the floor. The look in her eyes shifted from emotional to a mixture of hunger and desire. She was grateful that she wasn't the only one who was hungry because suddenly, she was starving.

Elina took control. She leaned forward and kissed Alex with fierce, probing passion. She rolled Alex over on her back, straddled her hips, and pinned her arms above her head without breaking the kiss. With a firm grip on her wrist, she guided one of Alex's hands between her legs. The last couple of days had been so unexpectedly intense that she just wanted to forget about all of it with a powerful, commanding fuck. She pushed her hips into Alex's hand and expected strong fingers to plunge deep inside of her. She was surprised when Alex pulled her hand back and broke away from the kiss.

"What's the rush? Slow down. Enjoy the moment with me." Alex stroked her cheek gently with her fingertips.

Elina had no idea how Alex could say so much by simply looking at her. The emotional expression on her face and the passionate look in her eyes sent tingling jolts of electricity throughout her body. She wondered if Alex saw any emotion in her expression. Was the need for raw physical gratification an emotion? Or was she simply a broken soul? She drew in a deep breath and let it out slowly. She hadn't always been like this.

"Come here. Lie down next to me." Alex held her arms open.

The throbbing need between her legs made her want to stay right where she was. A few strong thrusts of her hips and she'd feel a whole lot better. Elina ignored it as best she could and lifted herself off Alex. She snuggled in along the length of her body and rested her head in that sweet spot on Alex's shoulder. She lifted her arm and ran her fingertips from just above Alex's knee, up her thigh and over her hips and stomach and then between her breasts and up her neck. She was rewarded with a full body shiver. Alex adjusted her body so that she was on her side. She moved down in the bed slightly and kissed her. Elina's eyes closed and she was swept away to that magical kiss on the porch swing. Alex's kiss was filled with so much passion that her knees would have buckled if she'd been standing. Her tongue teased Elina's with the perfect amount of possessive need that made her nipples ache and created another rush of wet between her legs. She wanted nothing more than to take control again, but she resisted and let Alex set the pace.

Her hand trailed down Elina's neck and over her shoulder and then all along the length of her arm. She teased her way up her waist and then to her breast. Elina gasped for air when Alex's warm hand cupped her breast and she applied just the right amount of pressure to her nipple by squeezing it between two fingers. She took the move as an invitation to explore Alex's body and reveled in her reactions to her teasing touches.

Alex rolled Elina over on her back, bent down, and captured her nipple in her mouth. She covered her nipple and flicked it with the tip of her tongue. Oh, and what talented command she had over that tongue. Elina could think of so many places for that tongue to explore and savor, but first it was her turn.

She used her entire body to shift Alex onto her back. She worked her way down Alex's body, enjoying her responses to delicate nibbles on her ear and kisses on her neck. She captured Alex's nipple in her mouth and was rewarded with a sharp intake of air and a deep-throated groan. She held the back of Elina's head while her thumb stroked the side of Elina's neck. Elina could resist no more. She slid off to the side, straddling Alex's thigh and then ran her hand up the inside of Alex's leg. She was so wet. Elina slid farther down Alex's body, leaving behind a trail of kisses. She maneuvered her body between Alex's legs and started a new trail of kisses up Alex's inner thigh.

"Wait."

Elina froze. She lifted herself up on her hands and knees so she could see Alex's eyes. "What's wrong?"

"I've never had anyone want to do that for me." She half sat up and pushed hair out of Elina's eyes. "Or maybe I've never been vulnerable enough to allow it."

"May I be the first?" Elina smiled. Alex couldn't get any more adorable in such a sexy way.

Alex smiled and nodded and then rested her head back down on the pillow. "I'm so embarrassed." She covered her face with her hands.

Elina climbed back up her body and lay on top of her. "Please don't feel embarrassed. We could save that for another time if you'd prefer."

The sheer honesty of the confession and the trust it took to share it touched Elina on a profoundly deep emotional level. Everything about the experience shifted in an instant and her impatient physical need to be fucked into oblivion evaporated. Instead, the intimacy of the moment tugged at her heart and made her want to be in the moment with Alex.

"You wouldn't mind?"

Elina cupped Alex's face in her hands and looked into her eyes. "Not at all." She couldn't find the words to express how much Alex's confession meant to her. Even if she didn't climax. Right now, this would be enough. Elina kissed her tenderly.

Alex responded immediately with that perfectly possessive kiss. Elina slid over onto her side and trailed her hand from Alex's cheek down to the warmth between her legs. She slid her fingers against Alex and let her push where she wanted pressure. Elina bent her knee and opened herself up when Alex reached down between her legs. The pace picked up and Elina thrust into Alex's fingers when they were at just the perfect spot. Alex did the same when Elina applied a touch of pressure with her fingertips. All of her inhibitions seemed to be gone for the moment. Elina could feel Alex tightening and knew she was getting close. She circled herself on the heel of Alex's palm, putting a little extra pressure where she needed it most, and just like that, she was right there too. They gasped and shuddered in each other's arms. It was tender and incredible and everything she'd cherish about their first time together.

She kissed Alex and then stared into her beautiful eyes.

"So much better than a drink."

Alex smiled. "So much better."

Elina snuggled into her arms. She had every intention of a round two, but she blinked twice and drifted contently off to sleep.

## CHAPTER SEVENTEEN

Alex's eyes fluttered open. Somewhere close by a phone was ringing and ringing and ringing. It wasn't her ringtone. Thankfully, the call went to voice mail and the ringing finally stopped. She looked around the bright, sunlit room and smiled. Thank goodness, it hadn't been a dream after all. Elina shifted a bit in bed and snuggled in closer. Their naked bodies fit perfectly together. She wasn't ready to move. She didn't want this moment to end.

The stupid phone started ringing again. Whoever was calling was persistent. Elina stirred and lifted her head off that sweet spot on her shoulder. The sun streaming in the window added a deep golden glow to Elina's eyes. The way they lit up when she recognized who was in bed with her and then that sleepy smile which made those beautiful eyes sparkle was something Alex could get used to seeing every single morning. Talk about a great way to start a day.

"Good morning, or is it afternoon?" Elina leaned over and kissed Alex tenderly on the lips.

The phone started ringing again for a third time.

"I think it's afternoon and it seems that someone really wants to talk to you."

"Let it go to voice mail." Elina lifted herself up and straddled Alex's hips. "I have something else entirely on my mind."

Her hair cascaded forward and draped over her perfect breasts. Alex reached up and lifted her hair back behind her shoulders. She wanted to see as much silky skin as possible. The phone started ringing for the fourth time.

"Hold that thought." Elina shook her head and lifted herself off Alex.

She pulled a tank top over her head and tugged on the white fabric with one hand until it kind of covered one of her breasts. Alex propped herself up on her elbow and enjoyed the show.

"Hello," Elina said into the phone.

"We need to put Gina Holt back in play."

The words were slightly muffled, but that wasn't what concerned Alex. It was the fact that the color drained out of Elina's face. Whoever was on the phone wasn't anyone Elina seemed to want to talk to.

"No, find someone else. I can't go through that again."

Alex couldn't make out the caller's response.

"Hang on." Elina set the phone down and pulled on a pair of shorts. She straightened her tank top and pulled it down over her stomach. "Alex, I'll be right back." Elina picked the phone up and walked out of the room.

Alex dressed quickly and walked into the living room. It was quiet. She caught movement out of the corner of her eye. Elina was out on the back deck, pacing back and forth with the phone pressed against her ear. What she wouldn't give to hear the conversation. Alex watched for a few more seconds and then decided to go into the kitchen and put on a pot of coffee. Once that was started, she filled the tea kettle with water and set that on the stove on high. She finally looked at a clock to see that it was three eighteen in the afternoon. At least they'd gotten some decent sleep.

The door to the deck clicked open and then closed again. Scout and Hunter ran past the kitchen and down the hall, likely headed to the laundry room. Must be time for breakfast. Elina walked past the doorway too. She heard the two bowls being filled and then footsteps coming back up the hall. Elina kept on walking across the house and up the hall to her room.

Alex stayed in the kitchen and gave her some space. She pulled two cups down from the cupboard and dropped a tea bag into one.

The water wasn't hot enough yet, so she poured herself a cup of coffee, added cream and sugar and sipped on it while waiting for the kettle to whistle. When it did, she filled the mug and took it out to the dining room. She placed it on a coaster where Elina had sat for dinner on the night she arrived. She walked around the table and sat in her chair across from Elina's. It had only been a few days since that evening and yet it seemed as if weeks had passed.

Her second cup of coffee was empty and the tea was likely cold when Elina emerged from her room. Alex's heart sank. Elina was dressed in jeans and a blouse, and her hair was pulled back and braided, but that wasn't what knocked Alex off her feet. It was the fact that she had her suitcase in one hand, and her go bag in the other. She set them down on the floor behind the couch and marched toward the table.

"These meant so much to me when I thought they were from you, even though I hadn't thanked you for them yet." Elina picked up the vase of flowers and walked into the kitchen. "You'll be seeing me soon all right, bitch." She yanked the flowers from the vase and stuffed them into the garbage can and then dumped the water out of the vase before throwing it in the garbage on top of the flowers.

"I should have throat-punched Bobby Conner for pulling me into that news story. I knew better than to let my face get on camera. It's all my fault. The plane, the kidnapping, the ravine, all of it happened because she saw me on the evening news and Bobby just had to mention the ranch. I am so sincerely sorry. My being here has put you and Néiwóó in so much danger."

"Who saw you on the news? What's going on?" Alex asked.

"It doesn't matter. I'll fix it."

"It matters to me. I'm here. Let me help. Please, tell me what we need to do to fix it. Don't just disappear." Alex suddenly felt helpless. She wasn't ready to say good-bye.

"It's my mess and I have to clean it up."

"Fair enough. But if you're saying bad guys know about the ranch, then it falls into my professional area too. Please?" Maybe appealing to Elina's professional side would get through easier than an appeal to her emotional one.

Elina walked over to a side table in the living room, opened a drawer and pulled out a pen and a piece of paper. She wrote something down and then returned to the dining table and laid the piece of paper on the table. She tugged on Alex's hand. "Come on, let's go for a walk."

Alex glanced at the paper first. It was a note to Mary letting her know they were out back. She accepted Elina's hand and followed her outside.

"What I'm about to share with you is highly classified and confidential. It's also important to me that you know the truth."

"I'm a little nervous to hear what you have to say, but thank you for trusting me enough to tell me." Alex squeezed Elina's hand.

"You've asked me a few times what it is that I do. Over the years, my skills have evolved, and I've become somewhat of a federal bounty hunter for hire."

"A *federal* bounty hunter? There's no such thing. Bounty hunters work strictly at the state level and can only operate in the state where they're licensed."

"It's not an official title. It's simply the best way to describe what it is that I do. I'm an independent contractor and my work is sought after and sanctioned across several agencies. The cases I'm recruited for are strictly federal. It started out because of my SAR career and the fact that fugitives like to hide in remote settings, but then it evolved, and I became the person who could help when the rule of law was working against those sworn to uphold it. Technically, I'm not law enforcement and more like a bounty hunter in the sense that I don't need to worry too much about rules and warrants. I can collect evidence if it *happens* to end up out in the open. Once visible, it falls under the plain view doctrine and it's admissible in court. I'm granted quite a bit of latitude because my success rate is so high."

"Is that what the deputy director meant when he said you had to color in the lines? When Candice said they wanted you contracted for what went on here, were you contracted as a law enforcement consultant or were you contracted in your bounty hunter role?"

"The contract for this issue was just the deputy director's way of protecting you and the sanctuary. A nondisclosure of sorts.

Normally, I'm given an objective and while I'm working on that objective, I'm protected by the agency who requested my assistance. Believe me when I say that nobody wants my objectives in writing, so I don't really sign contracts. I either accept a job or I don't. Candice mentioned a contract, so I went with it."

"Okay, so help me understand the comment about coloring in the lines."

"You'll understand more in a moment." Elina looked up. She had tears in her eyes. "Honestly, I became arrogant. I thought I'd trained for it all, anything and everything. I thought there wasn't a situation I couldn't handle, and the truth is, I couldn't have been more wrong. I took a job that I wasn't at all prepared for and I allowed myself to be swept up in the insanity."

"Can you tell me about it?" Alex asked.

"I don't want to, but I feel like I need to. I'm afraid of what you'll think of me when I do. You may not want anything to do with me when you know what I did." Elina wiped tears from her face.

Alex couldn't help but wonder what Elina had done that would make her think that. Candice had shared that they were friends and her bar was set pretty high. Besides, the person Alex was getting to know seemed to have a line she wouldn't cross either. She looked over at Elina. "There isn't much you could say that would turn me away."

"I hope that's the case. We'll see." She half smiled. "About a year ago, I was hired as support for an operation that was already in progress. An undercover agent had gone missing and they wanted me to find her. It was a covert assignment. No one knew about my role. Everything about it was completely off-book. I memorized a phone number and that was my only contact. The target owned a lesbian bar and according to intel, it was a front for all sorts of illegal enterprises. Drugs, escort services and so much more. You name it and she seemed to dabble in it. They suspected that she had people in her pocket. A judge, law enforcement, someone high up in the chain somewhere feeding her intel because somehow, the evidence would disappear and she'd avoid arrest.

"My role was simple. I was supposed to go in, find the missing agent and if she was still alive, bring her to safety. If I happened upon some solid evidence of illegal activity, there would be a hefty bonus. I thought it would be like any other job, only this time I was rescuing one of the good guys instead of capturing a fugitive."

Elina released Alex's hand and wrapped her arm around her waist. Alex lifted her arm up around Elina's shoulders and held her close. The contact felt good. They fit together nicely. Alex was beginning to see the yin and yang between them and how they complemented each other.

"Tracking fugitives is a game of hide-and-seek. They hide, I seek, and when I catch them, I get paid, it's as simple as that. I study their patterns, their behaviors, but I never get to know them as a person with feelings and emotions. What I failed to understand was that undercover work to find someone that someone else is hiding, is completely different. There's a relationship that's needed to earn that kind of trust. You have to get to know your target as a person and make them believe you care."

Elina was quiet for a moment.

"I'd like to hear more." Alex squeezed her shoulder.

"There was an opening for a bartender and a dancer. My persona applied for the bartender role. The agency created a rock-solid identity for me too with an arrest record, a troubled past, the whole bit."

"Gina Holt?" Alex asked. "I heard them tell you on the phone that they needed to put Gina Holt back in play."

Elina nodded. "Yeah, Gina Holt. She's a little rough around the edges. The target apparently had a thing for dark skinned women. I'm sure the agency knew that, but they neglected to clue me in on that tidbit. I got the job. She flirted with me at first and before long we were together around the clock. From what I'd gathered, she'd been raised in a twisted and manipulative world. She felt screwed over by her family and made it her mission to make a name for herself. She wanted to create her own legacy by edging in on the family's enterprises. Believe me, she's no innocent victim. She loved to mind-fuck people. She totally mind-fucked me. I wasn't prepared for it. I started to forget which way was up. I began to care about her. I thought perhaps she could be saved, maybe even wanted out of that life. She made me think I was the center of her universe. The lines blur when you're undercover and you end up doing things that you know to be wrong, but your handler tells you to do them anyway, so your persona is believable."

"Like what? What happened? What did you do to make Gina believable?" Alex wasn't sure she wanted to know the answer. Was this where she'd learn that Elina could kill for a living? Could she care about someone who was a killer?

"One night, I was closing up the bar. She asked for a drink and told me to pour whatever I liked too, on the house. I made the drinks and told her I'd be right back. I had to put the cash drawer and the earnings in the safe. When I came back, we had a drink... and then another and another. The world started to swim and I felt a little weird. The next thing I knew we were naked and doing body shots on the bar. I swear that I could smell colors and the music that came out of the speakers was emanating from my soul. The lights in the club pulsed like a heartbeat. It was a sensory overload unlike anything I'd ever known and the desire to keep experiencing it almost consumed me."

Elina leaned her head on Alex's shoulder. Alex wasn't so sure she wanted to hear anymore. Drugs and body shots and mind-blowing sex with a lesbian crime boss. Alex had never felt like more of a small-town hick. Hell, she wouldn't even let Elina go down on her last night. She wondered if it wouldn't have been easier to hear that Elina really was a contract killer. She ignored the feelings of inadequacy and focused on listening.

"It was Molly, Ecstasy. She'd slipped it in my drink. It was in my system pretty much from that night until I got out months later. I lived in a euphoric haze, and coming down from it was a torturous hell that I never want to experience again. I was in the hospital for a week. When you take that shit, you forget to eat or drink or sleep. I was so messed up. My persona almost devoured the person I was before that job. The sad part is...I was played from both sides. The missing agent was found a few days after I'd gone under. She'd been murdered and her body had been dumped, but my contact never bothered to tell me. He kept me under for five months, hoping that I'd find information to take down the enterprise. But what he didn't know was that I had started to care about her and had stopped looking, maybe even stopped caring that what she was doing was illegal. I knew I needed out, so I missed a couple of check-in calls on purpose, and that's when they cast the net."

Elina stopped walking for a moment and stared off into the foothills. Alex waited to see if there was more to the story.

"Anyway, that's what the deputy director meant when he said I had to color in the lines. My once rock-solid reputation took a big hit. It was the first and only time I'd ever gone off the rails like that. There are times that I still battle Gina's needs, but then you came into my life when I needed you the most. You have no idea how important your phone calls became. Getting to know you helped pull me out of that darkness. Even last night, you slowed me down and reminded me that sex can be special and deserves to be savored. Alex, being with you felt wonderful. Getting to know you has helped me find my balance and heal my spirit. Thanks to you and Néiwóó and even helping my mom through the divorce, I'm getting closer to being whole again."

Elina sat beneath a small tree in the shade.

Alex sat down next to her. "If you're finally healing from all of that then why on earth would you ever consider going back into play? Why not let them hunt her down like any other fugitive?"

"Like I said, she's slippery. Technically, she's not a fugitive from the law, but there's a contract out on her life. That's what she's hiding from. They want me to flip her and take down the family empire. Her bar was owned by a shell company that they haven't been able to trace back to her directly. A lot of arrests were made, including my persona, but she skated free and clear. All assets associated with the bar were seized and her various enterprises shut down. There was a ton of cash in the safe and she's claiming to be broke so I'm betting she didn't get the heads-up in time to prepare."

Elina turned to face Alex. She reached over and held Alex's hand. "I have to deflect her focus away from Hawkins Ranch. There's a good chance she knows my alias was a lie, since she tracked me to the house and there's no Gina Holt associated with it. Those flowers were from her, a kind of calling card to let me know I'm in her crosshairs. And the agency that wants me to go back in somehow knows that she wants to be back in touch with me. I'm still not clear on that part. But everything that's happened these past few days is only the tip of the iceberg if she feels ignored. It's me she's after. If I go, then you and Néiwóó will be safe. I need to clean up this mess."

"She's the sister, the one who stole the money from the family cartel and was getting it laundered. And they just happened to drop that money on your family's land."

"Nothing just happens in her world. I'm certain that the money was dropped here on purpose. I don't have all of the details yet."

Alex's mind was spinning. She never thought she'd consider suggesting the end of someone's life and yet here she was thinking that everything would be over if someone would just take this mystery woman out.

"Where are you going? What's the plan? How can I help?"

"The less you know, the better right now. I did insist that USMS lead the op. I trust the deputy director and Candice much more than my old handler. You can help by keeping Néiwóó safe. Knowing you two are safe will let me focus on the mission."

"Can I have a general direction? I'd like to be prepared in case you need me."

Elina looked up and smiled. "I'll be a little north of Great Falls. It makes my appearance on the news make sense and takes the focus away from Wolfbend. My persona talked about a dream of having her own bar somewhere in Montana. I can make it work on the slim chance she doesn't know my alias is a fake."

"There has to be something more I can do to help."

"There is. Would you hide my truck and trailer? They'll provide me with an older model truck the same color and licensed to Gina. Could you also take care of my brood while I'm gone? And then, there's one more request and this one is the most important. I wonder if you would be my lifeline? No one needs to know we have a way to communicate, but knowing you're there for me will help keep me grounded." Elina leaned over a bit and pulled her phone out of her pocket. She shook her head and stuffed it back in her pocket. "Transport is only twenty minutes out and we have a lot to go over before I leave. Please tell me that you're in my corner."

Alex nodded. Without a doubt she was in Elina's corner. She'd love nothing more than to go undercover with her and be at her side. She tried to listen carefully, but it was difficult to focus given the fact that Elina would be leaving soon to willingly leap into piranha-infested waters without a protective cage.

## Chapter Eighteen

The small bar was dark and musty. It was a little hole-in-the-wall place that maybe seated twenty at most. One of the two overhead lights flickered occasionally. Elina fought the urge to climb up on top of the bar and unscrew the offending bulb altogether. The place reeked of stale cigarette smoke even though smoking inside had been banned for years. She wiped down the bar for what seemed like the four-hundredth time. At least it was no longer sticky to the touch.

Bells jingled above the front entrance when the door was pushed open. Late afternoon sun streamed in behind a silhouette until the door closed and stole any indication of the time of day. Gabby looked like a shell of her former self. Life on the run didn't seem to agree with her at all. There was at least an inch of gray roots peeking out of her rich, jet-black hair. Her trendy clothes, leather skirts, and stiletto heels had been replaced with jeans, a dainty floral blouse, and white canvas sneakers. She was almost unrecognizable without her perfectly applied makeup and notorious perfume. The contrast couldn't have been more striking.

She looked around the bar, most certainly taking a quick evaluation of her surroundings. There wasn't much to take in. The bar wasn't even open. Technically, it was closed for renovations when it was rented for the op. They'd set up a few ladders for show, although, if it were really her place, she would have had a bulldozer on site and started over. She dropped the towel on the edge of the sink behind the bar and then walked past Gabby and locked the front door.

"Are we alone?"

"It's not that big a place, feel free to check it out. Like I said on the phone, just me and the dog." Elina motioned behind the bar. Hunter was curled up on his dog bed.

"What brought you to this two-bit town?"

"Unlike you, I don't have unrestricted access to cash. It's not much, but it's a start." Elina tried to play it cool, but her blood boiled with rage. She'd have loved nothing more than to launch herself across that bar and choke the life out of that smug face.

"Aren't you going to offer me a drink?" Gabby walked up to the bar and sat on a stool. "You look good. How've you been?"

"Aside from being interrogated for days on end after you disappeared and hung me out to dry? Just fuckin' dandy. Something I've been wondering though, are you that lucky or did you have a heads-up?" Elina asked.

She pulled an olive jar out of a tiny fridge behind the bar and stabbed two olives onto a martini pick. She pretended the olives were Gabby's eyeballs and that made her smile. She set the olives in the glass along with a splash of olive brine. She poured Gabby's favorite vodka and a drop of vermouth into an ice-cold shaker, swirled it around, and poured the contents over the olives. Gabby smiled at her, likely because she remembered exactly how she liked her martinis made. She wouldn't be smiling if she could read her mind, that's for sure.

"A girl never divulges her secrets."

"You will if you want my help."

Gabby sat there and stared at her. Elina held the martini glass and waited.

"Okay, fine. No, I'm not that lucky, although I'm afraid many bridges have been burned. People stop being friendly when you can't pay them, and the fucking feds seized everything I had, including the cash in my safe. I'm running out of owed favors too. I guess Dominick has more power or better dirt on those I had under my thumb. Any chance you'd teach me to bartend?" Gabby accepted the martini glass and then drained it in one swig. "Oh, that hit the spot. I haven't had a drink in longer than I care to admit."

"I take it you'd like another?" Elina asked. She hoped the booze would loosen her up enough to confess something they could use as leverage. The mics scattered around the bar would record every word.

She turned for the olives, already certain of the answer. She made a double in the shaker and poured half into Gabby's glass and placed the shaker in the fridge for cold keeping.

"There's something else I haven't enjoyed in quite some time. You could take me right here on the bar, just like old times." Gabby smiled over the rim of her glass. "I've missed the way you make me feel."

The seductive tone of her voice lit Elina's body on fire. That night in the club happened just like she'd shared with Alex. The drugs made everything so incredibly intense. Just the sound of Gabby's voice brought it all back and Elina had to step back and think about the torture of climbing out of that haze to fight off the urge to honor the request. She closed her eyes and counted to five before she dared to open them again.

"Let's stick with the drinks," Elina said.

"What happened to you, Gina? You used to be a lot more fun. What, haven't you been able to find a decent Molly supplier in this hell-hole? Or are these frumpy clothes too much of a turnoff?"

Elina had never tried drugs before that job. Coming out of that fog wasn't anything she wanted to experience again, although her body remembered the intensity of every single touch while under its spell. Thankfully, being with Alex was every bit as intense, if not more so, because of the feelings and emotions involved. She focused on that to keep her out of trouble.

"I'm not playing this cat-and-mouse game with you. Why are you here? What do you want from me?" Elina asked.

She poured herself a whiskey neat. She kept the glass safely in her hand and walked around the bar to sit on the barstool next to Gabby.

"You were the only person who never asked me for a favor. You never asked for money. You didn't try to blackmail me or hold anything over my head. I tested you more than I've tested anyone else, and you stayed by my side. You looked at me like you could really see who I was. Those fucking eyes of yours. Talk about addictive. I really felt like you saw me and not the family bullshit. That, and you didn't put up with my shit. Instead, you called me out on it and kept me honest, so to speak."

"I did all that for you and how do you repay me? You disappear and let me take the fall. Remind me why I should help you, because what I'd like to do is feed you to my dog." Elina scowled at her and then tipped back the whiskey.

"I was on my way back to the bar when I got the heads-up. There was no way I could have warned you in time."

"You could have tried."

"I could have done a thousand things differently. I could have had Dominick taken out when Dad was sent upstate and then I'd be the one running the family empire."

"Yeah, and you were what, sixteen back then? Dominick's five years older and was already established in the family business. Like you had the balls or the people to take him out. You were probably worried about who your prom date was going to be or whether or not you had front row tickets to the Bieber concert."

"Fuck you."

"Struck a nerve, must be some truth in there."

"It would have been Destiny's Child, not Bieber."

"Come on, why'd you reach out? What do you want from me?"

Gabby's eyes narrowed and the facade of playfulness was gone. In its place was the gaze of a ruthless criminal. "When you were swept up, why weren't you charged? I hid a decent stash of Molly in your backpack. There was enough to be charged with dealing too, not just plain ol' possession. You should have gotten a few years away. Unless they used it for leverage to get information from you, but then again, your name wasn't on the rat list. Come to think of it, there wasn't a name I didn't recognize on the rat list either. I gave you some very specific dirt too. You could have tied me to a few things anyway, but then there was no warrant for my arrest. I'm intrigued to know why. Why not share what you knew?"

"What makes you think I didn't find the drugs and flush them down the drain? No need to share anything if there was no leverage. Why would you set me up like that?" Elina's pulse raced, but she kept her face blank. Gabby wasn't fishing for information. She knew.

"I don't think you found it, just like I don't think your name is Gina. Your cover was good, but not charging you when all of the other girls were charged was a big faux pas. The thing I can't figure out is what agency you're with, and believe me, I've tried." Gabby held up her empty glass. "If I haven't offended you too much, may I have what's left in the shaker?"

Elina got up and walked behind the bar. She refilled the olives on Gabby's martini pick, dropped the splash of olive brine into the glass and emptied the shaker. She hadn't shared because, at the time, she'd had feelings for Gabby. Not only that, she'd been way too out of it when they pulled her. The drugs had done a number on her body and brain, and any testimony she was able to give would have been muddied by the drug use. She didn't want to share any of that with Gabby. She was still fighting off the urge to launch across the bar and beat the living shit out of her for all she'd endured in those five months and in the months after as she learned to live again. She slid the glass across the bar and poured herself another shot of whiskey.

"You still haven't told me what it is you want. Why are you here fucking with my life all over again?"

Gabby nodded as if Elina had confirmed the conclusion she'd come to. "The people I had in my pocket are now avoiding me like the plague. I thought I had it all figured out. I had a passport ready, a clean ID, and a pilot who would fly me to a nice little island in the pacific. All that was left was to figure out how to pay for it since the feds seized my getaway money. Stealing four million from my brother might have worked, and that town seemed like a great place to drop it once I saw you on the news. I could get my girl back and have a place to organize the rest of my plans while also using the local money launderer. But then shit went wrong, didn't it?" She sipped her drink, her eyes cold and hard. "That's my bad and now

I'm not sure whether Dom's angrier that I stole the money or that I lost some of our crew to the feds. I tried to smooth things over, but his response was a photograph of them killing my pilot along with a nice little note about what he'll do to me when he finds me." Gabby tipped up the martini glass and drained it. "I sold off all of my jewelry for what seems like pittance, you know how much I loved my jewelry, and went into hiding, but that money is almost gone. Dominick's patient, and worse yet, he's persistent. It's only a matter of time unless I can figure out another option. So, that's why I'm here, because I feel like I can trust you to help me out of this mess. I think you can perhaps coordinate another option."

Trust didn't seem like a word they should use with one another. "When did you eat last?" Elina asked. Without a doubt, Gabby was feeling the three martinis, and Elina needed time to think. "There's a pretty decent pizza place in town. I can have something delivered."

"If I have a slice, do I earn another martini?"

"Two slices and a glass of water and then you will have earned another martini. Is a supreme okay?"

"No mushrooms, I don't eat fungus." Gabby twisted her stool until she was facing Elina. "You never told me which agency you work for. Could you get me into my safety deposit box?" She reached across the bar and touched Elina's cheek. "What's your real name?"

They both knew she wasn't about to answer that. She moved away from Gabby's touch. Elina finished ordering the pizza and then set her phone on the counter and looked into Gabby's eyes. "What's in your safety deposit box?"

"Evidence." Gabby plucked the last olive off the tiny skewer and popped it in her mouth.

"Evidence against whom?"

"Everyone, all of them. Specifically, my brother and everyone on the take. If my life has to change, then I want all of them to pay a price too. Recordings, paper, photographs, videos…all sorts of stuff."

Elina looked at Gabby. She no longer felt the connection between them that she thought existed back then. Had her feelings for Gabby developed because of the drugs? Perhaps her perception that Gabby had wanted out had been skewed by the drug-induced haze too. Or, had she been spot-on back then in thinking that Gabby could change? Was Gabby suggesting a life outside of the family business, or just trying to save her own ass?

"If you could do your life over, what would you do differently?" Elina asked.

"What do you mean? Other than my brother dominating the family empire, my life wasn't so bad."

"Say you weren't a Manbessee. Say you were born into the Cooper family with parents who worked normal jobs in an office somewhere. If you could pick a new life and be anyone you wanted to be, what would you do? What kind of career would you pick? Clean slate, anything."

"Couldn't the Cooper name carry some weight? I like a name that opens doors. Besides, isn't being rich a career? I liked life best when I was simply rich."

"Yeah, but in the real world, people have to earn money by working at a job. It's not too late to learn how to be a bartender." Elina pushed to see if she could get beyond the snarky answers that were typical of Gabby's first line of defense. Witness protection wouldn't offer the lifestyle she'd known all her life. Would she simply find a new criminal avenue to take once she'd taken her brother down?

"I'd like my club back. I enjoyed owning the club."

Elina shook her head. Gabby wasn't looking to change. She simply wanted to make others responsible for losing her way of life. "That's simply another way to choose rich as a career. You never really did anything at the club besides pass out drugs and have sex with anyone you wanted. You didn't even pretend to hire people or pay bills."

"Isn't that what a bar manager is for? What if I had a huge amount of evidence? Could there be a way for me to be rich again?"

It didn't appear that Gabby was the lost soul that Elina once thought she was. Instead, it seemed that she was every bit the spoiled, self-serving bitch in the briefing report. Elina decided to ask the questions a different way. She was certain she already knew the answers, but it was worth getting it voiced in a recording.

"Could you be rich and not break the law? No drugs, no operating an escort service, none of the stuff that went on at the club. If you have the right kind of evidence, you might be able to sway something close to the life you want. Could you simply enjoy being wealthy and park your ass on a beach somewhere?"

"Would you be able—"

The knob on the front door turned and then there was a loud thud. Wow, that was fast, she'd just placed the order not ten minutes ago. Elina smiled and silently hoped the delivery guy hadn't smashed the pizza when he tried to walk through a locked door. She made it to the end of the bar when the blacked-out front windows shattered into a million pieces. Rapid-fire shots from an automatic weapon sent splintered chunks of wood and glass flying in all directions. Elina shoved two stools out of her way and yanked Gabby down behind the bar.

## CHAPTER NINETEEN

The late evening sun blanketed the landscape in a tranquil blend of deep reds and oranges and a hint of purple where the clouds met small patches of deep blue sky. Alex sat in the saddle on the highest point of the pasture and savored the stillness of the moment. It felt good to be back in the saddle, and it seemed that Dutch felt the same way. He had a little bounce to his step now that he was no longer confined to a box stall and small paddock. The bison herd looked good too. The calves were growing quickly and beginning to develop the humps in their shoulders, and now had tiny nubs of horn on the top of their heads. Alex hoped to get the herd sorted and the bulls off to auction before they got much bigger.

There hadn't been too many still moments lately. The insanity of it all still had her a little rattled. Seeing a pilot run the herd and the intruders in the sanctuary searching for the four bags of cash was one for the books. But then to have Mary kidnapped and to have to find those bags and exchange them for her safety was something she wouldn't have believed if she hadn't lived it. To think that all of it was because of some criminal who was obsessed with Elina was the icing on the unbelievable cake. Too curious to let it go, she'd done some digging of her own. Details were sparse, given how undercover the operation was, but she'd found out a little.

Dan Williams, the local money launderer, had lived in the area for several years. He was the broker for his own real estate office and then operated as a registered agent setting up shell corporations out of the same location. The property out on Dry Gulch Road was listed as a high-end horse ranch. He cleaned the money by theoretically selling horses to and from people who didn't exist. He had local law enforcement in his pocket too, paying them to look the other way and to provide assistance when it was needed. It surprised her to learn that the three guys Elina took down at the exchange were, in fact, the county sheriff and two of his deputies. No wonder the first two intruders asked for the sheriff so they could get on with their day. She'd still be oblivious to the whole thing if they had recovered the money on their own. She sat there in the saddle wondering what else was going on out there right under her nose. Was the series of events a typical week in Elina's world?

Alex's phone rang, pulling her out of her thoughts.

"Hey, Candice. How's the op going? Please tell me it's over and that the target has offered to confess or testify. It's been a long week and we just want her home."

"Are you up at the house?" Candice asked.

"No, I'm out with the herd on horseback. Why?"

"There's been a situation. I think you should head back and take Mary out to the sanctuary until we know what's going on. I can't imagine why anyone would come up to the house, but better safe."

"Is Elina all right?" Alex's heart hammered in her chest.

"I honestly don't know. Alex, she's missing, and so is the target. We don't know if they're on the run or if they were captured. We're still piecing it all together. The bar took heavy fire. We lost eyes and ears. There was a breach inside and there's blood, but it could be that Hunter did his job. It looks like she took a couple of them out, but the place is shot to hell. Forensics should help us piece it all together."

"Was Hunter hurt?"

"They haven't found him either."

"What did you get off the mics before audio was lost? Did she say anything? Where in the fuck was the backup?" Alex asked. She turned Dutch's head and urged him into a full gallop.

"They were in position, but it all happened so fast. From what I gather, she thought it was a pizza being delivered. Once the bullets started flying, you can't hear anything else. The shooters were well armed and gave the team a hell of a firefight once we followed them in. One of ours had to be air-lifted out. At this point, we're not even sure we got all of the shooters or if some escaped."

"Shit, I should have been there with her. I'm holding you responsible if anything happens to her. How on earth did they even find them? The site was supposed to be secure!"

"I can't answer that yet, but I'm looking at all possibilities. I won't rule anything out."

"Do you think it was a leak? I knew I should have done the setup."

"Nothing is off the table."

"Call me back the second you have something."

Once again, Alex felt completely useless as a law enforcement officer. She should have been there. Logically, she understood the reasoning. Elina had the relationship with the target, a level of trust already established, which, jealousy aside, was unnerving in its own way, but she understood it. She also knew that she had to stay at the ranch. It was her assigned post. Then there was Mary. She'd sworn she'd protect her and had already failed to do so once. She bypassed the barn and rode Dutch all the way up to the main house. She slid from his back and tied his reins to the deck railing on her way up the steps and ran into the house.

"Mary? Mary, where are you?" Alex ran from room to room. "Mary!"

Alex spun around in the kitchen. No sounds, no Mary, no Scout. *What the fuck!*

A door clicked in the hallway. Alex ran out of the kitchen so fast that she almost knocked Mary flat on her back.

"What are you fussing about? Can't I take a shower? I had the dog with me, told him the command, just like you asked." Mary stood there, wrapped up in a fuzzy bath robe with water dripping from her semi-soapy hair.

"Something's happened. Finish up your shower, quick. We need to grab the go bag and head up to the sanctuary."

"Alex, I've about had it with this shit. What's going on now? Is Elina all right?"

"I don't have a status on Elina yet, but she's a badass, so we're going to assume she's okay. For now, please, rinse the soap off and let's go or I'll toss you in the truck sudsy, I don't much care."

"If it's that serious, I'll go sudsy. I can shower there. My bag's all packed, just like you asked. It's there, at the foot of my bed."

Alex grabbed the handles on Mary's overnight bag. She ran into the laundry room and grabbed the go bag that she made for Scout too. Her truck was down at the barn. Shit, shit, shit!

She had a small all-electric utility vehicle parked out back. She kept it there as a quick escape for Mary if needed. Something she could climb into easily enough, unplug and drive by simply pressing the pedal. Bonus with this little cart was that it was super quiet. Alex looked out the front windows for any vehicles pulling in, any movement at all. It was getting too dark to see. She didn't notice any headlights, but then again, Montana was wide-open range and rifle scopes offered plenty of reach. All the more reason to get to the cover of the sanctuary. She'd come back for Dutch once Mary was tucked away safe.

She had her shoes on, waiting patiently at the back door. Scout sat right at her side. Alex helped her down the steps and into the passenger seat of the side-by-side. Scout sat in the tiny bed with the luggage. She'd feel better when they were behind the fence line. She kept the lights off and navigated the path with the last bit of twilight.

After they passed through the first gate and it closed successfully behind them, Alex finally felt a tiny bit of relief.

"Besides the fence, what makes this any different than being in my house?" Mary asked.

"I've changed a lot over the years. Out here, I know when someone's coming way before they get close enough to be a threat. The fences have sensors and cameras that alert me on my phone. The fences around each cabin can be electrified too. Trust me, it packs a serious wallop. There are other security measures too."

"I want this setup around my house. Could you do that for me?"

"Absolutely." She disliked the thought that Mary would need this kind of security around her home, but whatever helped her feel safe. "Well, here we are, cabin four. I set it up, just in case. I even have a bottle of your favorite whiskey if you need a nip."

"You're a good girl, Alex."

Alex helped Mary inside. She heated up a bowl of soup and set up a small side plate with a few slices of cheese and some crackers while Mary finished her shower and got dressed.

"We have to go over a few things before I go."

"Where are you going? It's safest here. That's what you said."

"Mary, I left Dutch tied to your back deck. I need to take care of him and check on the other horses before I come out here for the night."

"Well then, you take Scout."

"Not a chance. Elina left him here to protect you."

"Bullshit, she left him here to protect *us*! You take Scout or we'll all go together, the three of us."

"Fine, I'll take Scout, but I'm going to juice the fence the second I close the gate. Don't get any harebrained idea that you can mosey out there and touch anything. I don't want to find you flat on your back by the gate."

"Fine by me. When you get back, you're going to tell me what's going on, and I mean everything. Now, show me what all I can do with this gizmo." Mary held up the tablet that controlled the security around the cabin.

Alex reviewed a few things with her and urged her not to touch any of it unless serious warning bells were sounding. She wrote down Candice's number on a piece of paper and then unzipped Scout's go bag and pulled out his vest.

All of Elina's instructions about Scout were covered at a rapid-fire pace on her way out the door. She hoped she remembered everything. His commands were all in the Arapaho language except one and that was a takedown command. There was a card inside his vest. She had to protect it as if his life depended on it. That's the part she remembered. After that, it was all a blur. Alex unzipped the pouch and pulled out the card. She gave it a quick overview and silently repeated the few commands she'd need to know for tonight. More than anything, she wished she knew the hand signals. Voice commands would give away her position. No time now. She slid the card back into his vest and got him ready to go to work.

She pulled the cart off to the side of the trail and stashed it as best as possible behind a small outcropping of rocks. She could walk the quarter mile from there.

"Heeteniihi," Alex said, and Scout silently took off. Shit, she hoped she pronounced "protect me" properly.

She stayed out of the light once she was close to the main house. She watched for any activity. Dutch's ears flickered from side to side, but perhaps he was simply responding to her presence behind him or maybe Scout's. Horses had incredible hearing. She crept closer to the horse and listened. Someone would have to be blasting a radio to get louder than her heartbeat, which was steadily thumping in her ears. She'd be surprised if she had any adrenaline left when all of this was finally over.

"Hey, Dutch, it's just me," Alex whispered.

She knew better than to sneak up behind a horse without saying anything. She'd learned that lesson with a swift hoof to the side of her knee when she was a youngster. She patted his neck while releasing the reins from the deck railing. She felt bad for riding him so hard and then just leaving him without a cooldown or a brush out. Luckily, the temperatures had been mild and the ride back wasn't that long. One of these days, she'd make it up to him. She fixed her boot into the left stirrup and swung herself up into the saddle. She turned him out into the yard, away from the light streaming out of the windows, and made her way slowly toward the barn.

So far, so good. She halted him at the hitching rail and slid down out of the saddle. She wondered if Scout had stayed with her, or if he was still up protecting the house. She was so out of her league. She tried to remember the commands on the card, but for the life of her she couldn't remember how to call him back. Maybe it was as simple as saying "come here." It was worth a shot anyway.

"Neheicoo," Alex whispered. She almost jumped out of her skin when Scout stuck his cold nose into the palm of her hand which was hanging at her side. She scratched his ear and then asked him to protect her again. At least she knew he was close.

She opened the small barn door and stayed off to the side and listened for a moment. When she didn't hear anything, she reached in and flipped the light switch and then stepped off to the side again. Nothing. Jesus, she was freaking herself out. Still, Candice told her to be careful. She pulled her side arm and cleared the building. Once she was comfortable that no one was in the barn or anywhere up in the loft, she sat on a hay bale and drew in a cleansing breath. She wondered if Elina was okay. She pulled out the prepaid phone that she'd given her and opened it to see if anything had come in. Nothing new. It was too risky to send something off. They agreed that Elina would initiate contact. Waiting, helplessly, was a living hell. Was Elina hurt? Was she okay? Had she been taken? All of this just needed to be over. Alex unsaddled Dutch, filled the water troughs, and threw hay to the horses before she called lights out and made her way back to cabin four with Scout at her side. Thankfully, without issue.

## Chapter Twenty

Gina, st-stop." Gabby gasped for breath. "I can't—" She tilted her head back and took a few ragged breaths. "Run anymore."

Elina scanned their surroundings for a place to hide. They seemed to be in a neighborhood on the edge of town. She tugged Gabby away from the illumination of a streetlight, to the cover of a garage behind a large two-story house. How in the hell did they find the bar? Either Gabby was being tracked or there was a leak. She prayed it wasn't the latter. Thankfully, it was dark, which offered a bit of cover. She spotted a loaded clothesline in a nearby yard. She ran over and pulled a variety of clothes off the line and then ran back to Gabby.

"Strip, everything off."

"Oh, now you want me naked? Fuck you."

"Shhh, quiet. Gabby, we can't risk that they tracked you somehow. Clearly you were the target. They could have taken me out at the bar anytime." Elina dropped the armload of clothes on the ground. "Come on, get changed. I'll be right back."

She ran over to an overflowing recycle bin on the back steps of the house. She quietly lifted several items out before she found a few empty bottles with the caps still on. She uncapped them and sniffed. Cola. Perfect. There was a spigot on the side of the house. She turned it on so that it wasn't much more than a trickle. No need to wake the occupants of the house with the sound of running water.

A quick rinse before she filled the bottles and then stuffed them into her go bag.

Gabby had yet to change a single article of clothing. She was sitting on the ground with her arms crossed. Apparently, the gravity of the situation had somehow escaped her.

"I'm serious. Strip, now, and give me your shoes."

Gabby scowled up at her and huffed her protest. She removed her shoes and handed them up. Elina pulled out the insoles and felt for anything out of the ordinary. Nothing unusual that she could find. The soles were flexible, no lumps or bumps. Nothing on the laces. These shoes would have to do until they could be replaced. She threw the shoes on the ground and tossed the insoles next to them in front of Gabby.

"Bra and panties too. I mean it, fucking naked."

"I am *not* wearing someone else's underwear! Do you know how much this shit cost?" Gabby held her arms out showing off the matching bra and panties.

"Go bare for all I care, but ditch the underwear."

Gabby started giggling.

"What is so funny?"

"You're a poet and didn't even know it." Her giggling intensified.

"I forgot what vodka does to you. I knew I shouldn't have made you martinis. Come on, strip, we gotta keep moving."

Gabby snapped her underwear like a slingshot directly into Elina's face. The familiar sweet, musky scent didn't escape her. Elina inhaled deeply before she pulled the fine silk away from her skin. It was every bit as sensually soft as she remembered. Her body buzzed with an instant, intense craving. She drew in a deep breath of clean air and pushed the desire off to the side. Gabby fanned her arms out and spun around. She was, in fact, completely naked. Perfect, perky breasts and voluptuous, full hips that begged to be savored, begged to be explored, not to mention legs that went on for days leading to a sweet, savory spot where she'd once spent hours at a time. Another wave of desire hit. Elina tried her best to ignore it. Gabby wiggled her hips and cupped her breasts with her hands.

"Happy now? There's a nice little grassy patch back here behind the garage. You know how to make me feel so good." Gabby slid her fingers between her legs. "Tell me you don't want to taste this."

Want, yes, without a doubt, but there was no future with Gabby. There never had been. Besides, her memories with Gabby were clouded by a drug-induced haze of pleasure. Those days were over. What she really wanted was so much more. An image of Alex appeared in her mind's eye. Yes, she could envision a future with Alex someday, but right now, she had to focus on simply surviving.

"Stop screwing around. Take your watch and earrings off too. Hurry up and get dressed."

"You have become such a fuddy-duddy. Not too long ago, you would have taken me right here, out in the open. Danger be damned. Baby, I can come quietly if I have to."

"Have you forgotten about the thousands of bullets that tried to take us out?"

"No, I haven't forgotten. Something else that I haven't forgotten is what it felt like to have your face buried between my legs. There could be worse ways to go. Besides, we got away. No one is chasing us now."

"You don't know that. Please, stop talking and get dressed or I'll leave without you. At this point, I don't much care. Survive on your own."

Elina needed to concentrate on something else. She took a moment to check Hunter for any injuries. She didn't feel any wet fur and he didn't flinch regardless of where she touched. She let out a sigh of relief. Everything happened so fast. She managed to grab her go bag, but that was about it. There was a lot of firepower at the front of the bar. It was definitely a coordinated attack with a kill mission. She'd never been more grateful that she locked the front door of the bar. That one small act was the only reason the two of them were alive. She wasn't sure how many guns were out front, but thankfully, only two men came around the back of the bar, each with handguns and not automatic rifles. She'd sent Hunter out the door and felt a beacon of hope when one of the guys yelled at the other not to shoot the cute dog. Hunter circled around and grabbed one of them from behind. It was just the distraction she needed to drop both men. Her two shots blended in with the onslaught from the front of the building. It was just too bad they hadn't also left an idling car back there. That would have been helpful.

"Did you tell *anyone* where you were going today? Do you have *any* idea how they could have tracked you here?"

"No, I didn't tell anyone. Who in the hell am I going to tell? Let's not forget that my own brother wants me dead. It's not like I have a bunch of friends. I took the bus, just like you told me to. I got off in town and walked to the bar. I wore these frumpy ass clothes, so I'd blend in. No car, no phone. I have a small wallet with the fake ID that I picked up right before I left and some cash. I did everything you asked."

"That's got to be it. Let me see your ID."

Elina ran the card between her finger and her thumb. There was something beneath the laminate. It was thin and about a half inch wide by an inch long. Could be a lamination error or it could be a tracking device. She'd seen some wafers that were thin like that. While the license was likely how they found Gabby, she wouldn't eliminate the possibility of a leak. Dominick would stop at nothing to protect his empire even if that meant killing his only sibling. She wouldn't put it past him if he got wind that his sister was looking to cooperate.

She pulled a multi-tool out of her go bag and cut the license in quarters. She tried to peel back the layers, but it was too dark to tell if it was really a tracker or just layers of the license. One way or another, she hoped she'd found the source of how they'd been located.

"Hey, asshole, do you know how much that stupid piece of plastic cost me? I'm out of fucking money, how am I going to get another ID?"

"Hey, asshole, it held a tracking chip and almost cost us our lives. Do you really want it back?" Elina piled Gabby's clothes together and lit the small pile on fire with a lighter. She tossed the pieces of the license on top of the pile. "Let's go."

"The least you could do is give me back my bra and panties before you burn everything. I wore them just for you. The last of my finest silk. Clearly, there wasn't a bug planted in them. Believe me, I would have felt that."

Elina had the two items concealed in her hand. She resisted the urge to inhale Gabby's sweet musky fragrance again. She focused on her experience with Alex and tried to push Gabby out of her mind.

"You can have them back once we're away from the fire and out of sight." Elina stuffed them into her front pocket.

"Bless you. You do have a heart after all." Gabby held the slightly oversized pants in place while she jogged to catch up.

Elina pushed Gabby to keep walking until they were a good five miles or so out of town. It was getting late and she could hear Gabby huffing and puffing with each step. Her stomach grumbled and reminded her that they never did get that pizza. She hadn't seen headlights or any type of movement in several miles. A sliver of moon finally rose and gave her a shadowy outline of their surroundings.

"Let's take a break here. I'll see if I can find us a place to hide until we can figure out what's going on." Elina removed the go bag and dug into the front pocket for the prepaid phone.

When the device was powered up, she launched the map app. She knew they were a little over two hundred and fifty miles away from the sanctuary. Okay, so not walking distance with two granola bars and one and a half bottles of water left. She zoomed in on the map. There were a couple of ranches nearby where she could likely procure a vehicle. Stealing a car was an option, but having law enforcement after them wasn't ideal. Especially when she wasn't sure who all she could trust. She zoomed in on the map and switched it to satellite view. It looked as if the terrain transitioned from prairie grass to some taller trees. There was a driveway into what looked like a hunting camp. If unoccupied, that might be the perfect place to hide until she could figure out what to do next.

Gabby was sitting on the ground leaning up against a small boulder. Elina made sure the phone was silenced and pulled up the texting app. She typed in the phone number to the prepaid phone she'd given Alex and then tapped down in the message field.

*Nebii'o'oo, yonootiseenoo yonooho*

She hit send. Now Alex would at least know they were alive and hiding. The first word, "my sweetheart," would confirm to Alex that it was in fact Elina who was texting, since it was the code word she'd suggested before she left. The tender smile and long embrace from Alex showed her how touched she was by the suggestion.

Elina powered down the phone and looked over to Gabby. Her eyes were closed. She needed to get them moving again before Gabby fell asleep.

"A couple more miles and you can rest," Elina said.

She put the phone back into the pocket of her go bag before slipping her arms into the straps and standing up. The camp, if that's what it was, looked to be a few miles to the northwest. Montana had some tricky terrain, and she hoped it was a simple climb in elevation and there would be no canyon walls involved.

What a mess this job had turned out to be, but then, had she really expected it to go any other way with Gabby involved? Was this the kind of career she wanted? Was it worth the risk of her own life to save someone who only cared about herself? Would she ever do enough to repair the hit her reputation took? Did she even care anymore? Maybe it was time to consider a new career. If she got through this job alive, she vowed to take some time for some serious soul-searching.

## CHAPTER TWENTY-ONE

Alex carefully opened the cabin door and ushered Scout inside. She hoped that Mary had fallen asleep, but no such luck. Mary sat on the end of the sofa, tapping her fingers on the armrest. Apparently, there was no getting out of this conversation.

"I'm glad you're back. I've tried to be patient, Alex, but time's up. I need you to tell me what's really going on. I'm no fool. Elina wouldn't go back to work without her rig and her horses, and she wouldn't take only one of the two dogs. Not to mention the fact that we wouldn't be out here in security jail if everything was over. I've trusted you. I kept the bag packed like you asked. Now it's time for you to return the favor and tell me what in the hell is really going on."

Alex sat down at the small dining table and rubbed her face with her hands. What could she really say without revealing the entire operation?

"What the dogs did on the night I was rescued, the way they took those two guys down, they're trained much differently than her hounds were. Does she even do search and rescue anymore?" Mary lifted herself from the couch and walked into the kitchen.

Alex smiled when she understood what she was after. Mary pulled two juice glasses down from the cabinet and poured a strong shot of Irish whiskey in each. She set one down in front of Alex and then sat down in the chair next to her.

"Is my Elina alive?" Mary asked.

"Yes. She's alive." Alex lifted the juice glass to her lips and took a sip.

"So, you've heard from her? You know where she is?"

"I know she's alive, but I don't know exactly where she is right now." Alex knew she'd already admitted too much.

"She's undercover? Who does she work for if not search and rescue in Wyoming?"

"Mary, you're putting me in a pickle. I don't want to lie to you, so I'll ask you to accept that there are some things that I'm not at liberty to share." Alex leaned back in her seat.

"I was married to a marshal, Alex. I understand that, but I also want some answers. Is she in danger? Whatever happened that has us hiding out here, is it because of what happened to us before she left? It's not really over, is it? Or is there a new threat?"

Mary was one sharp cookie. She was also relentless and wouldn't stop needling until Alex cracked like a soft-boiled egg tapped with the edge of a spoon. Her phone buzzed twice and then chirped in her pocket. A perimeter alarm alert. *That can't be good news.* What now?

Alex pulled the phone out of her pocket. Pressure sensors at the back fence were going off. She pulled up the camera app. It was the Suburban licensed to the ranch. Same bumper stickers, same two canoes strapped to the top. Why hadn't she been notified? The driver's door opened, and a person stepped out of the vehicle and waved at the camera. Alex zoomed in. Was that Candice? She zoomed in some more. Yep, that was Candice. Why hadn't she called or texted? Shit, something was seriously wrong.

"Mary, I'm not avoiding your questions, but I've gotta check this out. The fence will be electrified again. Please stay inside with Scout. I'm not asking." Alex walked across the room toward the front door. Without saying another word, she stepped outside.

She toggled off the electricity to the fence and opened the gate. Once the gate was closed and secured behind her, she reenergized the fence. She jogged through the trees and across the narrow grass-covered path that the truck used. Alex ran all the way to the tree line that hid the sanctuary from the back fence. She pulled her service weapon and flipped off the safety. Better to be safe than sorry.

"What are you doing here?" Alex remained hidden in the underbrush.

"I need to talk to you. No technology beyond your network, even the phones aren't safe."

"Is there anyone else in the rig?"

"No, just me. I can leave the truck outside the wire if you wish."

"Better to have it in the wire. I'll open the gate."

Things had to be completely upside down for her to wonder whether or not she could trust Candice. If she could trust anyone, it was Candice. She tapped the app on her phone and opened the back fence until the truck pulled through and then closed it again. She stepped out into the truck's path when Candice pulled behind the tree line onto the grassy path to the cabins.

"You can pull the truck up over here beneath the big pines. I hide my truck there when I clean the cabins."

Candice nodded and pulled the truck under cover.

"You're freaking me out. What's going on?" Alex asked the moment Candice stepped out of the truck. "Now our phones aren't safe?"

"Do you remember when we were looking for the money in the ravine and I told you about how I met Elina?"

"Yeah, what about it?"

"My partner that day?"

"Ken Smith, mister stick in the mud. Is he behind the leak? I swear to G—"

"Alex, shut up and listen. Ken's peculiar no doubt, but he's a stickler for the rules and as loyal as they come. A lot like you actually. Anyway, that day, when he was hit in the vest, it broke some ribs and injured his lung. He was in a lot of pain. Elina had been shot too, but she had enough medical training to triage. She patched him up until we could get him out of there. He's always been grateful."

"So, why exactly are we talking about Ken Smith?"

"Because he left the field after that hit and got into technology. I believe he was one of your instructors?"

"Yep, he rode me hard in class. I still don't see where this is going."

"This op was kept close to the vest, just a handful of people knew about it, but because of the technology needed, the director had to put a requisition in with the IT folks. Side note, Ken had been monitoring some anomalies with a few confidential files and how the tech was configured for those associated operations. He was concerned that someone internal had been compromised but wanted to figure out exactly who was screwing with the equipment and files. He wanted to have solid proof before he took it up the ranks, but a recently compromised file showed up in his scans and he saw Elina's name when he dug into what had been accessed, so he came directly to me with a heads-up. Someone accessed the footage of the plane that you submitted, the tail number, all of it. Someone accessed the file on Dan and the money and then accessed every single detail about this op. That's not all. An old file was accessed this morning. A twenty-five-year-old file. The testimony file on the Marco Manbessee trial." She hesitated. "Your testimony file."

Alex's brain went into overdrive trying to connect the dots. "What does my file have to do with anything about this operation?"

"You asked me if Elina could know everything about you, and now I'm asking you if you told her."

"No, I haven't. Even if I'd wanted to, there wasn't really a chance to have that conversation. She left less than twenty-four hours after getting Mary back. Why?"

"Did she tell you the name of her target for this job?" Candice asked.

Annoyance flared. "No. She didn't say, and I didn't ask. Professional boundaries and all that shit. My patience is growing thin. Candice, out with it already."

"It's Gabriella Manbessee. Her brother, Dominick, the head of the Manbessee Cartel, has issued a contract on her life for stealing four million dollars from him and dropping the cash in Wolfbend, Montana. The pilot's been found dead too. The hope was that Elina could use that as leverage to get Gabby to flip on her brother in exchange for protection. Given that Gabby reached out to Elina first, we had a feeling she knew that Elina had been undercover."

Alex felt as if she'd been sucker-punched and wasn't entirely sure her legs would continue to support her. She never expected to hear the Manbessee name again. "Are you telling me that Elina's on the run with the daughter of the man I put in prison? The daughter of the man who killed two marshals and took my mother? You took this operation on knowing the connections and I'm just finding out about it now?"

"Yes, but in my defense, there wasn't a link directly to you, Alexandria Trenton, until your witness file was accessed. It was just another undercover operation."

"Semantic bullshit and you know it. Is my WITSEC identity in the file that was accessed?"

"Not directly, but the associated WITSEC case file is referenced, and that file was also accessed. The two in custody should never have had access to those files."

Alex wanted to explode and yet she knew that now was a time for solutions and not reactions. Her training had taught her that much. "What department were they from?"

"The IT department. They tried to cover their tracks, but Ken said something about comparing timestamped backups to see what changed with security. He said he'd dig down to minute by minute if he had to. One suspect was a systems administrator and the other was a network engineer. Ken isn't sure yet if they worked together or if one used the other's credentials. They're both being interrogated now. The entire IT department is on lockdown. No one leaves until it's sorted out. Agents have their lives under a microscope as I'm sure you can imagine."

"I thought there were checks and balances to keep this kind of thing from happening. Super security and all that, but then again, if they set it up, then they could just as easily turn it off." Alex wanted to punch something. "How can I ever trust you again? You've kept so much from me. You should have told me. The moment Elina got the call to go back in, you should have told me about the connection.

They must have gone digging just to see what else was out here, and then saw my name."

"Alex, my role with the agency requires I keep some things close to the vest. I'll always care about you. You hold a special place in my heart, but you have to understand that I also have a job to do."

She listened to Candice's words. The logic was there but her heart still felt broken. "Elina needs to know. Her life is in danger because of what I did twenty-five years ago."

"Technically, the two are unrelated. Gina Holt owns a little bar north of Great Falls, Montana. Elina Hawkins is technically still the division lead for search and rescue. She lives in a cabin in the Grand Teton National Park in Wyoming—"

Anger boiled over and Alex no longer cared if Candice was a superior officer or if it cost her the post. She interrupted with all the rage that she felt inside. "And Alexandria Trenton, also known as the twelve-year-old witness Angela Carsen, happens to work on the Hawkins Ranch in Wolfbend, Montana, where the fucking four million dollars was dropped. Oh, and let's not forget that Elina Hawkins, from Wyoming, just happens to be their granddaughter. It's all in the case files. *You can't get more related!*" Alex had to get a grip. This wouldn't help Elina. "Okay, so the files were accessed. Was my information really leaked or is it still isolated to the agency personnel? Were the files copied to USB or emailed?"

"We're not sure what all was shared yet. There have been files sent, but they had a unique encryption key. Ken has a team that he trusts, and they are working on it. There's something else you need to know. The technology on this op was compromised. Any device that connected to the network in that bar was infected with some kind of code instantly making it a tracking device. Not only that, but somehow it captures in and outbound communication. If either of them has a phone and it's powered on, then they're being tracked."

Alex understood the gravity of what Candice was saying. Every single time Elina powered up that prepaid phone, she was broadcasting their location offering a direction of travel. Not only that, but also all in and outbound communication which could include any number of apps. A new round of nausea hit.

"I have a bag of burner phones in the truck. I bought them on my way to the airport. We can use those for now."

"We have to warn Elina. We have to go get her. Candice, she's a sitting duck out there!"

"Yeah, well, that's the crux of it. They may or may not have her location, but I know for a fact that we do not. The code sends the information to specific IP addresses and blocks ours. We lost sight the moment she left that bar. We're in the blind and she's more than two hundred miles away."

A twig snapped behind the Suburban. Candice and Alex each spun around and drew their weapons.

"I am armed. Identify yourself," Alex said.

"It's me. Jesus, Alex, don't shoot."

"Mary? What on earth are you doing? I told you to stay put."

"I saw Candice on the gizmo. You two aren't telling me shit, so I turned off the hot fence and snuck out here to say my piece."

"You shouldn't have done that. This is marshal business." Candice holstered her weapon.

"I consider myself an honorary member and I have a need to know." Mary had her hands on her hips and might as well have stomped her foot.

"How much did you hear?" Candice asked.

"Everything. The gizmo has a button on the camera that says, 'play audio.' Listen, you two, I know what undercover work can do to a person's spirit. It almost took my husband from me many years ago. Find those bastards and end this before it's too late."

Alex wanted to ask about Hawk, but now was not the time. Mary understood the effect it could have on a person. Elina had shared how it had almost consumed her soul. She didn't want that to happen again and would do everything in her power to protect her from that hell.

"Candice, we're not completely blind. I have a way to communicate. Elina insisted on it given how the last undercover op went." Alex pulled the prepaid phone out of her pocket. "It's likely been compromised on her end, but I could still warn her and have her ditch the phone. Maybe she can give us a sense of where she's headed."

"They'll see every word you type."

"How many of them do you suppose can read Arapaho? Now, where can we stash Mary? There's zero chance I'm sitting this one out."

Alex was an internal whirlwind of emotions. There were so many more questions than answers. She knew it was time to rely on the years of training. One way or another, she'd make sure there was a conclusion to this Manbessee madness. The biggest question was, would she be Alexandria Trenton or Angela Carsen when it was all over? Elina didn't know anything about Angela Carsen. For the first time in as long as she could remember, she didn't miss who she used to be. No, she was most definitely Alexandria Trenton, a badass federal agent and it was time to end this and bring Elina home.

## Chapter Twenty-two

The cabin, if that's indeed what it was, was much farther than it looked on the map. The good part was that it was perched high up on a hill. It looked deserted, but it was difficult to be sure until she got inside. She kept them walking until they were well past the structure, almost to the top of the hill, primarily so she could see it from as many different angles as possible.

"Tell me we're almost there. I swear I can't take one more step." Gabby flopped down on the ground next to Elina.

"Can I trust you to wait here while I go and check it out?"

"Happily. I hope this hotel has room service. I'm famished."

"If we're lucky, we'll find a can of beans or something. Stay put and please be quiet."

"Yes, ma'am." Gabby leaned up against a rock and stretched her legs out in front of her.

Elina made her way back to the small structure. In the faint moonlight, it didn't look like much more than an oversized shed. Any shelter would be better than nothing for a quick nap. No vehicle in sight, that was a good sign. She tiptoed up to the building for a closer look. It was too dark to see in the two windows on either side, but there was a padlock on the outside of the double doors, a pretty solid indication that it wasn't occupied by people, unless they were prisoners.

She pulled the multi-tool out of her go bag along with a penlight. The screws were simple Phillips head. The hinge side was the most accessible, so she removed those four screws and carefully pulled the door open. She stayed still and listened for a moment. No movement. She used the pen light to inspect the inside. It looked like a tiny house. There was a ladder up to a large loft bed. The space below included a table with two chairs, a small sofa, a tall dresser, and a tiny kitchenette. If there was a water source, they just might be set for a day or two.

She decided to check her phone before she went back for Gabby. Maybe Alex had some information for her. Maybe they could actually talk for a minute. It would be good to hear her voice. She pressed the power button and waited while the phone came to life.

There was an unread text waiting for her. It was written in Arapaho, as she expected, but the message was the last thing she expected to read.

*My sweetheart, your telephone tracks you. Kill it. Tell me where to look and I will find you. I will protect you both.*

She had no time to think about it. She pulled up a map app quickly and then typed up a response.

*My sweetheart, 47.6857 north by 111 west. From here I will take a direct path to a native tribal land in the northwest.*

At least Alex would have the same starting point that those tracking her had. She didn't even worry about translating the coordinate numbers, just her greeting and destination. She sent the text.

Elina spotted a backpack hanging on a hook by the door. She grabbed it and dumped the contents out on the sofa. A couple of empty water bottles, a couple of emergency foil-type fabric blankets, and a compass. She shoved the compass and emergency blankets into her go bag and then took the empty backpack over to the small kitchenette. She pushed back the curtains and inspected what was on the shelves. A few gallons of water and some canned goods. She cleared most of the food items off the shelf, except for the water chestnuts. She couldn't imagine anyone packing up for a remote getaway and thinking that they needed water chestnuts for a special meal. Yuck. She pulled out a small, sealed tote and added a can opener, a few spoons and forks and a small stack of napkins to her bounty. The weight of the pack was tolerable. She could still manage with a gallon of water strapped on either side.

She set the water and the pack by the door and then ran up to inspect the loft. She threw back the mattress. Nothing. She looked down below. There was no locked cabinet, maybe she'd find what she was looking for in the sofa. That always seemed to be a favorite hiding place. She pulled the cushion off. It was a sofa bed. Fingers crossed. She tugged on the frame and lifted it out into the room, folding out the last half of the bed. Bingo! A long gun case. She opened it. One of her favorites, a .308 Winchester with a scope and a shoulder sling. This would work brilliantly as long as she could also find ammunition. She lifted the gun from the case and pulled the bolt back. Empty. Hopefully there was something in the dresser since that was about the only place she hadn't looked. She started with the bottom drawer, but it was filled with linens and towels. She hit paydirt in the second to the bottom drawer, two metal ammo boxes. She popped the top on each. One held boxes of empty brass and the other live shells. No sense in arming the bad guys. *Thank you, Great Spirit!*

She checked the other drawers but only found clothes. She grabbed a couple of hooded sweatshirts to fend off the cool of the night and a few other clothing items that would fit Gabby better than what she was wearing. Once the rifle was loaded, she stuffed a few boxes of ammo into her go bag.

Elina took an extra couple of minutes to close the gun case and stash it back in the sofa. She stuffed some pillows beneath a blanket so it would look like someone was curled up on the couch sleeping. She removed her go bag and fed her arms into the straps such that the bag rested on her chest and belly. Then, she hoisted up the pack with the food onto her back. It balanced out better than she expected. She secured the water to straps on either side which were likely for a bed roll, but did the trick just the same, and found she could still move fairly fluidly. Lastly, she left the phone on the countertop and kept it powered on, and then disconnected the grill sized propane tank from the hose beneath the counter. She propped a smaller propane tank, for a lantern, in the tiny kitchen window on the far right-hand side. A target, if needed, that she could hit from the position where she'd left Gabby. She opened the valve on the larger propane tank under the counter and picked up the rifle. She carefully closed the shed doors and left the hinge side dangling down as if someone were inside. If a hunter was coming after them, she wanted to be sure to leave them a nice little surprise.

"Gina. Headlights on the road down below." Gabby hollered from the edge of the clearing.

Elina peeked around the side of the building and spotted the glow just before the car disappeared behind the lower tree line. She didn't worry about whether or not it was climbing up the hill. Chances were good that it was. Elina ran toward Gabby.

"Go, run. We need to crest the top of the hill before they spot us." Elina captured Gabby's hand and tugged her along.

"How are they still following us? I thought you found the tracking thingy?"

"Stop talking and run!"

The top of the hill was a mix of boulders and scrub brush. She kept pushing until they'd crested the peak and were on a path down the other side heading slightly southwest. She looked for the rock formation that she saw on the satellite view of the map. It would make the perfect perch, as if someone had made a fortress out of boulders. She spotted it and sent Hunter in to check it out. No good surprising a bobcat or a snake staying warm on the rocks. Hunter appeared on the top of the boulder and then ran back down into the nest in the center, an all-clear.

"Come on, climb up and over. We'll hide here."

Gabby didn't say a word. She climbed up over the rocks and then slid down into the center. Elina removed the pack with the food and water. She pushed it up the rocks ahead of her.

"Gabs, take this and set it on the ground for me." Elina pushed the pack closer to Gabby's outstretched arms.

"Got it."

She opened her go bag and pulled out one of the two survival foil blankets. She opened the package and carefully unfolded the metalized polyester.

"Here, keep the silver side facing you. Lean up against the rocks and completely hide beneath the blanket. It will keep you warm and hide you from a gun scope that can see heat. I'll be back for—"

"You can't leave me out here! What if they find me?"

"Shhhhh, I won't leave you, but I can't protect you from here either. Promise me that you will stay right here. *Do not leave this spot.* I have to hurry, or I'll lose my window. Now, cover up and be quiet. I'll be back for you."

Elina gave Hunter a hand signal to follow along and be ready. He disappeared into the night. She rearranged her go bag on her back and then slid down from the rocks and climbed back to the top of the hill. There was a good position on the ground between two large boulders that would offer her a great view and decent coverage. She unfolded the other survival blanket and draped it over her body so that just the barrel of the gun and the edge of the scope were exposed. She flipped the power switch on for the scope. Night vision scopes were a wonderful invention. She still wished for her waist belt with her thermal scope, but that had been well out of reach in the rush to exit the bar.

She could just make out the front corner of the car. It was parked about three-quarters of the way up the drive. She scanned the area for any movement. If she were the hunter, she'd be in the shadows, assessing the situation too. She didn't mind waiting. *Come out, come out, wherever you are.*

Two figures finally emerged from the shadows dressed in dark clothing. They wore night vision headsets, high-end gear, likely dual use with thermal vision. She was grateful for her perch and the protection provided by the foil blanket. She watched as they crept closer to the shed. Luckily, thermal imaging couldn't see through glass or walls. Night vision could see in the windows, but all they'd see was a shape beneath a blanket. If they wanted confirmation of living souls, they'd have to open the door to see any heat signatures. The hand signals they used weren't military, perhaps something they'd made up. One stayed at the side of the shed, peeking in the windows, while the other went around by the door. She took aim at the propane bottle in the window and squeezed the trigger.

*KABOOM!*

The shed exploded into a huge ball of fire. She shielded her eyes from the brilliant light. The bolt pulled back easily and ejected the spent brass. A fresh shell entered the chamber when she closed the bolt. She looked through the scope again and scanned the area while burning debris rained down from the sky. The two assassins were lying on the ground not far from what was left of the structure, which wasn't much, and their clothing was on fire. She stayed still, slowly scanning the area, watching for any movement at all.

A third person ran up from the car in the driveway. He wasn't wearing the night vision equipment. Good thing, or he'd have been blinded by the flames. He spun around in circles, a pistol at the ready, and kept looking back at the car. He nodded in the direction of the car and then began to fire aimlessly into the terrain around the remains of the shed. Aha, he was trying to get her to fire and give away her position. There had to be a fourth down there somewhere. She was certain he wasn't only trying to draw fire, but also trying to give another shooter time to get into a good position. A stray shot hit close. She kept watch. He was out of ammo and ran over to one of the men on the ground. He picked up the pistol that lay next to him and dropped it instantly. Apparently, the nearby flames had made it too hot to hold.

She needed to move if she wanted a better view of the car and whoever was wanting the distraction. She used the foil blanket as cover and sat up behind one of the two boulders. If she made her way just a bit more to the north, perhaps she could gain the upper hand. She held the foil blanket up and draped it over her so she could crawl about three hundred feet. She found another spot that afforded her some protection and held the blanket out in front of her as she dropped and then let it drape over her as she lay on her stomach. She lifted the scope to her eye. The car was empty. She scanned the area again. The two men were still down from the blast. The third was running back toward the car. She focused once again on the car. Slowly scanning the area... *Aha gotcha.* There was movement by the trunk.

The trunk lid opened and then closed. This person had a long gun. *Come on, one more step.* But instead of stepping out into the open, he ducked into the woods. She traced his movements through the scope. The other three must have been grunts because this one knew how to use the landscape for cover. This hunter would be a problem if not dealt with now. She was glad she stayed still and waited. She was also grateful she hadn't taken the bait and fired after that initial shot.

His body was behind a tree. She focused on the rifle and kept her finger steady on the trigger. He drew the weapon up, slowly scanning the landscape. Exactly what she would do. She waited for the glass of the scope to become almost a full circle in her crosshairs, and then she lifted her sight slightly above his scope, centered on his forehead, and pulled the trigger.

His body fell backward and lay motionless on the ground. She ejected the shell and actioned another round into the chamber. The distraction guy ran toward the woods. He stood there, staring at what was left of the hunter's skull. She silently hoped he wouldn't bend down and pick up the rifle on the ground next to the body. She took aim at the grill of the car and fired. Steam erupted from the radiator. No one would get far in that vehicle anytime soon.

She aimed the scope back on the distraction guy. He picked up the rifle and looked through the scope in her direction. Once again, the scope was a full circle. She didn't want to shoot him, but he was leaving her no choice. She actioned the bolt, ejecting the spent shell, and loaded the last round into the chamber. She watched as his finger moved to the trigger. *Don't do it, don't do it, don't. ...* She fired before he had a chance to do so.

Elina reloaded the rifle while pondering the bigger question. How many more people out there who were trying to fulfill the contract on Gabby's life, had the coordinates of this location? It was time to get out of the area and head northwest. Hopefully, Candice and Alex could find them before it was too late.

## CHAPTER TWENTY-THREE

Luckily, the risk to Mary was minimal given that Gabby was the focus at this point. She agreed to go and stay with a friend in a neighboring town until she got the call that it was safe to come home. Although she made it very clear that she still expected to be read in on everything that happened when Alex returned. Maybe Candice could offer some insight on how to handle that one. Another phone call and the animals were covered. Alex's best buddy, Trapper, would use his stock trailer to pick up the horses. He'd make sure there was enough feed for the chickens for a few days and she could monitor the bison fence from anywhere. She thanked him for helping her out and offered to cover the bar at some point so they could get away. Maybe Elina would give her pointers on how to make drinks.

Their plane was less than an hour out. Alex pulled out the last of her tech totes and flipped off the lid. There was one last piece of equipment she needed for her plan to work. She dug through the tote and when she still couldn't find it, she simply dumped the contents out on the floor. She'd clean the mess up later. There wasn't much time to configure the equipment to report to the new cell phones that Candice had brought with her. Aha. There was the missing item. Now, she could set everything up and test it before it was time to go.

The GPS trackers were fully charged and would have power for about a hundred and forty hours, almost six days. She hoped and prayed that they wouldn't need more than twenty-four hours, but better to be safe than sorry. She wrote a quick note and stuffed it into a small Ziploc bag and then hid it beneath an upside-down patch on Scout's vest. She knew Elina well enough to know that she was meticulous about the dog's gear. No way she'd tolerate an upside-down patch and Scout wouldn't let anyone but her touch the vest. This way, Elina would know to look in the hidden pouch where the command card had been kept.

She tucked a portable phone charger and one of the configured phones into the pocket and zipped it closed. Any applications that might be needed were already installed and tested. She called Scout over and confirmed the fit of the vest to make sure the bulge from the extra gear wouldn't press into his rib cage or create pressure that would rub and make it difficult for him to run. Everything fit perfectly, especially since the expansion was on the outside of the vest. She clipped a GPS tracker onto the D-ring on the back of his vest and covered it with a wide Velcro strap to keep it from swinging or snagging on anything and being ripped off the vest. Time for a quick test. She offered Candice's scent and sent him outside.

He took off to find his target. Alex opened the application she'd installed on her new burner phone and smiled when the map zoomed in on a red blinking dot. It was great when things worked as planned. Scout had already found Candice and his treat. X marked the spot. Damn, that dog was well trained. She called him back and finished prepping her gear, making sure to take along the shirt with Elina's scent. There were a lot of moving parts to the last leg of this operation, and she hoped they all aligned as planned.

Her phone chirped. An incoming text from Candice.

*Plane is inbound. Time to get over to the airstrip.*

*On my way.*

Alex tucked the phone into her pocket and hoisted up her own version of a go bag. She doubled-checked her side arm and touched the spare clips of ammunition on her belt. She slung two rifles over her shoulder, grabbed the strap on a go bag for Candice, and ran out to the Suburban. Scout jumped in before she had the door barely open, as if he knew he was an important part of the plan. Alex situated the two rifles on the floor behind the front seat and then closed the back door.

"Here, this bag is for you. Ammo for the rifle. Let me see your phone real quick. I need to install the app while we're on my network." Alex got in the passenger seat and exchanged the backpack for Candice's phone. She installed the tracking software and verified that it could see Scout's GPS tracker and the one broadcasting from her phone. Two blinking lights, a red dot for Scout and a green one for Alex's phone. Both showed up exactly where she expected to see them on the map. She handed the phone back to Candice. "All set." She opened the app on her own phone and a blue dot appeared next to Scout's red dot. "Perfect, now I can see you too. Let's go."

"The flight to Great Falls will take about twenty minutes. The deputy director of that office assured me that they'll have a vehicle waiting for us capable of off-road travel. We should be boots on the ground in less than two hours of her last text. The scent will still be fresh," Candice said without taking her eyes off the road.

"You put all of this together in no time at all."

"You did the tech side. It was a team effort."

"Is this what it's like when you're on a manhunt?" Alex asked. "Is this the kind of coordination you set up when you work with Elina to find a fugitive?"

"Yes, things have to come together quickly. Elina says the trail gets weaker as time passes by. There was one case where we flew the horses in, tacked up and ready to go. It would have taken too long to trailer them, so we loaded them up in a plane and flew them across the country. It's something the marshal service excels at."

"I wish we could have brought the horses in for this," Alex said.

"Me too, but I couldn't get a plane big enough for that and land in an airport close enough to where we need to be. The terrain in that area can be a mix of flatland and rocky hills. The four-wheel drive vehicle will have to do."

Alex sat back in the seat. She wondered what a life with Elina might be like. Would she travel all the time to jobs all over the country? She thought about the sanctuary and wondered if the post would still exist when all of this was over. Was it still something she wanted to be a part of or would a life like this be more fulfilling?

There was nothing exciting about running the sanctuary. Certainly nothing that could compare to the fast-paced adventure of tracking a fugitive. The quick coordination of a million moving parts and then racing to meet an awaiting plane did have an exciting appeal. The uncertainty of what they would encounter once on the ground was a bit unnerving. She wondered if it ever became "old hat," so to speak.

Candice pressed a button on the visor and a tall garage door opened on the side of one of the hangars at the tiny airport. They no sooner pulled onto the concrete, near the door and a jet flew low over the top of the Suburban and landed on the runway.

"This hangar is another entity titled to Hawkins Ranch, LLC," Candice said and swung the truck inside.

The driver's door flung open well before the vehicle was even in park. Alex paid attention and followed her lead. Candice pressed the button again and closed the large garage door. She yanked the keys out of the ignition and tossed them down on the floor mat beneath the steering wheel. Alex kept moving, collecting everything they needed to take on the plane with them, but it was interesting to see this side of it. She'd never been to the hangar and had no idea how all of this was handled. There wasn't a single window in the tall metal building. It was like a steel fortress.

Candice unlocked the main door, and once Alex and Scout were outside with her, she pulled the door closed and pressed a button that allowed the dead bolt to engage. Candice tested the door and then pointed to a twin-engine jet turning around on the runway.

"Hustle, that's our ride."

"How fast can that thing go? I expected a bigger plane." Alex ran up to the side door just as it opened and lowered, revealing five steps up into the plane.

"The Cessna Citation X may not be a huge jet, but this one can go seven hundred and seventeen miles per hour. It'll get us there in no time at all. Climb up and take a seat," Candice said from behind her. "There's a cubby up by the cockpit for the rifles and backpacks."

Alex stowed the weapons and packs. She turned around and made her way to what looked like large leather lounge chairs.

"Wow. Should he be on the furniture?" Alex pointed at Scout.

"He's flown many times before, that's his favorite window seat for takeoff." Candice smiled.

"Good to know." Alex felt a bit out of place in such a fancy plane.

"Hey, Candice, we're ready for takeoff."

"Thank you, Stacy. We're ready to go whenever you are." Candice clipped her seat belt and pulled on the strap.

"What about Scout? Do we buckle him in?" Alex asked.

"He's fine, notice which chair he jumped in. He'll lean into the back of the seat during takeoff and will jump in the opposite chair for landing. He's a pro. Besides, once we're cruising, he'll want to go say hi to the crew. Stacy has cookies for him hidden in the pilot's cabin." Candice leaned back in her seat. She looked so relaxed. Alex, however, was a bundle of nerves. She'd trained for field work extensively, but all the training in the world didn't prepare her for the real thing.

She leaned back in her seat and drew in a deep breath of air and then exhaled slowly. Her thoughts drifted to Elina. What was it like out there for her right now? Was she running scared? No, no way she was running; the thought alone was hard to imagine. Elina wasn't one to run, scared or otherwise. Perhaps she was hiding, doing her best to keep Gabby safe. Alex thought back to the conversation on the night of the rainstorm in the cab of the Suburban when she declared that she was a scout, a tracker, and a hunter. Was she hunting? How would that even work with a witness in tow? All of this was so foreign and yet she found it professionally interesting too. This operation may show her a path she never knew existed. Could she be a scout, a tracker, and a hunter and work at Elina's side or was she more suited to be a gatekeeper? It was time to find out.

## Chapter Twenty-four

G abby tripped and fell on her knees. She struggled back up onto her feet and trudged forward. She hadn't complained a bit since leaving the shed area. As a matter of fact, she hadn't said much of anything for over an hour. Elina held her hand out and helped Gabby down an eight-foot slope into a wide, sandy wash. It was surprisingly dry after the recent rains, and she didn't expect they'd have any unexpected deluges to carry them off before they could climb up the other side. Besides, it wasn't that deep of a wash and would be a perfect place to stay out of sight for a short break. Elina could use some food and water too.

"Let's stop here for a bit. Are you hungry? I found some food back at the shed." Elina set the rifle down and pulled the pack off her back and then let the go bag slide forward and set that down too. It felt good to shed the extra weight.

"I could eat something." Gabby sat down and crossed her legs in front of her.

Elina opened the backpack and pulled out a few cans. "Beef and bean chili, baked beans, a couple of kinds of chicken soup, corned beef hash, or Vienna sausages? If you're good, I have canned peaches for dessert."

"Chicken soup, please."

"Noodles or rice?"

"Noodles, thanks."

Elina dug down and finally found the can opener. She picked up the can of chicken noodle soup and spotted a pull top. She tossed the can of soup into Gabby's lap. She dug into the pack again and pulled out a spoon and a napkin. Gabby accepted the spoon and napkin. She set the soup can in her lap and stared at Elina.

"The epitome of life on the run, cold soup. Thanks."

"We can't risk a fire. It would give away our location. Besides, I wasn't carting around a pan. You're lucky to have something to eat."

Elina spotted a log a few feet away in the wash. She got up and walked over to it. The bark on the side was loose. She pulled a chunk free and walked back over to where Gabby was sitting. She created a soft bowl in the sand and laid the bark down as if it was a dish and then opened a can of tuna fish and dumped the contents onto the bark. She added a can of peas and carrots to the pile. Hunter wagged his tail. He wouldn't complain about dinner being cold.

"You didn't offer me tuna and veggies," Gabby said around a mouthful of noodles.

"No, I did not. You don't want the dog eating beans or noodles, trust me. Tuna, peas, and carrots are much better for him, and he needs to eat too. He works hard." Elina dipped her spoon into the can of cold chili.

"How long have you had the dog?" Gabby asked.

"Long enough for him to keep us safe. He's a good boy."

"What's his name?"

"Dog." Elina waited for a snappy comeback. Nothing. She watched Gabby for a moment. "You're not your snarky self. What's up?"

"Something occurred to me, back by the shed. The hired guns aren't going to stop coming after me until I'm dead. I know you told me to stay put, but I snuck back down the hill a bit and watched. What would I have done if you weren't with me? You took four guys out to keep me safe."

"Six."

"What?"

"I've taken six souls today in order to keep you safe."

"Okay, six. I thank you for that, but I can't run forever. I'm obviously not that good at it. What do I do?"

"You stop running. You stand up and take them down."

Gabby looked up into the night sky. "I've never done that either. I'm not a stand-up kind of person. I'm sorry that I dragged you into all of this." Gabby quietly ate another bite of soup. She lifted her spoon, pointing it at Elina. "Tell me the truth, was the bar really yours? Did my visit destroy your attempt at a fresh start?"

Elina leaned back into the sandy bank of the wash. It was surprisingly comfortable. She chewed on her mouthful of chili much longer than she needed to and pondered Gabby's question. She was walking a fine line. Would the truth help Gabby do the right thing? She wasn't so sure it would. Gabby had always done what was best for Gabby, period. There was no right or wrong, only what served her interest at the time. Still, if she wanted Gabby to trust her enough to testify against her brother and enter the witness program, she had to prove to be trustworthy. Shit, this could really backfire. *What to do...what to do.* She swallowed her mouthful of well chewed food.

"What difference does it make now? Are you offering to buy me a new bar?" Elina looked over at Gabby.

"I would if I could, but we both know that I can't afford much more than this can of soup." Gabby held up the can. "Can we cut the bullshit? Like I said, I watched you back there, by the shed. I don't know of any big city bartender who knows to hide under a foil blanket so some kind of scope can't see a heat signature, and then can take shots like you did. How'd you even know where to shoot so the shed would explode? You've kept me alive, and I appreciate that more than you know. So, I'm asking, who are you and why did you agree to meet with me? Can you help me out of this mess?"

Elina ate the last bite from her can of chili and sat up so she could look directly into Gabby's eyes. "No, the bar wasn't mine. It was simply a neutral place where we could talk, and yes, I know people who could likely help you out of this mess if you're willing to tell them everything you know. Who knows, you might even earn a clean slate, a fresh start."

"What, like witness protection?" Gabby was surprisingly direct. "Are you law enforcement?"

"No, I am not, but I trust some who are."

"So, you work with them?" Gabby asked.

"I've been known to coordinate introductions. If you have the leverage that you say you do then maybe you could negotiate a new life." Elina was honest without saying too much.

"Oh, I have the leverage. I have tons of shit on all sorts of people, especially my brother. It's all hidden in a safety deposit box where no one would think to look." Gabby set the empty soup can down. "What happened at the bar didn't bother me. I've been around gunfire like that. It's part of growing up in a family like mine. Lots of kabooms but you don't see anything. Even when you got us out of there, I had my eyes closed. I heard the gunshots, but I didn't look. I don't know what happened. I had no idea you shot anyone back there. I didn't want to know. Tonight, made it real. It scares the shit out of me to think of how he'd kill me. It wouldn't be a simple bullet to the head. It would be a slow and agonizing death. I know my brother and he would want to send a clear message. He's done it before, and you don't fuck with Dominick Manbessee."

"Even the mightiest giants can fall. Look at your dad. He's a feeble old man sitting on death row." Elina dug a deep hole in the sand with her hands. She filled the empty cans with sand and placed each one in the hole along with the lids and the bark bowl. She wiped off the two spoons with their napkins and tucked them back into the pack. The napkins went into the hole and then she filled it in with the pile of sand. A few more minutes of the light breeze and the wash would stop smelling like tuna fish.

"You don't think Dominick learned from my dad's mistakes? He has politicians, judges, police chiefs, shit, all sorts of people on his payroll. He's found a way to be above the law."

"Can you prove who all he has in his pocket?"

"Yes, at least who he had in his pocket when the bar was raided. The bugs may or may not still be recording. If they are, it's all being saved to the cloud. I don't really understand it, but a super cute little dyke had a crush on me. She told me what to put where and then made it all work. I made sure it was worth her while." Gabby smiled, but her spirit was showing the exhaustion of running, of everything.

"I have no doubt you made her very happy." Elina grimaced at the thought of what being happy with Gabby meant.

Gabby rubbed her face in her hands and then looked up into the star-filled sky. "What if I give up all of my leverage and someone that you trust really works for Dominick? I've seen it happen before. The leverage disappears and I'll end up shanked in my cell, or worse. I don't want to even think of the possibilities."

"The people I trust are not on your brother's radar, let alone his payroll. Of that, I'm certain."

"Will you protect me until it's over? I trust you."

"I can't promise that. It's not something I normally do."

Elina had no interest in protecting Gabby until a trial was over. The only reason she took on this job was to protect her grandmother and Alex. If it weren't for that news crew putting her on TV, Gabby wouldn't have found her at all. It dawned on her that Gabby stayed above it all by walking on top of those who dared to know her.

"I'd need that assurance before I'd be willing to share what I have. It's my life on the line. Maybe you could visit if I get a fresh start."

"Gabs, I hate to tell you this, but your life is already on the line. I could walk away right now and let you fend for yourself. Your games won't work on me. I don't do blackmail. I'll help you on one condition and that is, there are no conditions. You tell my people what you know. Turn over the evidence that you have. That's it."

Gabby blinked a couple of times, as if slapped across the face. "Okay, fine, if you get me out of here, I'll talk to the people you trust. I'll give them what I have."

"I'll do everything in my power to get you out of here safely."

Hunter crept over to Elina and tucked his nose in her hand and then crouched down.

"Shit, there's someone out there. Crawl over there and lie down on your stomach behind the log. There's just enough room for you between it and the side of the wash," Elina whispered, "I'll cover you."

Gabby's eyes were wide with fear, but she nodded and did exactly as Elina asked. She lay down on her side and tucked her arms in behind the log. Elina hid the food pack and what was left of the water at her feet and then covered her and the pack with one of the emergency blankets. She drizzled sand over the top of Gabby and the log to make it all more believable. Fingers crossed.

She gave Hunter a hand signal to arc out wide. There wasn't much cover for him, but the movement might distract whoever was out there and give her time to scan the area. Luckily, he didn't have a vest or a collar on. To most, he'd look like a tall coyote or a wolf from afar, and she hoped like crazy that whoever was out there was hunting for Gabby and not coyote.

Elina put her go bag on her back and picked up the rifle, and then snuck down the wash in the direction of Hunter's signal. She found an almost ninety-degree turn in the wash and held that position. She draped the other emergency blanket over herself, leaving just the barrel and the tip of the scope exposed. She scanned the area in a three-hundred-and-sixty-degree sweep. Everything was clear except the area Hunter had initially indicated.

What on earth was that? There were two men in a side-by-side UTV approaching from the direction of the shed. The vehicle moved along at a swift clip but was stealth quiet. She'd heard of long-range electric UTVs but hadn't seen one. What an impressive way to cover a lot of ground while remaining stalk-worthy quiet. The passenger was scanning the area in much the same way she was, through the rifle scope, likely night vision or thermal imaging, but at least his finger wasn't on the trigger. Thank goodness they had the cover of the wash. The more they traveled to the northwest, the more desolate the terrain became, at least for a little while yet. There was very little cover in the way of foliage or large boulders out here in the prairie.

The quad slowed to a stop. The passenger stepped out of his seat and held his scope off to her right. She could see them as clear as day but couldn't figure out what the passenger was so focused on. She stayed still and hoped like crazy that he would sit back down, and they would drive off. She'd taken enough souls and didn't want to take another. The scope scanned the area and locked on that same position off to her right again. She carefully scanned over to the area wondering what had the passenger's attention. Hunter. Shit. She should never have sent him out. She should have kept him down in the wash.

The driver of the UTV looked through a set of binoculars. "There's no one out here. I bet you five bucks you can't hit that coyote."

"That's not a coyote. The ears are too big. That's a cop dog."

She quickly returned her scope to the side-by-side. The passenger took aim and moved his finger off the trigger guard. *No, don't do it. Don't you dare. Why give away your position to senselessly shoot at a dog?* He clicked the safety off and tucked his finger inside the trigger guard.

BOOM! She fired before he had the chance. The shooter fell backward across the seat of the side-by-side and then slid down onto the floorboard. The driver jumped out of the seat and hid behind the vehicle. Luckily, the gun had fallen forward and was visible from her position. She waited and waited…and waited. The driver wasn't moving from his position. Elina was in no hurry. Patience would win this game. She watched and waited. The driver army-crawled behind the rear tires toward the rifle lying on the ground. *Don't do it. Please, don't do it. Stay there, stay hidden or jump behind the wheel and drive off.*

He refused to heed her silent warning and crawled to the rifle. He picked up the weapon and scanned the area. He had his finger on the trigger. She wished he'd stow the weapon and just go back the way they came. The circle of the scope closed in on her position. He was holding the rifle tight, preparing for the kick of the shot. She took the offensive and fired first. Damn it! It didn't have to end this way. He fell backward and landed on top of the first shooter. Idiot, he should have driven off and now it was too late.

"Neheic," Elina called Hunter back. She ran over to where Gabby was hiding behind the log and lifted the blanket off. "It's safe now, let's move."

There was a working vehicle begging for new occupants and zero threats in a three-hundred-and-sixty-degree sweep. Now was the time to put some distance between her last transmission and their current location.

## CHAPTER TWENTY-FIVE

The plane banked hard and did a one-eighty. Alex watched the approach from the side window. She couldn't make out anything that resembled an airport anywhere. She heard the landing gear come out and felt the plane tip the nose up for a landing. Where in the hell were they going to land? Bob's Hay Field, Airport and More? The tires squawked on impact and the pilots did whatever they knew how to do to stop the plane on what seemed like a postage-stamp-sized concrete pad. Jesus. Serious rock stars. They wasted no time either. The door was open before Alex had the rifles released from the clips in the cubby. She slung the go bags over her shoulder and followed Candice and Scout out of the plane.

A Rubicon edition four-door Jeep Wrangler with serious off-road tires was sitting there just beyond the wing of the plane. No doors and completely topless. Alex had always wanted to try rock crawling in a Jeep. She held both rifles and urged Scout into the back, as if he needed encouragement. Candice jumped into the driver's seat before Alex got around the back of the vehicle.

"Aren't you the crack shot with the long gun? I think maybe I should drive." Alex looked across the front seat.

"Fat chance. I'm calling rank."

"That's wrong on so many levels." Alex climbed into the passenger seat and buckled her seat belt. "Likely my one and only time in the field and you get to drive the cool car."

Candice pressed the engine start and smiled when the Jeep roared to life. She wiggled her eyebrows, shifted it into drive and hit the gas. Alex launched the navigation system and touched the icon for "where to" and then touched the feature for coordinates. She pulled the paper out of her pocket and typed in the latitude and longitude that Elina had sent. Once that was entered, she touched the screen for "view on map." At least now they would know where to start looking for a turnoff.

From the tiny airport, Candice navigated up to state highway eighty-seven headed northeast. The speed limit was fifty-five and she had the Jeep flying at least twenty miles per hour over the limit. Without the top on, the cool mountain air was frickin' freezing. Alex flipped the heat to high. She wasn't dressed for this. Luckily, the span on the interstate was short-lived. Candice slowed the vehicle when she turned onto a two-lane county road heading northwest. She punched the gas, ignoring the recommended thirty-five zone. Alex held on to the handle on the dashboard and said a silent prayer.

Candice finally slowed down a bit as they grew closer and closer to the dot on the map. Alex watched the left-hand side of the road for a driveway.

"There, turn there, after the rock," Alex said.

Candice killed the lights and guided the jeep up the drive. Thank goodness for moonlight. They stopped and parked just after pulling into the driveway.

"We'll walk in from here. No telling what we'll find up there." Candice walked around the back of the Jeep and opened the rear door. Scout jumped out and sat at attention. Candice unzipped a duffel bag and handed a headset to Alex.

"Where'd these come from? I couldn't get into the compartment in Elina's truck."

"I had the Great Falls office loan us some equipment."

"Sweet." Alex tightened the adjuster on the headset and flipped the power button. She could hear the mechanics inside hum to life. Displays seen from inside the device instructed her where to toggle for thermal or night vision. She tried thermal imaging. It was weird in a fun way. Sort of like walking in a neon-colored video game. The landscape all around them was various shades of blue and green.

Alex slung the rifle over her shoulder and walked up the driveway with her side arm at the ready. The bumper and then taillights of an older model sedan came into sight as they rounded a turn in the drive. It was at that moment that Alex wished thermal lenses could see through windows, but no luck. She flipped to night vision and motioned to Candice that she'd clear the right. Candice nodded and focused on the left. The car was empty.

She flipped her headset back to thermal vision and scanned the area for heat signatures. The first thing she noticed was a slight hint of steam wafting up from the front of the car. She bent down and spotted the bullet hole in the radiator. The ground directly beneath the radiator was yellow green color. The ground had been heated by the spray of the hot fluid. The steam rising from the radiator was dark red-orange and the hood was a faint yellow, signifying the degrees of warmth, but the ground all around the car was blue-green indicating it was much cooler.

She'd used these devices in training and watched the camera feed from her drones, but it was an adjustment to have your eyes covered when your brain was screaming to see reality. She tried to remember that it was simply a different perspective.

"Alex, recall all of your training. This is not an exercise," Candice whispered. "Follow me and please ask Scout to protect us."

"Heeteniihi," Alex whispered. Scout disappeared, and in that moment of pronunciation doubt she hoped she had said the command clearly. She shook it off and followed Candice up the hill.

Alex's heart thumped wildly. She'd trained to breach buildings and track fugitives, but out here, it wouldn't be a laser beam or a paint ball. Out here, the bad guys used real bullets and that was seriously scary shit. Her admiration for what Candice and Elina did, day in and day out, grew exponentially. Out here, the rules were different. She kept her focus in the moment and scanned the area looking for heat signatures. There was another vehicle up ahead, a truck with a flatbed trailer hooked up to the trailer hitch. The ramp on the trailer was down. Aggressive knobby tires had backed down the ramp and made their way up to the clearing ahead. Probably an ATV or something similar. The color of the engine beneath the hood of the truck was much brighter on this vehicle than it was on the car emitting steam. The truck had arrived sometime after the car. Like the car, it was empty. They kept working their way up the driveway.

Alex scanned the area from left to right and then right to left with each step in an effort to identify a threat before a threat could identify them. She crested the top of the driveway and froze in her tracks. She scanned the area twice to be sure of what she was seeing. She had to calm her racing heart. She watched for any movement. More than anything she wanted to rush over to each one and verify that none of them were Elina. *Focus on your training.*

"Four bodies. Two up ahead in the clearing by the burning structure. Two to the right at the edge of the clearing. So far, no movement," she whispered to Candice.

Alex switched her headset to night vision and walked over to the right at the edge of the clearing terrified of what she might see. She took in the scene. Two bodies, both appeared to be male. One was missing most of his skull, but the full beard was a helpful clue. She'd simulated what a high-powered rifle would do to a human skull in training and if anything, that lesson was an underestimate of the reality. She lifted the night vision goggles off her head and shook her phone twice for flashlight mode.

Brain matter, skin, bone, and hair was splattered on the trunks of the trees directly behind his body. Alex breathed through the nausea. The other man's death looked to be just as quick of an end. He was shot through the heart. The rifle he'd been holding was still in his hands. She heard Elina's voice in her head. *I prefer to capture whenever possible, but if my hand is forced, I'll always hope to be the last one standing. I don't know of anyone who would choose anything different.*

"She wouldn't have taken a life that wasn't trying to take hers or more importantly, the one she was assigned to protect," Candice said from behind her, as if she'd read her mind.

"I know. I understand that. It's just weird to have such powerful feelings for someone who does this for a living." Alex waved at the two dead bodies. She turned and looked up the soft slope to the smoldering remains of a building. There were two more bodies up there, close to the embers.

"The two up there are also male. The coroner will have to confirm that their identities match the ID in their wallets," Candice said.

Alex walked up the slope, closer to the bodies and then stepped back when her nose caught the scent of cooked flesh. "Is it wrong that they smell a bit like burnt chicken?"

"It smells that way to me too." Candice squeezed her shoulder. "Give Scout the scent and let's go. I think these four were together in the car. They died at about the same time based on heat signatures. There's still another team out there to deal with. We'll call this in from the trail."

Alex nodded. She pulled out a bag from her pack with Elina's scent. She called Scout in and offered the scent on the shirt. "Noowuhoot."

Scout lifted his muzzle in the air and ran up to the remnants of the small building. He ran to the closest side and then to the side facing the hill. He sniffed for a moment and then darted up the hill, quickly disappearing from sight. Thank goodness for the tracker. Alex and Candice turned and made their way back down the hill toward the Jeep.

"I'll follow the tire tracks and I'd like you to keep your headset on thermal vision for now. We don't need any surprises. Look near and far, keep us from looking like any of the four back there." Candice started the Jeep and dropped it into drive. She left the headlights off and started up the hill.

Once again, Alex's world was in the cartoon world of brilliant and bright neon colors. Luckily, most everything was illuminated in blues and greens with very little red and yellow. A desert rabbit and then a coyote on the hunt. She could deal with any four-legged critter. It was the ones with two legs that held rifles and pistols that she could go the rest of the night without seeing, well, except for a specific two-legged woman. Seeing her would be a welcome sight.

Then, about a half an hour or so into the ride, there were two more bodies, though not as much bright red-orange as they were light orange yellow. Dead bodies cooling in the low temps of the high desert. Hopefully, Elina's handywork and not Elina and Gabby.

"Slow, slow, stop. Two bodies on the right, zero threat," Alex said and lifted her goggles off. She peeked at her phone to see Scout's progress. His pace far outdid theirs given that he could hop up and over obstacles whereas they took their time driving the Jeep around those obstacles.

She shook her phone to flashlight mode. Two males, each shot once. A rifle was on the ground next to them. The quad or whatever they were driving was missing. Elina had procured wheels. Alex hoped Scout could still make headway and catch up.

"Pin the coordinates and we'll call it in. Let's keep moving." Candice interrupted her thoughts. "We don't know if any others are coming in from the north, east, west, or any number of intersection points. We can't assume they're following from the known direction of travel."

"Nope, can't assume shit." Alex was annoyed with being behind the eight ball. She wanted to be at Elina's side. She shook it off and jumped into the passenger seat of the Jeep. Goggles back on and in thermal mode.

"Ready, let's get at it."

Candice hit the gas with the urgency that Alex was feeling inside. The landscape looked wide-open, and Candice was letting the suspension of the Jeep absorb the many ruts and bumps.

Suddenly, the cartoon world had a deep, dark blue line approaching quickly. *Oh shit, that's not good. Nothing about that is good.*

"Stop, stop, stop…STOP!" Alex screamed. Without knowing it, she was pushing herself back in her seat as if that would save her from the fall.

The Jeep slid in the soft topsoil at the edge of the trench and turned slightly to the left. The right front tire dropped into a void and dangled in the air. Thank goodness the other three tires stayed on the ground. Alex exhaled her held breath and released her death grip on the dash handle.

"Backup. Please, back the fuck up."

"My bad." Candice laughed.

Not an appropriate response.

Candice backed the Jeep up and released her seat belt. She jumped out of the driver's seat and walked down into the wash. "It's pretty wide right here. It would have been a sketchy fall, but we wouldn't have died. We should be able to go down on an angle and crawl up the other side. We'll need momentum though, it's soft sand."

Candice returned to the Jeep. Alex was still sitting in the passenger seat. At the moment, she was grateful that it was Candice who would have to navigate the crawl. She backed the Jeep up a couple of car lengths, pulled a lever which Alex knew to be four-wheel drive, and then came in on a diagonal and kept up a decent speed. They angled down the side slope of the wash, crossed the bottom quickly, and then started climbing up the other side. Candice gave it a bit more gas and kept the momentum up. Sand flew everywhere. Alex smiled. After all, it was pretty damned cool.

"Good eye on seeing the wash. Keep it up. I'll keep following the tracks," Candice said and hit the gas.

"Candice, can I ask you something?" Alex watched ahead and didn't look over.

"What's up?"

"Do you know what happened to my mother?" The question had been in the back of her mind ever since she'd talked with Mary about it in the truck.

"Yes."

"Will you tell me?"

"Now's not the time, Alex. Focus on the work at hand."

"The Manbessees are the work at hand. Rocks, veer slightly left. We're still on the tracks. Look, just tell me if she's dead or alive?"

"She's dead."

She didn't even try to sugarcoat that one. Alex had suspected as much. "Was she buried somewhere?"

"That, I don't know."

"Fair enough. Thank you, for telling me the truth."

Her mom was really gone. There was a part of her that wanted her to be alive and then another part of her that thought she might hate her for disappearing if she was actually alive. At least she knew now and could stop wondering.

It was surreal to think that at some point in the next several hours she'd meet the daughter of the man she put in prison. The man who most certainly killed her mother. Would Gabriella know who she was? It didn't seem likely if her brother had a contract out on her life. Was she a victim in all of this, no different than Alex had been? Did Elina still care for her? Of all the questions, that one bothered her the most.

## Chapter Twenty-six

Hunter nudged Elina in the neck and barked once, right next to her ear. She slowed the battery-powered side-by-side to a stop. This was extremely unusual behavior. He knew it was quiet time, but something had his attention. What was Hunter trying to tell her? He pranced his front paws. His toenails clicked against the metal of the utility box with each step, and he whined loudly. She stood up on the seat and scanned the area in a three-hundred-and-sixty-degree sweep. She didn't see anything, but something or someone had to be out there. Wait, what was that? Barking? Was that Scout?

"Notikoniinen?" Elina asked Hunter if he heard Scout too. His whining grew more impatient. He looked from her to the distance behind them and then back to her. "Sooxoe." Hunter barked twice and then shot out of the tiny bed on the side-by-side.

"What did you say to the dog?" Gabby asked. "What language is that?"

"I told him to go and find his friend. My other dog is out there, we both heard him, which means my human friends are close too."

"You have two dogs? Is the other one named dog two, kind of like Thing One and Thing Two?"

"Hey, snarky Gabby is back. The food must have done the trick." Elina pushed in the locking brake on the UTV and then held up her hand to stop any response. "Wait, do you hear that?"

The chuff, chuff, chuff sound of a helicopter interrupted the silence of the night. Would Alex have access to a helicopter? It didn't seem likely if Scout was on the ground chasing her scent. Alex only had the one set of coordinates, and if Scout was behind her, it would suggest that she was somewhere back there too. The landscape had grown more and more sparse. There weren't any great places to lay low and hide.

Gabby looked up at Elina. "Seriously? A helicopter? How are we going to outrun that? Better yet, how do you shoot down a helicopter?"

"We don't know that it's even after us. Could be the shed fire or a med flight chopper."

Elina stood up in the seat, scanning the area through the rifle scope, trying to figure out what to do. There was nothing wrong with being prepared for the worst, even as she hoped for the best. She looked directly behind them just as Scout and Hunter crested the hill, running toward her. She smiled, inside and out. It really was Scout, which meant that Alex was somewhere close by. She ignored the helicopter for the moment and hopped down to the ground to greet her puppy.

Scout yipped and whined as if she'd been gone for months. She dropped to her knees and wrapped her arms around him. He smelled earthy and woodsy, just like Alex. Her heart fluttered in her chest, and she allowed herself a moment to enjoy the way that scent made her feel inside. The chuff, chuff, chuff of the helicopter grew steadily louder. She had to focus. She pulled away from Scout and something caught her eye. No way would Alex put a patch on his vest upside down. She pulled it back and a small baggie dropped down to the ground. *Alex, you crafty devil.* It was a note. The seal was tough to open so she dug a finger in the corner and ripped the baggie. Alex had kept to her word. It was written in Arapaho.

*Nebii'o'oo, notiitii, Notikoniinen's niisiyoonoo3oo.*

Her brain translated it as she read, *My sweetheart, look for it, Scout's pocket.* She gave Scout a hand signal to stand and unzipped his vest. She unzipped the pocket where his command card would normally be, and two devices fell the short distance to the ground. Each item had a label, one read "safe phone" and the other read "rapid charger." Alex had thought of everything. She pressed the power button on the phone and watched it come to life in her hand. She finally had a way to communicate again. Good thing too, because the helicopter was getting closer.

*My sweetheart, thank you for the gift. Helo coming at me. Is it friendly?*

The only word she couldn't translate was helo.

*Let me check.*

Alex sent the response in English. She must really trust this link. Elina zipped up Scout's vest and signaled the dogs back into the rear of the side-by-side. She tucked the charger into her go bag and the phone into her bra. She wanted to be certain to feel the vibration of a response. If she had to guess, it sounded as if the helicopter was approaching from the north. She jumped back into the driver's seat and whipped them around so she could follow her own tracks. If she could make it back to the wash, maybe they'd have a place to hide. Better yet, if they made it to Alex, she'd have the calvary with her.

The phone buzzed in her bra. She pulled it out and tapped the screen to display the text.

*Not ours. Not law enforcement. Come back. We're following your tire tracks. We're lights out in a Jeep.*

*K*

She didn't try for more than the one letter. The terrain was too bumpy, and she didn't want Gabby reading the messages. She darkened the screen and tucked it back into her bra. No longer worried about the vehicle's battery life, she decided to see how fast the little buggy could go.

"Why are we going back? All of the bad guys with guns came from back there. What if more have shown up?" Gabby asked.

"We're going back because the people I trust are back there and we don't know who's in the chopper." Elina looked across the seat into wide, worried looking eyes. "I'm doing my best to keep us alive."

"I know you are. I trust you more than anyone else right now." Gabby's hand rested on her shoulder. "Gina, I need to ask you a favor. It's a big one too. Please, don't let them take me alive. If they capture me and if you can't rescue me, then, well, if there's any way that you can manage a shot, please take me out. Kill me quick. Promise me that you won't let them torture me to death."

Elina turned and looked into Gabby's eyes. She looked serious, sincere even. Elina didn't know what to say. She'd already taken so many souls. It would take time for her own to heal. It was what was needed in order to keep Gabby safe. Taking a life that was trying to take yours was one thing, but shooting someone you once had feelings for, even as twisted as their time together was, was something completely different. Taking a soul that had once upon a time touched your soul, that would be a curse of a thousand deaths. A haunting that would last for all eternity.

"Let me focus on keeping you out of their hands. We'll cross any other bridge if we come to it, okay?"

Elina held the pedal to the floor, full throttle in an all-electric sort of way. The side-by-side absorbed most of the bumps and ruts, but every so often she'd hit one that would test the strength of the seat belt. Regardless of how hard she pushed the UTV, it was no match for the speed and maneuverability of the helicopter. The chuff, chuff, chuff was deafening as it grew closer to them. Dust swirled all around making it almost impossible to follow their own tracks. She looked in the tiny review mirror and watched the spotlight on the ground close in on them quickly and then it found them and there was no place to hide. The chopper hovered over them. The wind generated by the blades plumed dust everywhere and made it difficult to see and breathe.

"Found you, baby sister!" Speakers on the belly of the chopper bellowed out the booming male voice. "Did you really think you'd get away?"

"Don't let him take me. Promise that you won't let him take me." Gabby's voice was high with panic.

The chopper flew up alongside them and flashes erupted from a side cargo door. The only good thing was that now they were out of the spotlight. Elina swung the vehicle wide. With the light beneath the helicopter, she could see the bullets creating small mushroom plumes of dirt as each one struck the earth. She was so focused on watching the bullet track in the dirt that she hit something and almost ripped the steering wheel free from her grip.

"They are shooting at us!" Gabby strained against her seat belt trying to crawl across the seat. "Listen to me, Gina. Colorado First National in Dinosaur City, box fourteen."

A bullet or a rock at just the right angle hit the front tire. It popped loudly and caused the little vehicle to veer to the right. Elina tried to straighten it out, but the rim was digging into the dirt and leaving her with little control. And then they hit a back tire on the same side and there wasn't much she could do to control the vehicle.

Elina repeated the location of the safety deposit box in her mind. "Gabs, don't let him get in your head. Be the badass bitch in the leather skirt!"

The helicopter flew ahead of them and swung around, flying backward, putting them right back in the spotlight. Elina tried to make out how many were inside, but the dust and the spotlight was blinding. She had to figure something out fast. This wasn't going to end well.

"Gabriellaaaa, you spoiled little bitch. I'm going to cut you up into four million pieces," Dominick said through the speakers. "Do you hear me?"

"Gina, do something!"

"Dig in my small backpack. There are a few pistols. Find them."

"Don't let him cut me up."

"Focus!" Elina yelled so loud that Gabby recoiled.

Gabby dug in the bag and handed Elina a gun and held one in each of her hands too. "Okay, now what?"

Elina clicked the safety off on the pistol in her hand. "Here, trade me, use this one. It's ready to fire."

She exchanged guns with Gabby. "Aim at the glass windshield and keep pulling the trigger until there are no more bullets. Shoot as fast as you can. Now!"

She stopped the side-by-side and signaled for Scout and Hunter to spread out and be at the ready. They leapt from the utility box and disappeared into the engulfing dust storm. Gabby was already shooting. Elina took aim and emptied one of her pistols. The pilot tried to maneuver and tip the helicopter away from the onslaught of bullets. The shooter from the side door slipped and fell to the ground. His rifle landed somewhere behind his body. Elina wasn't taking any chances. She took aim and fired three shots into his upper body. He reacted to the impact of the first two, but not the third. She turned her focus back to the helo until both pistols were empty.

The whirl of the blades was winding down. The pilot had landed the chopper. Elina snagged her go bag from Gabby's lap and opened an inside pocket holding the extra ammunition clips for her pistol. She tossed the gun she'd taken from the men behind the bar, ejected the empty clip and replaced it with a full one. Once it was reloaded, she shifted the UTV into reverse and hit the pedal.

"Toss your gun. I don't have any more bullets for that one. Take off your seat belt and unhook mine too. I'm going to cut the tires hard. We'll both go out on your side. I need you to hold on to the rifle and the small backpack. We can't lose those two things. Got it?"

"Got it," Gabby shouted.

Elina forced the steering wheel to turn against the flat tires and swung the vehicle sideways. She stomped on the locking brake. The UTV rocked back and forth, the shocks absorbing the sudden stop of the momentum. She slid across the seat and followed Gabby out. "I need you to help me tip this thing up on its side. It's all I can think of to offer some protection. One, two, three, lift."

It didn't go as planned. Either the wheelbase was too wide, or they weren't strong enough to tip it up. Regardless, there wasn't time to try again.

"Forget it, hand me the rifle and crouch down by the back tire." Elina pointed to the spot between her and the side of the vehicle.

Without a word, Gabby crouched down as instructed. Elina tucked the pistol in the waist of her jeans, squatted down low and watched for movement with the rifle at the ready. The helicopter powered down and everything went dark. It was an eerily quiet moment. She willed her eyes to adjust to the lack of light. She looked into the chopper through the scope and both front seats were empty. She scanned the area around the chopper. Nothing. *Damn it, where did they go?*

"Look at the cowering little bitch. There's nowhere to hide, Gabriella."

Several flashlights clicked on behind them. Elina spun around and couldn't see anything behind the light. *How many had been in the chopper?* Gabby rose to her feet and stood next to Elina.

"Hiding and cowering are two completely different things." Gabby had attitude in her voice again. Good for her.

Elina swore she could hear another inbound helicopter. Hopefully, it was tactical support and not more of Dominick's people.

"I'll take that."

A man stepped forward with a pistol aimed at her chest and tried to take the rifle out of Elina's hand. She thrust the rifle at him and then swung it quickly to the side. The wood stock made contact with his wrist and knocked the gun out of his hand. She called out to the dogs and reached for her pistol in that moment of impact. She couldn't see another way out of this.

"Look out! Grizzly!"

The dogs came in fast and hard. The command served two purposes, the first to get the dogs to act, the second to install that touch of doubt in the bad guys that there was indeed a grizzly bear afoot. She didn't see who the dogs got, but whoever it was, the scream that followed was shrill. Two flashlights fell to the ground. Elina aimed the gun at the man who had tried to take the rifle and pulled the trigger twice. He fell to the ground. She grabbed Gabby's arm and pulled her out of the light. She was still uncertain how many men had been standing behind the flashlight beams. Hopefully only two. A couple of gunshots rang out. She needed her eyes to adjust so she could see what and who to aim at. Somewhere off to the side she heard the roar of a gas engine and then the horn was blaring. A bar of extremely bright lights clicked on and the entire area lit up as if it were daylight.

The dogs had two men on the ground. One still had a gun in his hand but thankfully, it was also the arm that the dog had ahold of, and he couldn't bend his wrist to get a clean shot.

"Freeze!" Elina had never been happier to hear Alex's voice.

"Gina, look out."

Gabby shoved her with the force of a linebacker but not before she felt the impact. She hit the ground hard and then everything went dark.

❖

A man glanced over his shoulder at Alex and suddenly she was twelve years old all over again. There was no doubt that he was Dominick Manbessee. He was the spitting image of his father. He turned away from her and lifted his arm. Alex looked at what he was focusing on and saw Elina and Gabby. She recognized her from the photos in the case file.

Gabby dove at Elina just as Dominick fired. She saw Gabby take the bullet and fall to the ground. It didn't look like Elina had been hit but was pushed into the shadows and Alex lost sight of her.

"US marshal. Drop your weapon and show me your hands!" Alex approached his position from the shadows, keeping her voice strong even as bile rose in her throat. "Drop your weapon now or I will shoot."

The man ignored her. He took one more step away from her and took aim. Alex wasn't going to ask again. She fired twice. She also saw a single muzzle flash in front of the man. It all happened in an instant. The man dropped his gun and fell forward. Alex approached his still body with the caution she'd learned in field training. She kicked his gun away from his hand, all the while keeping her weapon aimed at his heart. She reached down with her free hand and pulled her cuffs from the pouch on her belt. Once his hands were cuffed, she checked for a pulse. He was dead.

She rolled him over and shoved his body off to the side. Gabby was beneath him. She'd been shot in the chest. There was quite a bit of blood on her shirt, but that wasn't what killed her. The fatal shot wasn't bleeding at all. Dominick Manbessee gave up his life to shoot his own sister in the forehead. *How fucked up was that?* And yet, somehow, it was fitting.

Alex assessed the scene in a matter of seconds, but she still hadn't found the one person she was looking for. She shook her phone twice for flashlight mode and spotted Elina in the first sweeping pass about four feet away. She was face down and wasn't moving. *No, no, please no.* Alex took two steps and in one swift motion, she holstered her gun and dropped to her knees. She checked for a pulse and it was strong and steady. Why then, was she unconscious?

"Elina? Wake up. Can you hear me?" Alex ran her flashlight up and down the length of her. She found an entry and exit wound in the muscle just above her collarbone. She started to roll Elina on to her back but stopped the moment she spotted the blood on her head. She scanned the area around her head and spotted a large rock with blood on it.

"How is she?" Candice asked from behind her.

"Unconscious. Her pulse is strong. Looks like she smacked her head on that rock when she went down. Status?" Alex couldn't look away from her sleeping beauty. She had to be all right. She just had to be.

"The two guys that Scout and Hunter had are secured. Chopper is clear. All other hostiles are dead. We have two choppers inbound about a minute out. There's a medic on one of the inbound."

Alex nodded. She could hear the helos. They were close. She used her jacket to protect Elina's head while they landed.

"I want to go to the hospital with Elina." Alex wasn't sure Candice heard a word she'd said. Two helicopters touching down was deafening.

"Absolutely. Go with the medic. I'll secure the scene. Let me know when you have any info on her, okay?"

Alex nodded and then leaned down close to Elina's ear. "Please stay with me. Please be okay. I don't want to lose you."

## Chapter Twenty-seven

Elina delicately traced the pattern in the detailed beadwork on her grandfather's tobacco pouch. She was surprised to see it. It was one of the items that had been buried with him. She loosened the tie and opened the pouch just enough to draw in a deep breath. The ceremonial tobacco had a sweet, unique scent, one that reminded her of him. She clutched the pouch to her chest. *Wait.* These weren't the clothes she was wearing. Her jeans and blouse were gone. Come to think of it, she wasn't where she expected to be, either. She was at her grandparents' ranch, dressed in her ceremonial best.

The tanned buckskin was velvety soft, and the beadwork created an intricate pattern of white, turquois, red, and yellow. Long leather fringe ran the length of her arms and all around her knees. She loved the way it fanned out when she twirled. The beadwork on her moccasins matched the top of her ceremonial dress. She reached back to touch her hair and was surprised to feel the feathers woven into her braid.

She heard the delicate notes from her grandfather's tāhpeno. The sound of his flute had such a calming effect on her spirit. She remembered being entranced as a child whenever he would play. Still clutching the tobacco pouch, she walked through a field behind the barn and for some reason, she wasn't surprised to see his teepee set up right where it used to be when she was younger. Light wafts of smoke rose out of the top. She wondered what he'd look like if she went inside. Would he be the man she could see in her mind's eye, or would he be the hollowed shell that left this earth? She mentally prepared herself for either and lifted the flap of hide.

He was dressed in his ceremonial regalia too. Soft buckskin poncho-style shirt, buckskin leggings, and moccasins. His shirt had strips of tanned leather fringe around each arm at the shoulder and along the outside of his leggings. He wore a long necklace created from colorful beads that complemented the painting on the back of his poncho. He always looked so handsome, so regal and distinguished, especially in his native best. He was an elder, after all. He lowered the flute from his lips. She missed the music already. He stood and extended his arms to her. Without hesitation, she stepped into his warm embrace. It felt like heaven. He held her for some time and then stepped back and she wondered if a few seconds had passed or was it an eternity and time didn't matter here, in this place.

"Neisie, it has been too long." He spread out a buffalo hide on the ground next to his. "Please, join me."

Elina enjoyed hearing him call her neisie again. She relished being called "my grandchild" as much as her given name. No one called her that anymore. Her grandmother had never used the endearment, so it became something special between the two of them. She stepped around the fire and sat next to him on the soft, thick hide. He looked good. He looked like she remembered. Strong, capable of anything and physically fit. Come to think if it, she felt pretty good too. Nothing hurt. She felt strong and full of energy, as if she could tackle anything. She should be exhausted and sore. The past twenty-four hours had put her body through hell.

Her stomach sank and as much as she didn't want to know, she had to ask. "Neibésiiwóó, did Manitou, the Great Spirit, call to me? Am I dead? Is this the great teepee in the sky?"

"The great teepee in the sky, good one." He slapped his leg and chuckled. "Your heart still beats, child. It's your soul that beckoned my spirit."

"I don't understand."

"You will before our time is over."

He held out his hand for the tobacco pouch. His fingers brushed hers when he lifted it away. His hands were still calloused from years of hard work, which seemed odd since he was no longer physical.

"I am as you see me." He answered her unspoken thought. "I look differently, much younger when my sweet Mary beckons me and older when I chat with Mick or Alex. Everyone has their favorite version of who I am."

"You've visited all of them, even Alex?" Elina asked.

"I've been beckoned by their souls and now, I've been beckoned by yours. It took you long enough, young sprout." He looked up with smiling eyes.

"How does this work? Are you here to fix me?"

"Are you broken?" He rocked his arms like a scarecrow and laughed. "It's your dream. Ask what your soul might need from my spirit? Consolation, knowledge, wisdom, or maybe my presence and laughter?"

This was nothing more than a dream. Nothing more than a silly mind game? Disappointment washed over her.

"Don't be disappointed. It's not a silly mind game."

"Can you read my thoughts?"

"Your soul doesn't need you to use words to communicate with me in this place. It's not a mind game because the mind isn't involved at all. Souls roam anywhere they want to go when we sleep, and the experience is shown to us in our dream. It is very real."

"What happened to the souls that I took tonight?"

"Each transitioned into a spirit."

"Will I be punished for taking so many souls?"

"Did you take those souls out of malice or hate? If you could do it over, would you do anything differently?" he asked.

She thought about that for a moment. Was there anything she could have done differently? She could have let them all live, but they would have hunted her, hunted Gabby. She did what she had to do to stay alive and to keep Gabby alive. It wasn't hate, it was survival.

"It's never easy to take a life. It shouldn't be easy, even though there are times that it's necessary, but then you already know this truth. I sense that's not what concerns you."

No, that wasn't what was weighing her down. She accepted that there were times when taking a life was necessary. If she was honest, she was more concerned with how Alex felt about it. Would Alex judge her for taking so many souls? Would Alex think she was nothing more than a killer? Would Alex still care for her and want more?

"Close your eyes and inhale through your nose. Tell me what you smell."

Elina inhaled deeply. Ah, there was that earthy, woodsy scent that made her swoon. Alex's scent filled the teepee. Warmth wrapped around her hand.

"She hasn't left your side. The warmth you feel is her hands wrapped around yours."

Elina wished to be wrapped up in her arms, like she was the night they slept together. "I've done so many horrible things. How could she ever see past my failures? How could she ever love someone like me?"

"What do you mean someone like you? What have you done that was so horrible?"

"I'm too embarrassed to tell you. You are the very definition of honor, and this past year, I've lived the exact opposite of honor. I've brought shame to our people."

"Would it surprise you to learn that I already know? Souls are horrible at keeping secrets from spirits. You think if you don't say the words that you're keeping it from me, but you feel the emotion, so, I know. Don't be embarrassed, sprout. I once battled my own demons after a few undercover assignments. Everyone battles some kind of demon. The most important thing is the fight. We only lose when the demons win. You fought and won, so did I. The fight was difficult for each of us in our own way. Some souls are built for undercover work. You and I are not those souls."

"You went off the rails while working undercover too?"

"I wouldn't have used those words, but yes, I suppose I did. The person I had to pretend to be almost consumed who I was. I know that you understand that statement on a very deep level. I barely escaped that world and came here, to this land, to heal. That's when the sanctuary was created. It was a way for me to help people without having to live among those who are the darkest souls alive."

Elina stared into the campfire. She suddenly felt understood. She had so many questions and then, in an instant, the questions dissipated, and she was filled with answers. He had gone through something very similar. She could feel his emotional pain from that time and then the peace he found on the bison ranch.

"Your actions didn't bring shame to our people. So what if your reputation took a hit. You've been looking for a change anyway. You're the only one who is ashamed. Forgiveness has to start here and then change can happen." He lifted his hand and pointed at her heart.

"I do want change. I'm tired of living in the shadows and hunting people down, but it's more than that. I want to create a life with Alex like you and Néiwóó shared. When I'm with Alex, I feel seen. I also feel this overflowing desire to do anything and everything just to see her smile. I think I've fallen in love with her."

"My spirit smiled when you two started talking and then more so when you envisioned walking a new path with Alex. I'm proud of you and everything you've accomplished. The sanctuary is a place of strength and courage. A perfect fit for you and Alex. It helps all who stay there."

"It feels right. She feels right. I love her."

Neibésiiwóó added another small log to the fire and stirred the coals. The warmth from the flames felt good, like it was warming her up from the inside out. Or was that Alex's warmth? Regardless of the source, it felt like unconditional love.

He picked up a good-sized clay bowl and rested it in front of his crossed legs. He lifted various dried herbs from the bowl and placed them in his hand. "Sage to drive away the negative forces and heal your spirit. You've had a rough year, so I'll add extra." He smiled at her and then focused on the herbs again. "Braided sweetgrass is a cleansing healer and attracts positive energies. It's time to release the bad and welcome the good. Cedar will offer protection, and finally, the ceremonial tobacco. A sacred plant and a powerful healer for your soul."

Elina watched him place pieces of the herbs in a smaller dish and then wrap the remaining bundle up in cotton string. She removed an eagle feather from her braid and offered it to him. His eyes sparkled with appreciation for the gift. He held a twig close to the fire until the tip ignited and then lit the bowl of herbs with the small flame. The cleansing scent filled the teepee. He fanned the bowl with the eagle feather.

Neibésiiwóó offered her the healing effects of the smoke floating up from the bowl. She graciously accepted the gift. He used the eagle feather to lift and direct the smoke, starting with her head, to calm and cleanse her mind so that she could welcome good thoughts. Next, he cleansed her eyes so that she might see good things, see the good path. He sent the cleansing smoke to her ears so she could hear good things coming into her life and then cleansed her mouth, so her words came from kindness and compassion. Next, was her heart to lift away any negative feeling so that she could feel with kindness and consideration. Finally, she bathed the rest of her body in the smoke, so that she could journey down her path in a good way.

When the ceremony was finished, she felt centered, calm, and relaxed.

"This smudge stick will be waiting for you in my teepee, along with the eagle feather. It is up in the loft of the barn. A gift from me to you." He set the bowl of smoldering herbs down. "It's time for you to return to your body and let them know you're okay. There's great concern."

"I've missed you."

"Come and see me any time." He smiled and held her hand for a second.

"Thank you, I love you."

"I love you too, Neisie." He clapped his hands together and the teepee filled with a blinding light, erasing everything around her. A series of loud beeps kept repeating, over and over, in her ears and then it was drowned out by a sweet melody, one she'd like to dance to.

## CHAPTER TWENTY-EIGHT

Alex rubbed her eyes and fought against the exhaustion. Elina should be awake by now. The doctor said that the brain swelling was down. Her bullet wounds looked good too, so why wasn't she awake yet? It didn't make any sense.

The room was consumed with a litany of chirps and beeps. Two or three of them going off at once was a maddening event that seemed to last forever. She pulled out her phone and opened her music app. It might be sappy, but she had a playlist of all the slow songs that she wanted playing in a loop while she held Elina in her arms, swaying ever so slowly. She tapped shuffle and repeat and then touched the play icon and set the phone on the bed. This way, if she sang along, the real artist would help hide the fact that she was completely tone deaf. Singing was not her forte.

She held Elina's hand and leaned in close enough to feel Elina's breath. The fact that she was breathing on her own was comforting. She had to be okay, she just had to be. There was so much that needed to be said. So many experiences to share. She wanted a chance at all of it. Maybe now would be a good time to practice saying everything she wanted to say.

"Can I tell you a secret? I'm head over heels in love with you, Elina Hawkins. I think I've always been a little in love with you. Maybe you could have called it a crush, but over the last few months and especially the past few weeks, it's grown into an entirely different level of love. I think of something, and I want to share it with you. I see something amazing, and I want you to see it too. I love the way your eyes light up. I love hearing your thoughts about anything and everything. I can't imagine a life without you in it. It might seem fast, but I know how I feel." Alex watched her closely to see if she reacted at all. Did her eye twitch and had she moved her hand or had Alex moved it? This would have been a much better conversation on that first night out on the back deck while sipping on whiskey. She hadn't been ready then. Hell, she hadn't even known how she really felt then. Now, she knew, and she was ready. She'd tell Elina her story now, even if she had to repeat it later.

"First, you should know that I'm not who you think I am and yet, even when I say that, I think that's wrong too. I think you might know me better than I know myself. I've spent so long feeling like no one really knew me. As a child, I was erased from existence and then handed a script of new memories. It's a surreal feeling to be reinvented. It also creates a curse of lies and omissions. I've always struggled with the dishonesty of it and pushed people away. I know you said that understanding why we each have secrets is what could bind us instead of pushing us apart, but I'd rather you know the truth. I think the truth creates the strongest bond. You trusted me with your truth, and I trust you with mine." Alex watched once again for a reaction. She hoped Elina could hear her. The words were flowing perfectly.

"I don't know what to make of how intertwined our lives are. For example, did you know that you were trying to flip the daughter of the man I put on death row twenty-five years ago? You see, my mom wasn't really killed in a botched robbery. That's one of the reinvented stories I had to memorize. She was part of the evening housecleaning crew for the Manbessee complex. We both witnessed the night Marco Manbessee killed one of his rivals. She went to the police and we were moved to a safe house. Four men showed up the night before the trial was scheduled to start. The two marshals protecting us were killed and the men dragged my mom away. Obviously, they didn't know I'd seen it too."

Alex drew in a deep breath. She hadn't spoken of this day in all the years since it happened. She leaned down and rested her head on the pillow next to Elina's. The closeness felt comforting.

"My mom and I had argued earlier that night after dinner, and I was hiding in the closet crying. I saw the entire thing go down through the slats in the closet door. I was frozen with fear and couldn't move. I sat there all night staring at the dead bodies of those two US marshals. Candice found me the next morning. She was sent over when my mom failed to arrive at the courthouse. Then, I was sent to your grandfather's ranch for safekeeping until the trial started. My testimony put Marco Manbessee on death row. That man took so much away from me. He killed my mother and took me away from everything and everyone I knew. I've spent all this time focusing on what I lost in my childhood and failed to see what all I've gained. Yes, I lost my mom, but I gained a father I'd never had when Mick adopted me. I gained a whole new family and an entirely new life."

Alex closed her eyes and kept her head resting on the pillow right next to Elina. She listened to another song before she started talking again.

"I hadn't realized that until now. I mean, sure, logically I knew it, but it didn't really click until this whole ordeal happened. I spent so many years thinking I couldn't let anyone close because of all the secrets surrounding witness protection. I felt cheated out of sharing my life with someone special because of it. So, what did I do? I built on that and embraced a career of secrets wrapped up in more secrets, but then you helped me realize that the secrets are such a small part of who I am. I might have lost a name and the ability to share details about the real neighborhood I grew up in, but it could have been worse, and bonus, I fell in love with a woman who can know all of it."

Alex pulled back slowly, unsure if her brain was playing tricks on her. Had Elina just squeezed her hand? Elina's eyes fluttered and then she blinked. Alex smiled and her heart fluttered.

"This is a great playlist."

"You may not know this, but you owe me a lifetime of slow dances. We had that conversation yesterday." Alex caressed Elina's cheek.

"Hmmmm, that sounds nice. I bet you're—" She swallowed and drew in a deep breath. "A good dancer."

"How long have you been awake?" Alex asked. "You heard all of that, didn't you?"

Elina smiled and nodded slightly. "If I say no, will you say it all over again? I also have a confession. I'm head over heels in love with you too, Alex." She swallowed and licked her lips. "I'm sorry you went through all of that. I had no idea. I'm in love with the woman you've become in spite of it all. You're my Alex and there's no one like you."

Alex leaned down and kissed her gently on the lips. "I'm glad you came back to me. I've missed you. I'm so happy you're awake."

"I missed you too." Elina squeezed her hand. "Where am I?"

"The best trauma hospital in the state."

Elina was quiet for a few minutes. Her eyes were closed again. Maybe she'd drifted off. Alex leaned back in her seat.

"Hospital?" Elina asked. "Where?"

The delayed response surprised Alex. She sat forward in her chair again. "Yes, hospital. You're in Great Falls, Montana."

"Great Falls? How long have I been here?"

Alex wasn't sure what she was asking. How long in Great Falls or how long in the hospital? She decided to be specific and answer both. "A few days in Great Falls. More than twenty-four hours in the hospital."

Had she drifted off? Alex sat back in her chair again. She held Elina's hand and smiled when the next song started. It was a lovely ballad about how two people had hung out so much that rumors started around town that they were a couple. They stopped denying how they felt for each other and let the love blossom. She couldn't wait to get home and let the love blossom, with Elina.

"Gabby. Where's Gabby? Is she okay?" Elina mumbled.

Alex didn't want to talk about Gabby. She didn't want to see Elina's reaction to the news, but then, that wasn't for her to decide. Maybe it would offer some closure.

"Alex, what happened? How did I get hurt? Why am I here?"

Alex drew in a deep breath. "Dominick fired at you and Gabby pushed you out of the way. You were hit in the shoulder. You hit your head hard when you landed and have been unconscious since. Gabby was hit in the chest and didn't survive her injuries. She didn't suffer. Do you remember a helicopter chasing you?" Alex asked.

"Yes. It's all coming back in flashes." Elina turned her head slightly. "Was I driving a dune buggy?"

"Yeah, kind of." Alex chuckled.

"Manbessee. He was in the chopper?"

"Yes, he was in the helicopter."

"Did he get away?"

"Dominick is dead. I shot him."

"I remember more now. We were running. I heard you yell, and I turned back. He was aiming at me. She shoved me out of the way. That first bullet was meant for me."

"I'm grateful to her for that selfless act." Alex lifted Elina's hand and kissed the back of it.

"Her first and last." Elina held tightly onto her hand. She used her elbows and tried to sit up a bit, but she was too weak to lift herself more than an inch or so. She winced and flopped back onto the bed as if she'd raised herself a foot.

"What do you need? I'm here. Let me help." Alex hated feeling helpless.

"I want to sit up more. I need water."

Elina whispered so softly that Alex could barely make out the words. She reached across the hospital bed and used the remote to lift the head of the bed a little higher. Elina licked her lips and swallowed again. Alex poured some ice water into a glass and lifted out a few ice chips with a spoon. Elina opened her mouth and accepted the moisture. She licked her lips again.

"They tracked us and shot up the bar. We ran. How did they find us after I blew up the phone?" Elina asked. Her color was getting better. That had to be a good sign.

Alex could see Elina reliving the night in her mind.

"Dominick provided the equipment to the various hit teams tracking you two down. Everything had location trackers. From what we can figure out, he wanted to capture Gabby himself."

"That night, I took so many souls. I don't want you to look at me and see a killer." Tears welled up in Elina's eyes.

"Oh, sweetheart, you are not a killer. You're a defender and there's a difference. I would have taken each and every one of them down too, in order to protect you. They weren't innocent. Every single person that you took had a gun and wanted to take you and Gabby out first. I don't think less of you. Like I said, I love you."

Tears streamed down her cheeks. "I love you, too." Elina pulled on her hand. "Can you help me move over?"

"There are so many leads and tubes. I don't want to hurt you."

"Move the tubes and get into this bed. I need you to hold me."

Alex didn't hesitate. She lifted the covers and moved the leads and tubes off to the far side. She scooped Elina up and shifted her over in the tiny bed and then climbed in next to her. Heaven. It felt like heaven to hold her in her arms again.

"The work you do at the ranch. The sanctuary. Do you love it?" Elina asked.

"I do. Getting a taste of fieldwork proved to me how much I enjoy running the sanctuary. I hope it works out that they keep the post. I've learned things to make it better and safer. How about you? Are you ready to jump back into your work when you're better?"

"Honestly, no, I'm not." Elina rubbed the back of Alex's hand with her thumb. "It's time for a change. It's too hard on my spirit."

"Any thoughts on what might be next for you?" Alex squeezed her eyes shut. She didn't want to get her hopes up, but she had her fingers crossed.

"I had a chance to visit with Candice a bit on the night we freed Néiwóó while we were waiting for the apprehension teams to arrive. She mentioned that the sanctuary would benefit from a second marshal on site. If you like the work and plan on staying, then what would you think of me being that second badge? They would take my experience into consideration. I could be a US marshal right beside you."

"I think that all of my dreams might just come true."

Elina snuggled into her neck. Alex turned into her and fell asleep.

❖

The hospital room door clicked and then opened. Elina looked over to the tiny hallway into the room. She must have dozed off. She had no idea what time it was or, for that matter, what day of the week it was. She forgot to ask that question. One thing she did know was that she was still snuggled up in Alex's arms and that felt wonderful. She felt stronger and more awake than she had when Alex climbed in bed next to her. The toenails on the floor should have been a clue, but her heart smiled when she saw the two dark muzzles round the corner. Her smile grew even more when her grandmother, her mom, and Candice followed behind.

"If you all aren't a sight for sore eyes," Elina whispered.

"The doctor called and said that you were awake. We wanted to rush over before visiting hours were over." Néiwóó held her tightly in her arms. "I'm glad you're okay. We have some things to discuss when you're ready."

"Hey, sweetie, it's so good to see you." Her mother bent down and kissed her on the cheek.

Elina smiled. "Hey, Mom. It's good to see you too."

Alex lifted her head up from the pillow and rubbed her eyes. "Hey, Mary, Candice, and how did I not know Elina had a twin?"

Elina laughed. "Alex, this is my mom, Bly Hawkins."

"It's very nice to meet you. Now I know where she gets her incredible looks from. Congratulations on your move back to Wind River."

"Flattery will win you graces, sweet Alex. She got most everything from me except the eyes. Those are a gift from Hawk." Bly smiled and shook Alex's hand. "It's a pleasure to finally meet you too."

"I don't mean to interrupt, but there are two puppies over here that need to know you're okay," Candice said from across the room. Scout and Hunter strained against the leashes. Each was whining and stammering to get across the room.

Elina motioned for the dogs and held out her hand to Candice. The dogs ran up and hopped up, so their front paws were on the edge of the bed. Tons of puppy kisses covered her cheeks.

"How on earth did you get them in here?" Elina asked.

"A badge and couple of service dog patches goes a long way at the nurses' station. Besides, the nurse was cute. She gave me her number and winked at me. Who knows?" Candice leaned over the puppies and held Elina in her arms.

Elina pulled her in close. "Dinosaur City, Colorado. Safety deposit box fourteen. Colorado State Bank or Colorado First National. Get a warrant. It's where Gabby kept evidence against her brother and those in his pocket. There's stuff in the cloud too."

"Got it. Thank you, for taking the risk. My dear friend, I regret to inform you that your persona, Gina Holt, did not survive her injuries. It's over. No more undercover work if that's what you still want," she whispered into Elina's ear.

Elina turned and looked at Candice with a nod and a smile. She had everything she wanted in this room. She thought about her conversation with her grandfather in the teepee. She still wasn't entirely sure it really happened, but either way, she felt at peace inside. Without a doubt, she was done with her contract work, and more specifically, the undercover work. She was ready to walk a new path. One with Alex at her side. She rested her head on the pillow and cherished the love she felt in this bleak hospital room.

# CHAPTER TWENTY-NINE

Elina sat on the back deck sipping a hot cup of tea. It was hard to believe that she'd been home from the hospital almost a week already. At least the headaches were subsiding, and she could stand for more than ten minutes without getting dizzy. The doctor expected her to make a full recovery in another week or so. It would take a bit longer to build the strength back in her shoulder. She was grateful it hadn't been worse.

She wasn't accustomed to being on the sideline and had to fight the urge to just get back in the saddle. She smiled and shook her head slowly. She literally had to fight the urge to get in the saddle. While it had been fun watching Alex work the herd from afar, she would have enjoyed it more if she'd been able to be out there with her, especially when Alex looked so damned hot in leather chaps. Those were going to be put to good use when she could resume normal activities once again. Of all the things she wasn't allowed to do, why'd they have to take away sex? She craved the chance to share that experience with Alex again. Oh, the things she wanted to experience with Alex were almost endless. The doctor urged her to abstain while she recovered. Sadly, Alex heard it too and wasn't about to let her break the rules. No strenuous activities, including sex, until all symptoms were gone. Hopefully, only one more week of waiting. She wondered if Alex would indulge her and wear just the chaps and the hat. They wouldn't be on long. It conjured up a sexy image in her mind. She drew in a deep breath and let it out slowly. The next seven days might prove to be the longest week of her life.

The roundup and sorting were completed yesterday. Alex had a few friends from town come out to help. It was nice to meet people from Alex's world. Trapper and his wife, Tess, were fun and totally in love with one another. Elina imagined that they would be a nice couple to spend time with. She looked forward to getting to know them better.

"I brought you out a fresh cup of tea." Her grandmother handed her the mug and then sat in the chair next to her with a glass of whiskey in her hand.

"Thank you." Elina smiled. "Hey, why can't I have whiskey?"

"One more week won't kill you."

"It might." Elina laughed.

"So, are you still on vacation?" Néiwóó asked with a sideways glance.

"About that, I imagine you have questions." Elina turned in her chair so she could see her grandmother's expression.

"No, not really. I've pieced a few things together. Well, maybe one or two questions. First, where's home for you? Wyoming or Montana?"

Elina smiled at her grandmother. "That one's easy. I've decided to move to Montana. Two of my favorite people on earth live in Montana."

"That makes my heart happy, though I'm sure your mom will miss having you so close."

"I'll visit her often and I'm sure she'd love to come up here too."

"I'm sure she would." Néiwóó took a sip from her glass. "I wonder if I can offer a piece of unsolicited advice."

Elina wasn't entirely sure she wanted to hear any advice right now. She was still trying to come to terms with everything that happened over the past year, not to mention the past couple of weeks. She was still trying to stay steady on her own two feet. She had a feeling that her grandmother would say whatever she wanted no matter what.

"I'm listening."

"I don't know when your career transitioned, but the path you're on now is a dangerous one. Sweetheart, I don't want to lose you. I worry that your luck will run out."

"Would you feel better if I told you I was looking into a career change in addition to the move?" Elina asked.

"Depends on what you choose. Your next adventure could be even more dangerous than the last."

"I'm almost certain my next adventure will be less dangerous, though nothing's one hundred percent safe." Elina sipped her tea. "Turns out that the deputy director offered me a job with a badge. Seems there's an opening at a safehouse in Montana."

Elina looked over in time to see her grandmother smile.

"You don't say." Néiwóó sipped her whiskey.

"He also mentioned that the position was part of a certain lease negotiation. You wouldn't know anything about that, would you?" Elina asked.

"Alex can't keep doing everything on her own and you said you wanted to help with anything I needed." She looked over and winked.

As if on cue, Alex pulled up behind the house and parked in her spot beyond the back deck. She hopped out of her truck and bounded up the stairs.

"The calves went for a great price at auction. The trailer is all cleaned out and I stopped by the bank and deposited the check into your account, Mary."

"Thank you, Alex. You're a good egg, no matter what Elina says about you."

"Oh, is it happy hour?" Alex bent down and kissed Elina. "How are you feeling?"

"Better by the minute and a little jealous that I can't have happy hour too. I'm glad you're back."

"I'm glad you're back too. We have business to discuss." Mary stood from her chair and walked into the house. She returned a moment later with a large manilla envelope and two small glasses on a tray. She poured a drink for Alex and put a tiny splash in the second glass and handed it to Elina. "I'm not getting any younger and the recent events have made me realize that this spread is too much for me and maybe even too much for just Alex and me. To that end, I've made some phone calls and gotten my affairs in order, so to speak."

"Is everything okay, Mary? You're not sick, are you?" Alex pulled a chair over and sat facing Elina and Néiwóó.

"I'm fine, I'm fine. You can stop looking at me with sad puppy eyes. What I mean to say is that this spread needs younger hands than mine. It's time for the next generation to take it over, only I'm skipping a level. I want you two to own Hawkins Ranch, together. The work here needs to continue, and we can't exactly have new owners who don't know that the sanctuary exists. It serves a purpose and gives people hope when there's short supply. But it has one stipulation. You have to take care of this old woman until she dies or needs to go into a home. If that's something we can all agree to, then we have papers to sign."

Elina was shell-shocked. Staying on the ranch was one thing, but owning it was the last thing she expected to hear. She looked up and saw that Alex was just as shocked.

"I have money saved. I could probably qualify for a decent amount," Alex said.

Elina could see the gears turning behind her eyes.

"Nonsense. I'm transferring it to you, not selling it. If this land sells to anyone, it's the US Marshals Service. It's all in the paperwork. It's what Hawk wanted when the time came, but seeing as you two can run it, there's no sense rushing the sale. When it's time for you two to do something different, then they can accept the terms or decline, and you can put it on the market."

Her grandmother was indeed one sharp cookie. She'd thought of everything. It felt right too. Elina didn't feel any pressure, just excitement for a new future.

"So, what do you two say? Are you in or what?"

"I don't know what to say besides thank you. Yes, I'm in." Alex stood from her chair and bent down to give Néiwóó a hug.

"I'm in too and thank you. Your love means the world to me." Elina set her glass on the table and used the back of the chair for balance as she stood. Her grandmother stood too. Elina wrapped her arms around her two favorite people and when she closed her eyes, she was certain she could hear her grandfather's flute playing off in the distance. She found herself looking forward to life on this new path and to a future with Alex. Love was found at the sanctuary and with it came a freedom from secrets, at least with each other, and that was all that mattered.

# About the Author

A vivid imagination spurred Nance Sparks's desire to write lesbian romance. Nance lives in south central Wisconsin with her spouse. Her passion for photography, homesteading, hiking, gardening, and most anything outdoors comes through in her stories. When the sun is out and the sky is blue, especially during the golden hour, Nance can be found on the Wisconsin River with a camera in hand capturing shots of large birds in flight.

# Books Available from Bold Strokes Books

**A Champion for Tinker Creek** by D.C. Robeline. Lyle James has rescued his dad's auto repair business, but when city hall condemns his neighborhood, Lyle learns only trusting will save his life and help him find love. (978-1-63679-213-2)

**Closed-Door Policy** by Erin Zak. Going back to college is never easy, but Caroline Stevens is prepared to work hard and change her life for the better. What she's not prepared for is Dr. Atlanta Morris, her gorgeous new professor. (978-1-63679-181-4)

**Homeworld** by Gun Brooke. Headed by Captain Holly Crowe, the spaceship Velocity's crew journeys toward their alien ancestors' homeworld, and what they find is completely unexpected—and they're not safe. (978-1-63679-177-7)

**Outland** by Kristin Keppler & Allisa Bahney. Danielle Clark and Katelyn Turner can't seem to stay away from one another even as the war for the wastelands tests their loyalty to each other and to their people. (978-1-63679-154-8)

**Secret Sanctuary** by Nance Sparks. US Deputy Marshal Alex Trenton specializes in protecting those awaiting trial, but when danger threatens the woman she's falling for, Alex is in for the fight of her life. (978-1-63679-148-7)

**Stranded Hearts** by Kris Bryant, Amanda Radley, Emily Smith. In these novellas from award-winning authors, fate intervenes on behalf of love when characters are unexpectedly stuck together. With too much time and an irresistible attraction, anything could happen. (978-1-63679-182-1)

**The Last Lavender Sister** by Melissa Brayden. Aster Lavender sells her gourmet doughnuts and keeps a low profile; she never plans on the town's temporary veterinarian swooping in and making her feel like anything but a wallflower. (978-1-63679-130-2)

**The Probability of Love** by Dena Blake. As Blair and Rachel keep ending up in the same place despite the odds, can a one-night stand turn into forever? Or will the bet Blair never intended to make ruin their happily ever after? (978-1-63679-188-3)

**Worth a Fortune** by Sam Ledel. After placing a want ad for a personal secretary, a New York heiress is surprised when the woman who got away is the one interested in the position. (978-1-63679-175-3)

**A Fox in Shadow** by Jane Fletcher. Cassie's mission is to add new territory to the Kavillian empire—murder, betrayal, war, and the clash of cultures ensue. (978-1-63679-142-5)

**Embracing the Moon** by Jeannie Levig. Just as Gwen and Taylor are exploring the new love they've found, the present and past collide, threatening the future they long to share. (978-1-63555-462-5)

**Forever Comes in Threes** by D. Jackson Leigh. Efficiency expert Perry Chandler's ordered life is upended when she inherits three busy terriers, and the woman she's referred to for help turns out to be her bitter podcast rival, the very sexy Dr. Ming Lee. (978-1-63679-169-2)

**Heckin' Lewd: Trans and Nonbinary Erotica** by Mx. Nillin Lore. If you want smutty, fearless, gender-diverse erotica written by affirming own-voices folks who get it, then this is the book you've been looking for! (978-1-63679-240-8)

**Missed Conception** by Joy Argento. Maggie Walsh wants a relationship with Cassidy, the daughter she's only just discovered she has due to an in vitro mix-up. Heat kindles between Maggie and Cassidy's mother in a way neither expects. (978-1-63679-146-3)

**Private Equity** by Elle Spencer. Cassidy Bennett spends an unexpected evening at a lesbian nightclub with her notoriously reserved and demanding boss, Julia. After seeing a different side of Julia, Cassidy can't seem to shake her desire to know more. (978-1-63679-180-7)

**Racing the Dawn** by Sandra Barrett. After narrowly escaping a house fire, vampire Jade Murphy is unexpectedly intrigued by gorgeous firefighter Beth Jenssen, and her undead existence might just be perking up a bit. (978-1-63679-271-2)

**Reclaiming Love** by Amanda Radley. Sarah's tiny white lie means somehow convincing Pippa to pretend to be her girlfriend. Only the more time they spend faking it, the more real it feels. (978-1-63679-144-9)

**Sol Cycle** by Kimberly Cooper Griffin. An encounter in a park brings Ang and Krista together, but when Ang's attempts to help Krista go spectacularly wrong, their passion for each other might not be enough. (978-1-63679-137-1)

**Trial and Error** by Carsen Taite. Attorney Franco Rossi and Judge Nina Aguilar's reunion is fraught with courtroom conflict, undeniable chemistry, and danger. (978-1-63555-863-0)

**A Long Way to Fall** by Elle Spencer. A ski lodge, two strong-willed women, and a family feud that brings them together, but will it also tear them apart? (978-1-63679-005-3)

**Barnabas Bopwright Saves the City** by J. Marshall Freeman. When he uncovers a terror plot to destroy the city he loves, 15-year-old Barnabas Bopwright realizes it's up to him to save his home and bring deadly secrets into the light before it's too late. (978-1-63679-152-4)

**Forever** by Kris Bryant. When Savannah Edwards is invited to be the next bachelorette on the dating show When Sparks Fly, she'll show the world that finding true love on television can happen. (978-1-63679-029-9)

**Ice on Wheels** by Aurora Rey. All's fair in love and roller derby. That's Riley Fauchet's motto, until a new job lands her at the same company—and on the same team—as her rival Brooke Landry, the frosty jammer for the Big Easy Bruisers. (978-1-63679-179-1)

**Inherit the Lightning** by Bud Gundy. Darcy O'Brien and his sisters learn they are about to inherit an immense fortune, but a family mystery about to unravel after seventy years threatens to destroy everything. (978-1-63679-199-9)

**Perfect Rivalry** by Radclyffe. Two women set out to win the same career-making goal, but it's love that may turn out to be the final prize. (978-1-63679-216-3)

**Something to Talk About** by Ronica Black. Can quiet ranch owner Corey Durand give up her peaceful life and allow her feisty new neighbor into her heart? Or will past loss, present suitors, and town gossip ruin a long-awaited chance at love? (978-1-63679-114-2)

**With a Minor in Murder** by Karis Walsh. In the world of academia, police officer Clare Sawyer and professor Libby Hart team up to solve a murder. (978-1-63679-186-9)

**Writer's Block** by Ali Vali. Wyatt and Hayley might be made for each other if only they can get through nosy neighbors, the historic society, at-odds future plans, and all the secrets hidden in Wyatt's walls. (978-1-63679-021-3)

**Cold Blood** by Genevieve McCluer. Maybe together, Kalila and Dorenia have a chance of taking down the vampires who have eluded them all these years. And maybe, in each other, they can find a love worth living for. (978-1-63679-195-1)

**Greener Pastures** by Aurora Rey. When city girl and CPA Audrey Adams finds herself tending her aunt's farm, will Rowan Marshall—the charming cider maker next door—turn out to be her saving grace or the bane of her existence? (978-1-63679-116-6)

**Grounded** by Amanda Radley. For a second chance, Olivia and Emily will need to accept their mistakes, learn to communicate properly, and with a little help from five-year-old Henry, fall madly in love all over again. Sequel to Flight SQA016. (978-1-63679-241-5)

**Journey's End** by Amanda Radley. In this heartwarming conclusion to the Flight series, Olivia and Emily must finally decide what they want, what they need, and how to follow the dreams of their hearts. (978-1-63679-233-0)

**Pursued: Lillian's Story** by Felice Picano. Fleeing a disastrous marriage to the Lord Exchequer of England, Lillian of Ravenglass reveals an incident-filled, often bizarre, tale of great wealth and power, perfidy, and betrayal. (978-1-63679-197-5)

**Secret Agent** by Michelle Larkin. CIA agent Peyton North embarks on a global chase to apprehend rogue agent Zoey Blackwood, but her commitment to the mission is tested as the sparks between them ignite and their sizzling attraction approaches a point of no return. (978-1-63555-753-4)

**Something Between Us** by Krystina Rivers. A decade after her heart was broken under Don't Ask, Don't Tell, Kirby runs into her first love and has to decide if what's still between them is enough to heal her broken heart. (978-1-63679-135-7)

**Sugar Girl** by Emma L McGeown. Having traded in traditional romance for the perks of Sugar Dating, Ciara Reilly not only enjoys the no-strings-attached arrangement, she's also a hit with her clients. That is until she meets the beautiful entrepreneur Charlie Keller who makes her want to go sugar-free. (978-1-63679-156-2)

**The Business of Pleasure** by Ronica Black. Editor in chief Valerie Raffield is quickly becoming smitten by Lennox, the graphic artist she's hired to work remotely. But when Lennox doesn't show for their first face-to-face meeting, Valerie's heart and her business may be in jeopardy. (978-1-63679-134-0)

**The Hummingbird Sanctuary** by Erin Zak. The Hummingbird Sanctuary, Colorado's hottest resort destination: Come for the mountains, stay for the charm, and enjoy the drama as Olive, Eleanor, and Harriet figure out the meaning of true friendship. (978-1-63679-163-0)

**The Witch Queen's Mate** by Jennifer Karter. Barra and Silvi must overcome their ingrained hatred and prejudice to use Barra's magic and save both their peoples, not just from slavery, but destruction. (978-1-63679-202-6)

**With a Twist** by Georgia Beers. Starting over isn't easy for Amelia Martini. When the irritatingly cheerful Kirby Dupress comes into her life will Amelia be brave enough to go after the love she really wants? (978-1-63555-987-3)

**Business of the Heart** by Claire Forsythe. When a hopeless romantic meets a tough-as-nails cynic, they'll need to overcome the wounds of the past to discover that their hearts are the most important business of all. (978-1-63679-167-8)

**Dying for You** by Jenny Frame. Can Victorija Dred keep an age-old vow and fight the need to take blood from Daisy Macdougall? (978-1-63679-073-2)

**Exclusive** by Melissa Brayden. Skylar Ruiz lands the TV reporting job of a lifetime, but is she willing to sacrifice it all for the love of her longtime crush, anchorwoman Carolyn McNamara? (978-1-63679-112-8)

**Her Duchess to Desire** by Jane Walsh. An up-and-coming interior designer seeks to create a happily ever after with an intriguing duchess, proving that love never goes out of fashion. (978-1-63679-065-7)

**Murder on Monte Vista** by David S. Pederson. Private Detective Mason Adler's angst at turning fifty is forgotten when his "birthday present," the handsome, young Henry Bowtrickle, turns up dead, and it's up to Mason to figure out who did it, and why. (978-1-63679-124-1)

**Take Her Down** by Lauren Emily Whalen. Stakes are cutthroat, scheming is creative, and loyalty is ever-changing in this queer, female-driven YA retelling of Shakespeare's Julius Caesar. (978-1-63679-089-3)

**The Game** by Jan Gayle. Ryan Gibbs is a talented golfer, but her guilt means she may never leave her small town, even if Katherine Reese tempts her with competition and passion. (978-1-63679-126-5)

**Whereabouts Unknown** by Meredith Doench. While homicide detective Theodora Madsen recovers from a potentially career-ending injury, she scrambles to solve the cases of two missing sixteen-year-old girls from Ohio. (978-1-63555-647-6)